GILLIAN ARCHER

Lick It Up

A Long Licks Rock Stars Romance

First published by Gillian Archer 2026

Paperback ISBN 978-1-966830-09-2

ASIN B0GHZV8Y9B

Paperback Cover Design by Jillian Liota, Blue Moon Creative Studio

Edited by Dayna Hart

Proofread by Crystal Blanton, Luxe Ink Productions

gillianarcher.com

First edition

ISBN: 978-1-966830-09-2

This book was professionally typeset on Reedsy.
Find out more at reedsy.com

Contents

Lick It Up Playlist

Stream it here: https://bit.ly/4owPsGV
Better Man—Little Big Town
Drunk on a Plane—Dierks Bentley
Somewhere on a Beach—Dierks Bentley
I Just Got Back From Hell—Gary Allan
Every Little Thing—Carly Pearce
Cruel Summer—Taylor Swift
Love Ain't—Eli Young Band
Treat You Better—Shawn Mendes
Shake It Off—Taylor Swift
All Night—Brothers Osbourne
Lick It Up—Kiss
Your Song—Elton John
Marry You—Bruno Mars
Wanted Dead or Alive—Bon Jovi
Who Knew—P!nk
Troubadour—George Strait
Best Thing I Never Had—Beyoncé
Make You Feel My Love—Adele

Prologue

Saylor Tate

Las Vegas, Nevada

Four days before wedding date

My mind was a jumble of lists, tasks, and that nagging feeling I'd had for months that this all was a mistake. And I told police later that was the reason I didn't see it coming.

Trent had been acting weird for months. Mom wouldn't listen. She continued to chalk his behavior up to guys and weddings. She kept telling me that Trent was the smart decision. Trent was vice president of investments at a huge banking institution—the same one my stepdad worked at—older, stable, smart, and of course handsome. I was lucky to be with him. Not a single word or question about our love for one another. Mom prioritized stability over everything. Which, granted, made sense, given my dad's death when I was two left her completely unmoored. But still, why didn't my feelings factor into any of this?

Because I was having serious doubts.

So in addition to my nagging fear this all was a mistake, I was thinking about the cake delivery, who was going to pick up Aunt

Stacey at the airport tomorrow, the huge shopping list for the groom's dinner—because despite the name, it'd all fallen on my shoulders—and making sure my hairstylist had the correct address for the venue, and a million other things.

I just wanted to collapse into a heap and cry.

"Saylor Tate?" An accented male voice asked from behind me as I unlocked my car in my apartment building's garage.

"Yes?" I turned to him with a smile.

When—*BAM!*

Out of nowhere, the side of my face exploded in pain.

I bent over, clutching my cheek in my hands, as tears blurred my vision.

"You tell your fiancé, Trent Hale, that we're serious." His thick, accented words puffed so close to my face I could smell the nicotine on his breath. "He doesn't want me showing up at his wedding Saturday with extra guests. Screwing over the Aslanov Bratva is a serious fucking mistake. One his loved ones will pay in blood and pain."

His hand threaded through my hair and yanked until I fell to my knees.

A pained whimper left me, and then everything froze as I felt something large, cold, and metallic press into my uninjured cheek.

"It'd be a tragedy if we had to paint your parking spot with your blood. Maybe we can work out something in trade, instead. What do you think, *Kotyonok*? Want to be my little plaything?"

My breathing sounded more like wheezing as I stared into a pockmarked face with a huge scar splitting his right eyebrow and ending in the corner of his mouth. And it was somehow scarier as he grinned at me with his yellowed, crooked teeth.

Nothing about that smile was nice.

"*What was that?*" he yelled.

I flinched and my whole body trembled as I stared into his dark, pitiless eyes.

"I can't hear you, *Kotyonok!*"

"I-I-I, I'll tell him," I whispered through a pained whimper when he tugged on my hair.

He grunted. "See that you do. Otherwise, you'll be seeing me again—a whole lot more of me."

After one more vicious tug of my hair, he walked away.

I crumpled to the ground.

As his car pulled away, I covered my face with shaking hands and cried.

Chapter 1

Saylor

Three days after wedding date

I thought canceling the wedding would be the hard part—turned out going on the honeymoon alone was a whole new humiliating low. Everywhere I turned, people were asking where my husband was, from the desk agent at the airport to the flight attendant in first class.

Hence the alcohol in front of me.

I'd always loved Dierks Bentley's '*Drunk on a Plane*.' Little did I know it would turn into my anthem. I couldn't get my money back, so here I was drunk on a plane.

Destination Fiji.

It was the only part of the wedding Trent had been passionate about. He'd always wanted to stay on this certain island in a treehouse bure [boo-ray] overlooking the ocean to one side and the island on the other. The jungle side of the treehouse also had an outdoor shower.

It was the whole reason I'd taken out that extra student loan to cover the honeymoon—my gift to Trent. Although now I understood why he'd wanted control over the finances. Thank god I'd grown up on *Judge Judy* and pushed back on combining our accounts until *after* the wedding.

Although, in hindsight, I was wishing I'd waited to move in with the asshole.

"So what are you celebrating?" a deep voice asked above me.

I blinked and looked up at the older, surfer-looking attractive man standing next to my first-class pod. His long, dirty blond hair was pulled up in a man-bun, and his dark blue eyes twinkled down at me. Faint lines fanned out around the outside of his gorgeous eyes. At my hesitation, he grinned, and a dimple appeared in his scruff covered right cheek.

I literally lost all ability to talk or think for a second.

Technically, I had a thing for older men, considering Trent was thirty-seven to my twenty-two. And this guy was definitely in the same category.

Only hotter.

His eyes got smolder-y as we continued our staring contest.

All sorts of dirty things ran through my mind at that look. The mile high club featuring at the top of the list.

"You okay, baby girl?"

I swooned all over again. *Baby girl?* Gah. I'd had the hugest crush on Derek Morgan from *Criminal Minds* as a teenager. And this guy had all the swagger and intensity that had made me fall for the character.

After a deep breath, I managed to nod. "Uh, yeah. Just maybe didn't take the whole altitude thing into account when I ordered. Might be a little tipsier than I'd planned." Which I realized—after the words left me—was a stupid thing to admit to a stranger. I closed my eyes with a wince. "Sorry. That was an overshare."

He waved a hand. "Don't worry about it." He paused, and after a beat, he straightened and tipped his head. "Enjoy the rest of your flight."

Then he ducked into his pod, and I lost the opportunity to make all those dirty fantasies come to life due to my slow, alcohol-induced reaction time.

This being single thing was going to be harder than I remembered.

Although given that I'd hooked up with Trent during my freshman year of college and had been with him for almost four years, it wasn't surprising. I hadn't been single as an adult really. And definitely not since I'd been granted the ability to drink.

How did people balance alcohol and flirting? Was there a class I could take somewhere?

I groaned and pushed the bottles to the other side of my tray. After hitting the button to convert my seat into a bed, I closed my curtain for privacy. We had eight more hours on the flight. Might as well try to get some sleep.

My last thought before I passed out was that I really had to get a handle on this whole flirting thing if I wanted to make this a fun trip. Maybe my surfer could help me with that.

I dreamed of rolling around in a bed with Derek Morgan…and my surfer at the same time.

* * *

It was my moan that woke me up.

I blinked a few times, confused about my surroundings, and then I sat up with a start. The plane's cabin was still dark—*thank god*—and I believed that the engines covered my unfortunate outburst. Although I blamed that on not having sex for almost three months. Trent's left-field "save ourselves for marriage" request probably had more to do with impotence—due to his losing streak—than any religious beliefs.

Ass.

I scrubbed at my face with the heels of my hands then froze with a wince as I remembered my cheek. It didn't hurt too much anymore, but I was desperate for my concealer to cover the still green-yellow bruise.

Unbuckling my seatbelt, I leapt from my chair and headed for the tiny bathroom cubicle. Most of the seats I passed had their curtains closed.

But not my surfer.

His curtain was open as he reclined with his overhead light on so he could read—Ozzy Osbourne's autobiography, judging by the cover—with reading glasses.

I paused for a second to take the whole scene in, but when his eyes met mine, I booked it down the aisle and closed myself in the tiny bathroom.

Like a wuss.

Because I was all talk (or was it thought?) and literally zero follow through.

I took care of business then checked out my concealer in the wavy mirror. After touching up the coverage, I washed my hands and took a few deep breaths.

I should probably have a mantra or something to get through these next two weeks, but I'd never been a woo-woo type of girl. Straight forward, factual, over-achieving type A was more my style.

Shaking my head, I rolled my eyes at my reflection then reached for the door. I was hefting my purse over my shoulder, so I didn't notice someone was standing right in front of me.

"Ooomph!" I bounced off the person and went back on my back foot. "Sorry, I didn't—Ack!" My apology ended with a screech as my surfer—sans reading glasses—pushed into the tiny space, making me back up against the sink.

He slammed and locked the door behind himself then turned to me with a wolfish grin. "We should probably hurry. I don't think we have a lot of time."

My mind blanked for a second, and then I realized what he was implying.

"Whoa." I shook my head. Despite my fantasies and earlier drunken thoughts, I wouldn't ever do that.

He tipped his head. "You okay, baby girl?"

"Look, I don't know who you think I am, but I'm a good girl. I don't"—I waved a hand between us—"do this kind of a thing. Ever."

"Oh." The sparkle left his eyes, and he looked genuinely bummed out by my refusal.

Was it wrong that I liked that?

Oh, I was clearly screwed up in the head. Thanks so much, Trent.

And Mom.

And Dad.

I could go on, but I didn't want to get caught in here with him.

The tiny, confined space had me breathing a little funny. Or maybe it was him. Either way, I needed more room to breathe. "I also had a little episode where someone attacked me in a parking lot about a week ago, so this is giving me all sorts of anxiety. Do you mind opening the door, or should I press this little call button here?"

"Yeah. Right." He shook his head. "Sorry." He tossed me another searching look then unlocked and opened the bathroom door.

Once he disappeared down the aisle, I closed myself back into the restroom. No way I was going to be seen leaving at the same time. Leaning against the sink for a second, I laughed incredulously.

Did that seriously happen? Did he really think I'd hook up with him because I'd stared at him? Something told me that wasn't his first attempt at joining the mile high club—just the latest.

But maybe it was his first rejection.

Just when I thought this week couldn't get any crazier, the universe had to prove me wrong.

CHAPTER 1

Apparently there was always a new low for me. Yay.

Chapter 2

Malcolm Holt

Taveuni, Fiji

Fiji was made up of hundreds of islands, so what was the chance she'd be at the same tiny, privately owned resort island as me?

But she'd been doggedly at my heels through customs, baggage claim, and then on the connecting flight on the puddle jumper.

It was hella awkward.

But seriously, what was I supposed to think when she'd looked at me like that? So many women had over the years—groupies, in particular. The number of women who would've been swooning at the same opportunity were plentiful.

It was her loss, actually.

But then she got off the puddle jumper at the Taveuni island airport.

"Mister and Missus Hale! *Ni sa bula*!" An island man wearing a baby blue Ring Gold t-shirt and board shorts shouted ebulliently. He crossed the distance between us and anointed us with flowered leis. "Welcome to Fiji."

"We're not—" I started but was cut off by Mystery Woman.

"I'm not a Hale, and neither is he. I mean, I would've been a Hale if the wedding happened, but it didn't, so I'm not."

Both the resort escort and I stared at her with wide eyes for a moment.

That was...a lot.

"Err, sorry to hear that." The resort employee blinked a few times. "How would you like to be called?"

"Saylor is just fine. Saylor Tate."

The resort employee nodded. "Got it. Saylor. Miss Tate." The color in his cheeks probably had little to do with the heat. He nodded and turned to me. "Shit, you're Malcolm Holt."

I ducked my head and rubbed the back of my neck. He hadn't said it loud enough for anyone to hear, but I didn't want to take the chance. "I think you have a reservation for me under Logan Ecchols."

My assistant was a pain in my ass who thought it was funny to book my reservations under character names from her girlie shows. Last time it'd been Jess Marino from something called *Gilmore Girls*.

I didn't see the humor.

The resort employee nodded. "Right. Right. I think we were expecting you. I'm sorry, I'm new. Let me check." He pulled out his cell phone and tapped away at the screen. "Ah, we had you down for the later flight. But you're here now, so let's head to the van and then the boat."

"Boat?" Saylor repeated timidly.

"Yes, it's about a twenty-minute boat ride to the island and then your honey—er, vacation can begin. Let me grab your bags."

I hefted my backpack onto my shoulder and grabbed my roller. "I got these."

"Sure, sure." He bent over Saylor's two bags and arranged them so he could pull them. "Can I grab your other bag, miss?"

Saylor shook her head. "I'm good. I'm sorry, what was your name again?"

"It's Vili."

Saylor smiled. "Nice to meet you, Vili. Thanks for the help."

"*Sega na leqa.*" A hint of interest darkened his tone, and I gritted my teeth. He'd literally just found out about her heartbreak and was already signaling his interest?

Asshole.

I planned on giving her a day—or two at most—before…shit, I'd already forgotten how she'd turned me down on the plane.

Fuck.

It was an awkward ride across the island to the dock where a fishing boat with a canopy bobbed against the current.

I'd stayed at Ring Gold Island before, so it wasn't a surprise to me. But judging by the look on her face, Saylor had been expecting something…different.

I swallowed my chuckle and watched as Vili helped her aboard, then I helped him stow our luggage.

A few minutes later, we were bouncing across the water, a faint mist spraying our faces. I took a deep breath, closed my eyes, and just let the peace of the moment wash over me. Something about the water here just felt different. I might have a house on the beach in Cali, but nothing felt like the pristine beauty of the water in the South Pacific.

Saylor felt differently, judging by her shriek and the way she scrambled to get out of the spray.

My chuckle was lost in the roar of the outboard engine and the wind.

Since I'd been at the resort a year ago—for almost a month—I was welcomed by every employee we passed with back slaps and promises of great fishing.

I waved off an escort to my bungalow. "Same one, right? I know the way."

"Err actually, the Hales uh, I mean Miss Tate has booked that treehouse. We have you in the other one."

The other, *lesser* one he meant. I tried to hide my snarl of disappointment. I loved that treehouse. It had the most privacy. And a private plunge pool.

Vili gestured helplessly. "When the call came for your reservation, that one was already booked. Had been for almost a year. I'm so sorry."

Saylor studiously avoided looking in my direction.

No offer to switch.

No conciliary shrug of apology.

I might as well not exist.

I tipped my head at Vili. "I understand. I guess I'll take that escort after all. Don't wanna take a wrong turn."

"Great, great. Let's just get—" he gestured to one of the guys lingering near the dining area. "Jone! You mind helping Logan to his bure?"

Leaving Vili to escort Saylor? Oh hell no.

"Jone looks busy to me." I jerked my chin at the broom Jone clutched. "How about we all go together and drop Saylor off first?" My words might've been in the form of a question, but my tone definitely was not.

No way in hell was I leaving her to Vili and his leering

For the first time since we'd arrived, Saylor turned to me. She gave me a relieved look, and I nodded at her.

Our introduction might've ended awkwardly, but no way in hell did that mean I was going to hang her out to dry. Cleary, the woman had some heartache to work through. She didn't need me or Vili circling her when she was so vulnerable.

And then we were off to our bungalows with the promise of someone bringing our luggage to us later.

I waited at the top of the steps as Vili showed her around her treehouse bure—not present for the tour but still close enough to hear if she needed some help. But Vili was solicitous and stayed in his lane.

Then Saylor and her curves and wounded eyes were forgotten after we crossed the beach and climbed the stairs to my treehouse. This one might not have all the amenities as the other treehouse, but the deck was stellar.

I leaned against the railing and stared at the endless ocean as the sound of the gentle waves lapped against the sandy beach below, and that sense of peace I'd been chasing washed over me. Closing my eyes, I soaked it in.

Ten months, nineteen countries, and so much jet lag.

I hadn't been able to convince any of the guys to come with me. They thought I was nuts to immediately get on another plane and fly however many hours to get here. But this was something I just couldn't find anywhere else.

Peace.

"Would you like me to go through the amenities with you, sir?"

I jolted at Vili's voice. I'd forgotten he was here. Shaking my head, I answered, "No, I'm good, Vili." I reached into my pocket and pulled out my wallet.

Vili held up a hand. "You should include all gratuities in your final bill at checkout, sir."

I nodded as I opened my wallet and pulled out a mix of euros, Brazilian reais, and Canadian dollars. "But see, this isn't a gratuity." I folded the clutch of bills, grabbed Vili's hand, and pushed them into his hand. Stepping into his space, I dropped my tone into a menacing hiss as I stared directly into his eyes. "This is a promise that no one is to fuck with Saylor. Spread it around. Let everyone know she's off limits."

Vili visibly flinched then sprang back and batted at the bills spilling from his hands. "*Lo*, I…um, yes, sir. Enjoy your stay."

I didn't watch him flee.

I turned back to the view beyond the railing and soaked in all the peace I'd been missing for so long. It was everything.

After my luggage arrived, I changed into some board shorts and a tee and laid out on the lounger on my front deck. I could've reached for the book I'd been reading on the plane or my phone to check in to see what the guys were up to, but none of it sounded interesting.

I stared through the slats of the railing at the ocean beyond and thought about what had sent me running to Fiji in the first place. That restlessness I'd felt in all the guys toward the end of our tour. I mean, we all got sick of each other after a while, but something about this time felt different.

Heavier.

Gio had been hanging all over his new girl. Leif had been secretive and not around much. Ryker had been on the phone constantly with his mom and her doctors. Beau's new wife had been all over the greenrooms commanding everyone around her—including Beau.

And don't even get me started on the party scene. It'd been so intense the last few weeks, I had to retreat in defense of my sobriety. Even Beau's wife had snorted something in the greenroom right in front of me.

They were all either deep in their own business or crazy partying in a way I just couldn't anymore.

None of them had been interested in talking to me, let alone coming to Fiji to relax.

It just felt like everything was splintering.

Like maybe this was the beginning of the end of the Long Licks.

It was the kind of thing that in the past would make me reach for a drink or a hit of something to make it all go away and bring back the calm, but I was eight years sober, so that was out.

I'd talked it over with my sponsor, actor Caden Dawson, and he thought a solo trip was what I needed. Some time alone to decompress and just commune with nature. He was into all that chakra/crystal bullshit and more spiritual than me, but maybe he'd been onto something because this right here was pretty damn awesome.

We'd come here a year ago for Beau's wedding, and it'd been so awesome we'd stayed almost a month. Of course, for that trip we'd rented out the entire island, so being here with other guests was strange. There were appointed dinner times and no room service, which meant I was forced to head back to the main bungalow for dinner.

Most of the people here seemed to be couples on their honeymoon.

Which was…awkward.

Maybe I should've put more thought into my destination than I had.

Being the lone guy on an island of honeymooners was getting me more attention than I'd planned.

Until I saw Saylor sitting all alone on the edge of the dining room and the pitying looks she was getting from all the couples around her.

Talk about awkward. She was so uncomfortable, I could visibly see her tension as she tapped at her phone's screen.

Fuck that.

I jerked my chin at Jone at the entrance then crossed the room to Saylor's table, pulled out the empty chair opposite her, and sat. "Sorry I'm late."

She jerked in surprise and looked up from her phone. "What…?"

I tipped my head at the couple nearest us then asked, "Did you order already, baby girl?"

"Um, yeah." Her eyes flicked between the table and me before settling on me with more warmth than I'd seen before. "But I didn't know how long you'd be, so I didn't order anything for you."

"Sorry, baby. I'll do better." Lifting a hand at a nearby waitress in a floral top and skirt, I gestured to my empty end of the table.

She smiled at me then hustled back into the kitchen. A few seconds later, she returned with a place setting and wine glass. "*Bula,* Mr. Holt. Would you like wine like Ms. Tate or something else to drink?"

"No alcohol. Sparkling water, please."

"Yes, of course. I'm so sorry, I forgot. And for dinner tonight, you have a choice between a chicken tagine or a spicy tuna rice bowl. I believe Samu and some guests caught the tuna today."

"The tuna."

"*Vinaka.*" She bowed her head and left the table.

"So..." Saylor stared at me then shook her head like she couldn't believe I was sitting there. "This is awkward."

I tipped my head. "Awkward was what I walked in on here. Can't believe they don't have room service."

"Not true. You can get dessert delivered to your room." Saylor laughed.

I laughed with her, watching the way her eyes sparkled with life. Blue eyes had always been my weakness.

"Yeah, but considering I've only had airplane food for the last eighteen hours, I couldn't survive on chocolate alone. Although it has gotten me through the last few days."

I tipped my head. But before I could comment our waitress came back with my water. "Thanks."

She smiled and set my glass down. "Your meals will be out in just a few moments."

"Thanks."

Once she left, I turned back to Saylor. "So where are you from?"

She rolled her eyes. "Las Vegas. And I'm guessing from the way everyone welcomed you here, you're someone famous."

"You didn't look me up?"

She hitched a shoulder. That she had more important things on her mind was implied.

I mimicked her shrug. "I have a few fans."

She nodded but didn't press for more information. "Thank you for earlier. I didn't really think about traveling as a single woman. I haven't been single for...forever. High school really."

"You don't look like you're long in the tooth exactly." I smiled. "Be honest—how long ago was high school?"

"I'll have you know I just finished my bachelor's in education."

I muffled a groan. "So you're—what? Twenty-two?"

She nodded and raised her eyebrows as merriment danced in her eyes.

"Fuck me," I mumbled through my fingers as I rubbed my hands over my face. "I didn't think you were *that* young. I'm old enough to be your daddy."

She snickered. "I mean, I've never had a daddy kink, but if ever there was a guy made for it..."

I dropped my hands from my face and stared at her with wide eyes.

Her light blue eyes sparkled back at me and she tipped her head. "Oh, come on. You've never wanted to hear a girl call you daddy while you held her hair from behind while you...you know?"

I struggled for a second time to muffle my groan. I was uncomfortably hard in the middle of the dining room with her innocent eyes twinkling at me.

Maybe not that innocent...

Chapter 3

Saylor

I mean, I wasn't lying. I'd never had a daddy kink—but I was starting to see the appeal.

Malcolm was gorgeous. He had that whole scruffy surfer vibe down pat. His clearly toned body was beyond hot. And I'd always been a fan of a guy with a dimple. The combination had me flirting outrageously with this stranger.

Flirting that was clearly welcome, judging by the warmth in his dark blue eyes.

"Chicken tagine for the lady." A large bowl of stew-y chicken slid to a rest in front of me. "And a spicy tuna bowl for the gentleman. *Kana vinaka.* And we have a few choices for dessert later if you're interested." Our waitress melted into the background.

"And now I have meal envy." Malcolm nodded at my bowl.

"There's more than enough here. Feel free to help yourself."

He raised his eyebrows and gave me a smoldering look. "Noted."

My cheeks burned as I dug into my dinner. I hadn't meant *that.*

Or had I?

What had my bestie, Jayne, told me before I left? *'The best way to get over a guy is to get under another. Enjoy your trip.'* Complete with eyebrow wiggle.

I'd rolled my eyes at her, but now I was thinking her advice might just come in handy.

If I could ever find my courage to make a move.

But then again, maybe I wouldn't be the one making the move.

"Uh, how long are you staying on the island, Malcolm?" I asked before forking some of the tender chicken into my mouth.

He winced. "Call me Mal. Please."

I nodded.

"I think my booking is for two weeks. I need to doublecheck though. Last time I stayed here, I came with a group, and we had the run of the place. The whole couple-y vibe took me by surprise."

I bit my lip and dragged my fork through the sauce in my bowl. "I'm assuming from your solo attendance here and that little scene on the plane that you're single?"

He tipped his head. "No, I'm in a relationship. With myself. It's going really great."

I laughed. "I'll have to remember that one."

"But yes, I'm single." He shrugged. "Have been for a long time. By choice, of course."

"Clearly." My eyes widened as I realized how transparent I was being.

But Mal just smiled and then took a drink from his water glass.

And I might've watched him a beat longer than was socially acceptable.

Yeah, definitely going to have to learn some new social skills.

Clearing my throat, I picked up my fork and pretended to be interested in my meal when really I was just watching Mal out of the corner of my eye.

"So you're not going to even ask?" Mal asked me as he stabbed at his bowl with his chopsticks, leaving the conventional utensils on the table.

I watched, impressed, as he deftly carried rice and tuna to his mouth. His luscious lips parted and he made a growl-humming sound that had me clenching my thighs together.

"Ask what?" I murmured, spellbound and so freaking turned on. I couldn't remember the last time I'd felt this way with my ex, if ever. He'd been more of a lights off and under the covers kinda guy. Something told me Mal wasn't about that. He probably preferred an audience.

I shivered at the thought.

He chewed and swallowed before reaching for his water glass. "About what I do. You're not curious?"

I lifted a shoulder. "We can talk about it if you want."

"No." He shook his head. "I mean, I don't want to. It's why I'm here. To get away from that. From everything, really."

His babbling was endearing. I smiled at him.

He shrugged. "I'm just surprised. Most girls want to know what's up. Exploit it if they can. Get what they want from me—sex, clout, money." He shrugged again, staring down at his tuna bowl. "Can't remember the last time someone didn't look at me and mentally catalogue what I was worth."

"Well, that's sad."

He snorted in agreement and tipped his head. "It's the sad truth."

"If it's a contest—I can see your sad story and raise you an even sadder one. I guarantee you, I'll win by a mile." I sighed and traced my fork through my bowl. Just thinking about the whole scene I fled back home made my stomach knot. "But like you, I'm here trying to get away from everything."

"It's good to leave the heaviness of life behind and just be in the moment, huh?"

I nodded. "You have no idea."

"No, you have no idea, but thank you. I like you, Saylor Tate."

"Thanks." I smiled back at him. "I like you, Mal Whatever-Your-Last-Name-Is-Again."

He chuckled lightly then picked up his chopsticks and dug into his tuna bowl.

The earlier sexual tension fell away, and I felt a companionable warmth just being in Mal's company. It was hard to be annoyed at that.

Maybe I'd get a handle on this whole being single thing.

Eventually.

Once we'd stuffed ourselves with tuna, chicken, and a delicious chocolate cake, we stumbled across the dark beach, lit only by torches lining the path.

"Thank you for rescuing me back there." I jerked a thumb over my shoulder at the dining space we'd just left. "This whole being single thing is going to take some getting used to."

Mal nodded. "I think it's important to be okay with yourself before you try being part of a couple."

I groaned. "I'm not nearly drunk enough to get philosophical tonight."

"Noted." Mal laughed lightly. "Although if that was an invitation to have a drink back at your place, I should tell you that I'm sober."

"Really?"

"Yup. Going on eight years now."

"Wow. Congrats. That's a feat. You should be proud of yourself."

"Thanks."

"Is this a bad time to point out that eight years ago I was fourteen?"

Mal groaned and clutched at his chest. "You're killing me here, baby girl."

I snickered. Looking up at him, I was relieved to see that he was smiling back at me. I didn't want him to think the age difference was a deterrent in any way.

"First rule of dating an older man: do not continually point out what an old fart he is."

"I can safely say that I would never use those words to describe you." We stopped at the staircase leading up to my treehouse.

The words asking him to come up for a drink were on the tip of my tongue, but I bit them back because—one, he was sober so it was a horrible question, and two, despite my bravado, I wasn't ready for that just yet.

But hopefully I would be before the end of our two-week stay.

"Thanks again for dinner." I climbed the first step then turned back to face him. "How about I buy dinner tomorrow night?"

The resort was all-inclusive, but that wasn't the point.

"Only if you let me buy breakfast tomorrow morning." Mal tipped his head.

My lips quirked as I fought to hide my smile. "Sounds like a plan. Us silly singles have to stick together at this couple-y resort."

Mal closed the distance between us and stared straight into my eyes despite me standing one step up. "I plan on sticking as close as you'll let me, baby girl. Sleep tight."

I swayed toward him, but he sighed and took a step backward. He waited there a beat, still staring into my eyes. I held my breath at their smoldering promise. He inclined his head again and nodded at the stairs behind me, clearly waiting for me to go up.

I released a shuddering breath, turned, and climbed, aware of his eyes on my rear the whole way up.

No pressure.

My mind was a tangle of confusion as I got ready for bed—alone. All the new feelings Mal had brought out in me warred with my anger about my ex. I was still pissed at him, and as I took my makeup off, the vivid, yellowish-green bruise on my cheek was a stark reminder of why.

But underlying it all was a new sense of hope.

* * *

"You tell your fiancé, Trent Hale, that we're serious." His thick, accented words puffed so close to my face I could smell the nicotine on his breath as he bent next to me. "He doesn't want me showing up at his wedding Saturday with extra guests. Screwing over the Aslanov Bratva is a serious fucking mistake. One his loved ones will pay in blood and pain."

His hand threaded through my hair and yanked until I fell to my knees.

A pained whimper left me, and then everything froze as I felt something large, cold, and metallic press into my uninjured cheek.

I woke up with a muffled scream.

Because this time the gun went off.

Only I wasn't in my apartment building's garage.

Sunny skies highlighted the grass cloth wallpaper I spied through the wispy mosquito netting. The gentle sound of waves lapping at the beach below me came from the open window on my right.

It was so surreal. Just all quiet and peaceful.

So very different from my dream.

I slumped into my soft mattress with a groan.

And then my phone alerted with a new text message, piercing the calm.

Mom: *I can't believe you just left. It's so irresponsible.*

I sighed. I couldn't believe she was taking *his* side in this whole thing.

Actually, I could totally believe it.

Groaning, I staggered out of bed and padded to the bathroom to take care of business. I couldn't even look at myself in the mirror as I washed my hands and brushed my teeth.

Shame was a weird beast. I hadn't done anything to be ashamed of. But this cloud had hovered over me since I'd found out what Trent had been up to. When the police showed up, and I answered the door holding an icepack to my face. When I had to tell my parents I was canceling the wedding.

When I showed up here alone.

I sighed.

I really just wanted to hole up in my bed and mope, but the siren song of coffee called for me, and I didn't know how to operate the fancy espresso machine in my room. And really, I was too damn exhausted to try.

Throwing my hair into a messy bun, I pulled on some shorts and a tee. Pausing in my doorway, I tried to shake off the gloom of my mom's text and that fucking memory that continued to haunt me.

This was supposed to be a fun escape.

Leave that shit behind, Saylor.

I forced a skip to my step as I closed the door and headed for the stairs

"What the fuck happened to your face!" The words came from ten feet away, at the bottom of my treehouse stairs.

I froze, teetering about six steps from the bottom.

Shit. I forgot my concealer.

And that cloud of shame came roaring back.

Throwing a hand up to cover my cheek, I pivoted and tried to run back upstairs, but Mal's hand on my arm stopped me.

Without a thought, I cowered away from him, clutching my face in my free hand. "Don't!"

The hand on my arm disappeared, and a muffled curse came from behind me.

"I'm not going to hurt you, Saylor. I'm sorry I scared you."

My shoulders hunched up to my ears as I realized what I'd done—what I'd revealed.

Shaking my head mutely, I ran back up the stairs and slammed the door behind me. I flipped the two locks and dropped down onto my butt, covering my face with my hands.

And I cried.

It hurt. I hated that this was what I'd turned into. That I let him and that shitty situation scar me.

But it did.

And it hurt so much.

I should be stronger. I should be smarter than this.

But I wasn't.

And I was starting to think I might never be.

Once my tears slowed, I headed for the bathroom to do damage control.

It was probably twenty minutes later when I left my treehouse a second time, but it felt like an eon, judging by my grumbling stomach.

I didn't expect to see him sitting on my bottom step, waiting for me.

I paused in my open door and seriously contemplated calling the front desk and begging them to send me food.

Or sending someone to eject Mal.

But I didn't. I couldn't.

Sighing heavily, I pulled the door closed behind me and headed down the stairs.

Mal must've heard my approach as he stood up and turned to watch my progression. His eyes danced over my now concealed cheek before surveying the rest of my body—no doubt looking for more bruises.

Oh god. He'd probably come up with a logical assumption of why I had a bruised cheek.

A new sense of shame crawled down my spine.

I avoided his eyes and didn't even pause. I shouldered my way past him and headed for the beach path.

"Seriously, Saylor? You're not going to say anything to me?"

"It's none of your business." I pulled sunglasses out of my thin shoulder bag and slid them onto my face.

But Mal didn't get the hint. He fell into step with me on my right. "Disagree. Are you okay? Does… I mean, it looks like it hurt like a son of a bitch. Are you safe? When you go home, I mean?"

Remembering the pile of my belongings in Paige's spare room, my stomach twisted over how much was still up in the air. Was canceling the wedding and moving out enough for the Bratva to forget me? Because I wasn't ever going back. Threaten my life once…

I sighed. "One dinner together does not grant you access to everything in my life. And forget dinner tonight. I'm busy."

He snorted but didn't reply as we continued to walk down the combed path to the main hut.

And I really tried not to notice how good he smelled or how the breeze made his longish hair fan out. Or how some of his hair got caught in his stubble.

Gah. Why was that so attractive?

Asshole.

All men were assholes. Maybe I should take a vow and join a convent or something. Did they take non-Catholic women? And what was their stance on vibrators?

I snorted at the thought.

My cold shoulder routine continued as we entered the dining area. Since no one was at the little podium, I headed straight for the coffee urns and filled a mug.

"Caffeine freak, huh?" Mal rumbled at my side. "You must love those machines in our rooms."

"Don't know how to work it," I replied before I remembered that I was ignoring him.

Mal smirked. "I can always swing by and show you."

Despite how much I wanted to use that espresso machine, I went back to ignoring him. And I headed for the table ladened with fruit, pastries, and five different cereal options. I grabbed a plate and filled it with the most luscious looking fruit and a croissant loaded with chocolate.

No diet here anymore. I was going to eat what *I* wanted and enjoy this trip.

I carried my burden to an empty table and sat down.

Mal, of course, sat in the chair opposite me. Unlike me, he only had a glass of water and a tea, judging from the teabag still visibly floating inside.

Yeah, I wouldn't be taking any espresso machine lessons from the guy drinking tea. Hard pass.

I wanted to tell him to sit elsewhere, but that would mean talking to him. I also wanted to ask why he wasn't eating anything, but see above.

Jone stopped next to our table. "You still eating your egg white omelet with mushrooms and cheese?"

I looked at him in confusion before realizing he was talking to Mal.

"Yes, that sounds amazing. Can I get some sourdough toast with it?"

"Sure thing." Jone turned to me. "Can I interest you with anything from the kitchen? We'll cook eggs to order or pancakes or French toast. I can check what today's quiche is for you."

I shook my head mutely. I hadn't realized the spread wasn't all that was on offer. No way would I be able to eat all this and eggs or whatever. Tomorrow I'd plan better. "No, thank you."

Mal cleared his throat. "How about you add on an order of crispy bacon?"

Jone hesitated then nodded before leaving us alone at the table.

I focused on my plate and continued with my silent treatment. While the croissant was amazing, the company was awkward. Not that I was going to do anything about it.

Mal sighed heavily, and I knew without looking up that he was staring at me. I could feel the weight of his gaze, and it made me so uncomfortable. I wasn't ready to share what had happened. I didn't want to *think* about it, so I definitely didn't want to talk about it.

Mal sighed again. "Just…please tell me that you're not going back to that situation. I won't ask any questions, just…I really need to know that you'll be safe when you go home."

"In the poetic words of Taylor Swift, we are never ever, ever getting back together." I finally looked up to show Mal just how serious I was about that statement.

He smiled. "So you're a Swiftie?"

"Is this where you sneer at my taste in music?" I viciously stabbed at a piece of honeydew melon with my fork.

"Nah, she's awesome. I admire someone who lives their life out loud and in the open. Not to mention she's a fucking billionaire. Anyone who can take the shitty hand she was dealt by her label and turn it into the empire she's built has my respect. Plus, I really love '*Love Story*.'"

I rolled my eyes. Like hell did this guy love her gooey love song. "Yeah, sure."

"I do." He then proceeded to recite the lyrics to the first verse in a smooth, rich baritone.

I blinked. "That's…you sound amazing. And I totally take it back. You're clearly a Swiftie too."

"Thank you." He sat back with a genuine smile. "I did miss seeing her last tour, though. Still heartbroken over it, actually."

"I saw her in Vegas." I gloated.

He winced then clutched at his chest in feigned pain. "Please tell me you at least got a shirt."

I laughed and nodded.

And the rest of breakfast was just easy. We talked and laughed about our favorite artists and concerts. It was fun. Comfortable. Peaceful.

And exactly what I needed.

Chapter 4

Mal

I craved distraction in the same way I craved alcohol.

I needed something—anything—to occupy my mind and keep me from obsessing about my bleak future. And Saylor's bruise was the thing my addict brain latched onto. I knew, *I knew,* I should call my sponsor to keep me from spiraling. But that would mean admitting that I was out of control.

And I wasn't. Not really.

I hadn't felt the need for a drink or a hit since we'd left the tour behind.

And I'd turned down Samu's invitation to meet up and drink cava. Not that it was alcohol, but it could be a trigger, with its numbing affects and social drinking aspect.

I wasn't going to relapse. I was just a nosy asshole.

Or at least, that was what I told myself.

And it was killing me that Saylor wasn't spilling about her situation. Was she safe? Would that asshole come for her?

I hated seeing women abused. It brought back long buried childhood trauma I thought I was over. But apparently not.

Still, I knew better than to bring it up to Saylor again. She wasn't gonna budge.

So if I couldn't exhaust my mind, maybe exhausting my body would help.

As Saylor and I left the dining hut, I turned to her with what I hoped was a charming smile. "How about we grab a kayak and check out the island from the water?"

She bit her bottom lip as her eyes danced between me and the calm water behind me. "I've never done it before. Is it hard?"

"Nah, you just gotta be smart about it. Take the current into consideration and try not to brain your partner with your oar. Piece of cake."

"Okay." She didn't sound sure, but she followed me to the equipment desk, and we checked out a kayak, life vests, and oars. Samu helped me carry it down to the beach and gave us the usual safety spiel.

Saylor's eyes grew wider the longer he talked.

I cleared my throat, and when Samu looked my way, I shook my head slightly.

His speech ended abruptly. "Yeah. So that's it. Just wear your life vests at all times, and have fun. And don't forget to sign up for some fishing later, Mal. I gotta get back on the water. She's calling my name."

"Sure thing, Samu. Thanks."

He left with a wave and once he was a safe distance away, Saylor turned to me with a weird expression. "Who is she?"

"What?" I looked up from buckling my life vest.

"He said: 'She's calling my name.' Who's she?"

"Ah, *waitui* [wye-too-ee]." I reached toward her and finished clipping the buckles on her vest.

Her eyes widened even more.

"You ever see *Moana*?"

She nodded.

"Kinda like that. Samu has a deep cultural connection with the water." I stepped back and picked up an oar. "You want front or back?"

She blinked a few times then shook her head. "Uh, whichever you don't want."

"I should probably take back, so we get where we wanna go."

"Okay."

After a shaky start, we pushed off from the beach, and before long were stroking against the current but parallel to the beach. I'd learned from my last time that you didn't want to go the other way. Nothing was worse than trying to row against the current once you were already gassed.

Saylor was quiet at first. She paddled smoothly with me, careful not to collide oars. But since I was mostly steering now, there was little danger of tangling.

Suddenly she laughed.

I smiled at the sound. "What's so funny?"

She shrugged. "I just never would've labeled you a Disney fan, that's all."

"I feel like I should be insulted."

"Well, just with the whole man-bun, tattoos, and lithe muscles, I would've pegged you as anti-corporation, anti-billionaires, and maybe a yoga enthusiast."

I cracked up. Pulling my oar out of the water because I didn't want to lose it, I bent over in my seat and laughed so hard tears burned my eyes. "Shit, that's funny. Me, a yogi." I laughed some more as I put my oar back in the water to steer. "I can't wait to tell Gio."

And then I sobered. Gio hadn't been taking my calls or replying to my texts since we got off tour. He'd gone underground. I really hoped he hadn't relapsed. Maybe he and his girl had gone to Vegas and were living it up like he'd been talking about weeks ago.

Just without me.

"Gio? Is that a friend?"

"Only way I'll answer that is if you answer a question from me. Tit for tat."

Saylor's whole body went rigid in front of me. It didn't take a genius to get that she wasn't keen on the idea.

I sighed. "And like for like. So if you wanna know who Gio is, I'll ask who your best friend is. I won't take it any deeper than you go. Deal?"

She studied the handle of her oar for a long minute before finally nodding. "Sure."

"Gio is...complicated. He's a friend. A coworker. A pain in my ass. But I guess I'll settle on friend. We've known each other since middle school. He's also the best drummer I've ever seen."

The tension leaked out of her shoulders the longer I talked until finally she put her oar back into the water. "He's in a band?"

"Yeah... Yeah, he is. Uh, who's your best friend?" That was a smooth transition.

"Paige. But unlike you two, I've known her since grade school. We grew up on the same street. Graduated high school together. Went to UNLV together. Only she went for hospitality, so she's working at Oasis at their arena. She organizes the suites and 'gladhands the uber rich assholes who need help wiping their behinds.' That's a direct quote, by the way."

"Sounds like a fun job," I said sardonically.

Saylor scoffed. "Paige has a fancy title, but that's essentially the job. Most days it sounds like a huge headache." She stroked her oar through the water a few times. "Some days I wonder if I should've gone into hospitality too."

"What did you go to school for again?"

"Elementary education. I still have to pass a test, but then I'll be certified as a teacher. I just finished my student teaching session in a third-grade classroom." She sighed. "I mean, I like the kids, but the administration and some of the parents make the job not so fun. And don't even get me started with cell phones in the classroom."

"Hence the butt-wiping envy?"

She laughed. "Exactly. I could be wiping bigwigs' butts instead of runny kids' noses."

"Sounds messy either way."

"Truth." She sighed deeply. The sound was sad and contemplative. "I really wanted to design clothes. But my parents refused to help me with college if that was going to be my major. I got so many lectures from my mom about picking something that had a career at the end of the degree. She'd tell me: 'clothing design is a pipe dream.' Or: 'no one makes money as a designer.' I swear she was more thrilled than I was when Trent proposed. She wanted me to get my MRS and didn't care about my BA at all."

That was more truth than I'd expected from her today. But before I could even absorb it, she chattered on.

"Uh, that was a lot of word vomit. It's your turn. So what's your super-secret job you won't tell me about?"

"Um, that wasn't my question. I asked what did you go to college for. And I didn't go to school, so that's my answer."

"Oh, come on. I told you all about my bestie, my mom's disappointment in me, my dream job, and what my job actually is. You gotta give me more than 'I didn't go to college.' That's a cop out."

I didn't want everything to change between us. But I was more than aware that the longer I waited to tell, the more wounded she'd feel that I kept it from her.

I didn't know what the best move to make here was.

I wanted to spend more time with Saylor.

But I didn't want to lie to her either.

And rigorous truth-telling was a pillar of my sobriety.

Shit.

I put my oar back in the water and stroked determinedly, keeping my eyes on the shoreline and away from her body in front of me. "I'm the lead guitarist for the Long Licks. Gio is our drummer. We just finished a two-year international tour and are on break for a few months. But I'm pretty sure our lead singer, Leif, is going to screw us and go solo. We only have one album left on our contract, which will probably be a 'Best of' album if Leif goes solo. So this might be the end of the Long Licks."

That was more truth than I'd faced in a long time. I hadn't even dared to say that last part out loud until now.

And judging from the stillness in the front half of the kayak, my answer had hit with all the subtlety of a nuclear bomb.

Shit.

Finally, after the longest moment of my life Saylor asked, "And you never went to college for that, huh?"

I smiled and went back to stroking my oar in the water. "Nope."

"Huh, I guess my mom was wrong. College doesn't always spell success."

My smile grew into a grin.

We went back to our banter so smoothly I don't know why I ever worried about her reaction.

"Do you use a cleaning service back home?" I asked. "Or are you a control freak?"

"That's a not-so-subtle change of topic." She tipped her head, and I would've given anything to see her expression about now. Then she laughed softly and I relaxed. "Or do you have a secret Cinderella kink, and this is your way of telling me?"

I laughed with her. "Nah, I just tried to hire one for my mom while I was on tour, and she yelled at me for a solid ten minutes, going on about wasting my money and how keeping a woman's home is a point of pride. I don't know. I was wondering if it's a generational thing, or if my mom is just weird."

"I guess it's one of those things that sounds amazing but is kinda weird in practice for some people. And I might be one of those people. My ex used a service which kinda freaked me out when I moved in with him. I ran around and hid my underwear before they came over every time." She made this cute sounding snort. "Like they cared what my panties look like."

I was a total dog because I was wondering what her panties looked like. Was she a boy shorts girl? A thong wearer? Maybe hipsters?

"What about you?" she asked, jolting me out of my mini-fantasy. "You have to have a cleaning service for your big mansion in California, right?"

I hitched a shoulder and then drug my paddle through the clear water. "I lock up my closet and my office on days that they're scheduled. Honestly, I'd lock my whole bedroom suite, but then I'd have to clean my bathroom, and that's not happening." I smiled at her cute snort again. "I guess like you, I like my privacy, and maybe I have a hard time trusting people too."

"Huh."

"And I never thought about it from that perspective before. So thank you."

Saylor nodded and didn't say anything after that, but I could tell by the tilt of her head, she was taking what I said in.

I smoothly turned our kayak in the water and let the current carry us most of the way back to the main beach where we'd started. Once we beached, I hopped out and went to help Saylor, but she was already stepping out on her own. "That was fun. Thanks for talking me into it."

"Thanks for being a good sport. I love being on the water, not as much as Samu, but still."

The smile slipped off her face. "I guess I get now why you laughed about being anti-billionaire."

"I'm not a billionaire. I'm nowhere near billionaire status."

She didn't look like she believed me.

I gestured to the beach around us. "Billionaires own their own beaches, hell they own their own airplanes. They don't accidentally book a vacation at a couples resort."

Her shoulders dropped away from her ears. "You got me there. I mean, I know you didn't fly private, since you tried to seduce me into joining the mile high club."

I laughed, totally unashamed now. "In my defense, women throw themselves at me on a regular basis. I thought you recognized me and were interested. You were giving me all these signals."

"I was going to pee and made eye contact with you." She scoffed. "How was that a signal?"

I gestured helplessly. "I was horny and you're hot."

She rolled her eyes and turned to leave.

"Again, in my defense, I'm going through a dry spell, and I was vulnerable because I'm pretty sure this is the end of my whole career."

She turned back to me and narrowed her eyes. "Seriously? You just told me you just ended a two-year international tour. What's your idea of a dry spell? One day?"

"More like eleven months."

Her eyes widened. "*Months?* You don't mean days?"

I shook my head.

"But you're...you. Why would you... I don't get it."

It was my turn to hunch my shoulders. "Shit, this is more truth telling than I was planning on doing today." I rubbed a hand over my face. "You know how I've been sober for eight years? Some parts of my lifestyle are triggering, so I needed to make some sacrifices to maintain my sobriety. It kinda drove a wedge between me and most of the guys on this last tour. Our bassist, Beau, was off with his bride most of the time, so all the single guys would hang out together, but I didn't—I couldn't. By the end of the tour, Leif wasn't talking to me, Gio was avoiding me like *I* was the problem, and Ryker wasn't much better. Shit was awkward. Welcome to life as an addict."

She nodded, but I could tell that she didn't really understand it. That she couldn't relate.

I sighed. Clearly all this truth telling was a mistake. "Come on. Let's go return our gear."

She stepped around me and moved to grab one of the struts on the kayak.

"Ah, they'll grab the kayak. We've just got to return the oars and vests."

She nodded again then turned and head for the main building, leaving me to follow and watch her swinging little ass in those tiny shorts.

Fuck.

Fuck!

It felt like I screwed everything up. She wasn't ready to hear about my job. Or my insane life. And really wasn't ready to face what life with an addict meant.

Not that we were planning a life together.

This was just some vacation fun. Although I did travel to Vegas a lot…

Jone was manning the desk now and took our vests and oars with little patter. He must've read our body language and knew not to bother us.

We walked side by side away from the equipment rental hut toward the general direction of our treehouses.

Finally, I cleared my throat roughly. "You got any plans for the day?"

She huffed. "I'm gonna put on a swimsuit, avoid my phone, and probably read by my private pool. Get some sun. Maybe take a nap."

"Sounds like fun." I waited a beat but no invite to join her came.

"Um, what are you gonna do today?"

That was only a polite social return. There had been zero interest in her tone.

I definitely screwed this up. "Probably the same minus the pool, since I don't have one. Maybe I'll check out my outdoor shower instead."

Her breath hitched, and I watched her out of the corner of my eye as her cheeks flushed.

Maybe all wasn't lost after all.

"Maybe I'll break out my guitar and work on some songs and my fingering. Gotta keep the digits nimble." I wiggled my fingers in front of me.

She made a whimpering sound that she tried to cover with a cough.

I grinned.

"Uh, yeah. That sounds like a fun day. This is me." The *thank god* was clear in her tone, and then it was my turn to muffle my reaction as I literally wiped my smile off my face.

"We still on for dinner?"

Her gaze slid to the side before she nodded. "Of course."

"Great. And just warning, I plan to dress for dinner tonight, so be prepared to be wowed."

"Isn't that my line?" She gave me a funny look.

I shook my head. "I'm wowed every time I see you, baby girl. I just want you to know that I'm here and willing to put in the work. See you at six."

Chapter 5

Saylor

I debated way too long over what I was going to wear tonight. Concealer was a given. I'd learned that lesson. But dresses? I'd brought three of my own creations, and two of them felt too casual given Mal's warning.

And that look he'd given me when he'd called me baby girl?

I swooned just remembering.

But this blood-red dress with the high neck, bare arms, and high thigh slit just felt… Obvious?

Mal wasn't the only one in the middle of a dry spell.

Hopefully nearing the end.

I had matching strappy sandals to wear with the dress, and I just hoped I didn't twist my ankles walking down the stairs before the night even began.

I could do this.

I wanted to do this.

Trent was done screwing up my life.

Making me feel bad about my decisions.

I was moving on.

The best way to get over a man was to get under a new one, after all.

And Mal seemed oh so very willing to me.

I could do this.

It was my mantra as I left my treehouse and walked down the stairs. I really tried not to stumble when I caught sight of Mal waiting for me at the bottom step.

"I was just coming up to get you."

My smile felt wobbly. "I'm starving. Plus, I doubt you need more cardio after our morning."

Really it was hard to walk down the remaining stairs without tripping as I took in all that was him.

His idea of dressing up was a long-sleeved black button-up shirt and black pants. But he'd done that thing guys did where they rolled their sleeves back to their elbows and the tattoos peeping out from his rolled sleeves and on his neck were delicious. All tough guy hard warring with that gentle look in his eyes.

I was spellbound.

When I reached the bottom step, I just stood there and stared.

But that was okay, because Mal was staring back at me.

"Wow," he finally murmured. "You look amazing."

"Thanks." I looked down at my hem and brushed some imaginary lint off my dress. "Um, you do too. Look nice, I mean." Awesome. *So smooth, Saylor.*

He chuckled lightly. "You make me feel underdressed. I should've tried harder."

"No!" The word shot out overly loud and obvious. "I meant it. You look nice too. God, I'm so awkward. I'm sorry, it's just been a minute since I've done this." I gestured between us.

Mal grinned. "Apparently you weren't listening earlier. It's been a minute for me too. Longer than, actually. Meaningless hookups aren't the same as what we're doing here."

"It's not?"

"Of course not. I'm trying to show you how much I'm trying here. And apparently doing a shit job of it."

I swayed toward him unconsciously. I wanted him to know I felt that too, but I didn't know how. Lord knew I couldn't actually say it.

So I decided to show him.

Closing the small distance between us, I reached up and kissed him. And in less than a heartbeat, Mal was kissing me back.

His lips moved over mine with a mastery I'd never felt before. My arms twined around his shoulders, and his big paws clutched the small amount of fabric on the back of my dress. In three seconds, he had me trying to climb him like a contestant in a lumberjack competition. I'd never felt so aroused so quickly. I just needed a little friction, and I could totally get off right now.

Mal broke our kiss with a harsh groan. "Fuck me, baby. You've got me harder than I've ever been. It's gonna be embarrassing here in a minute. Give me a second."

I frowned, confused why he'd stopped. But when he stepped away from me and the huge bulge in the front of his pants stood out, I got what he meant.

I couldn't help it—I laughed. I just felt so powerful and in control of my life for the first time in so long.

I was punch drunk happy.

"Yeah, laugh it up," Mal grumbled. "It'll be hella funny if I walk into the dining room with a visible wet spot on the front of my pants."

Screw dinner. We should just go up to my treehouse. I was just opening my mouth to say as much when my stomach let out a loud rumble. Clutching it in embarrassment, my shoulders hunched a little. "Sorry. It's been a minute since we ate."

Mal blinked a few times. "Unless you have a mouse in your pocket, I'm assuming we means me and you?"

I nodded.

"You haven't eaten since breakfast?"

I shook my head.

"You didn't go down for lunch?" His voice rose.

"I fell asleep by my pool. And by the time I woke up, lunch was over. I raided my mini-bar, but Tim Tams can only do so much."

"Fuck. Those don't even have nuts in them." He grabbed my hand and pulled me in the direction of the dining hall. "You need protein to fill you up. Nuts. Meat. Lentils. Soy. Tim Tams are just calories."

"Sweet, delicious calories. But thank you for the nutrition lecture, *Daddy*."

He groaned and muttered under his breath something about, "trying to kill me." Then he coughed and said louder, "Let's get some food in you before you fall over."

"Okay." I followed his lead and enjoyed the feeling of him being all grrr and worrying about me. "But for the record, it was the sight of you like that that made me unsteady on these sandals, not lack of nutrition."

"Ditto, baby girl. Ditto."

Anticipation sang through my bloodstream. I had a feeling this was going to be the quickest meal of my life. I had more important things to do.

Mostly him.

But apparently he didn't get that memo.

He chatted with our server over the two fish options, drawing it out until my stomach rumbled again.

"Wahoo. I'll have the wahoo," Mal finally answered.

"*Vinaka*." She bowed her head and left the table.

All around us couples talked softly over candlelit tables as the bamboo ceiling fans above us twirled, cooling the open aired hut. Despite the humidity and the lack of air conditioning, I hadn't felt overly hot at all during my stay.

Until I looked across the table at the heated stare Mal was giving me.

"Any chance we can get dessert to go?" I asked innocently.

Mal closed his eyes briefly and muttered a curse. "You gotta tone it down a little, baby girl. I'm trying to keep it PG considering the audience we have here."

My eyes flicked to the table next to us where the couple were sitting next to each other and alternating between kissing and feeding each other bites. It was sickly sweet.

I felt a distant pang as I realized but for that bookie, that would've been me and Trent.

Was this too soon?

Was I making a mistake?

No. Trent was an asshole, and I was better off without him.

I looked back at Mal and his head was tilted, his eyes narrowed as he stared back at me. It felt like he knew exactly what was going on in my head.

After a shuddery breath, I blinked innocently. "We wouldn't be the only ones acting inappropriately."

He regarded me quietly for a moment then shook his head. "I hope they have a dentist on the island because all this is so sugary sweet I'm liable to get a cavity."

I rolled my eyes at his weak joke. And then our server returned to the table with our dinner, saving me from having to come up with a reply.

Once she left, I leaned over the table and asked, "So what's the wildest thing you've ever done on tour?"

Mal had been mid drink and he choked. Sputtering water shot across the table before he bent over the side of the table with huge hacking coughs.

"Oh my god. Are you okay?" I asked as his face turned red.

Everyone in the room turned to watch him cough.

"Is he choking?"

"Does he need to be Heimliched?"

"I volunteer as tribute!"

I glared at the overeager blonde giggling into her wine glass.

Mal raised his hand. "Sorry. Just went down the wrong tube." He coughed a few times. "I'm fine. *Really*."

A few servers came over to check on him, and he waved them off with a charismatic smile. After a few more murmurs and long glances, everyone returned to their dinners.

"Um, sorry about that." I bit my lip as he wiped his face with his cloth napkin.

"No, I am. Didn't mean to give you a shower." He dipped his head charmingly. "Just really wasn't expecting that from you."

I picked up my fork and twirled it in my pasta. "Does that mean some things in your life are off limits too?"

"You want to go tit for tat again?"

I snorted, took a bite, then gestured between us with my fork as I chewed and swallowed. "This is the wildest thing I've ever done, and I haven't even done you yet."

His eyes twinkled. "You have some wild stuff planned?"

"I mean, I hope? If you're game, that is."

"Definitely." His eyes burned with sexual promise.

My heart pounded in my ears. Having all of Mal's energy directed my way was almost overwhelming. I shifted on my chair as I felt an answering throb between my legs.

Was I ready for Mal's idea of wild?

Could I keep up with him?

And then my earlier doubts returned.

Was this too soon?

Was I making a mistake?

"I can hear the overthinking from here. We haven't done anything. We don't have to do anything. This can move as fast or as slow as you want. We're both here for ten more days, right?"

I took another bite of my dinner, despite my churning stomach. "Um, so what do you want to talk about?"

"I'm guessing that's a no to the tit for tat then?"

I shrugged. "I mean, to be fair, I did answer the question. You, however, did not."

"No you didn't. Your answer can't be nothing. You've done things. You've had sex." He blinked before dropping his tone to ask quietly, "You have had sex, right?"

I rolled my eyes. "Yes. Sorry to burst your bubble, but I am not a virgin."

"Right. No. That's good. I mean, not that it matters. Purity is a social construct. I just wanted to make sure. It's just... What were we talking about?"

I snickered. "About how I haven't done anything wild."

"Right. I still maintain that 'nothing' isn't an acceptable answer. One person's tame is another's wild. This isn't a contest."

"Okay." I took another bite of my pasta and a thought swirled in my head so devious, I couldn't not do it. "How about we play a game?"

"Oh, now you're talking my speed." He grinned back at me before taking a bite of his fish. "I'm in."

"No questions? You're just in?"

"You're being all cute and flirty and confident. Of course I'm in."

"Great. So you know the rules of never have I ever, right?"

He paused, his fork held in midair. He blinked at me a few times then lowered his fork to his plate. "This feels like a trap."

I rolled my eyes. "It's just a game."

"But I'm sober. So I'm not going to drink."

"You can drink water. Think of it as a reverse tit for tat. We're just getting to know each other."

"It still feels like a trap."

"Hey, we don't have to play if you're afraid. It's fine."

He huffed. "I know what fine really means." He huffed again. "Fine, let's play."

I snickered. "That wasn't telling at all."

He laughed too, and the look in his eyes made the butterflies in my stomach come out in full force.

I rolled my eyes and felt so giddy. I couldn't think. "You go first."

"Fine. Never have I ever…seen my best friend naked."

I tipped my head then picked up my water and took a sip.

So did he.

"You're supposed to say things you haven't done." I pointed out, laughing.

He shrugged. "That's not exactly easy to do."

"Right." Maybe this wasn't the best idea. But still, there were things I wanted to know. "Never have I ever had a threesome…"

He took a sip.

"…with my best friend."

He kept drinking.

My eyes widened. "Really?"

He shrugged. "It was a long time ago. Back when we were first touring. Before we even were a name. And technically that was two questions, so I get the same."

"It's not my fault if you drank too soon. I wasn't done asking my question."

"Sure, sure." He laughed. "Never have I ever…thought about someone else during sex."

I took a sip.

So did he.

I laughed. "Never have I ever…cheated on my significant other."

I fully expected him to drink. I mean, he was a rock star—god really. They weren't faithful.

Right?

Mal lifted his eyebrows and set his glass down.

I boggled. "Seriously? I said significant other. So not just wives—"

"Technically there's only been one of those. Well, maybe one and a half, but that's a whole different story."

I blinked a few times as I wondered how someone had half a wife, but he went on.

"I'm not a cheater. Girlfriends, wives, whatever. Once I commit, that's it. I keep it zipped. I'm a faithful guy."

"I…didn't expect you to say that."

Mal shrugged. "It's not really newsworthy. Despite what some people want you to think, it's not that hard to keep it in your pants, really."

"Really?" I repeated. "When you have all those women and groupies just throwing themselves at you?"

"Sure they're hot, but at the end of the day they're not the person I want—the person I care about. Some things are more important than getting off. And honestly, sex like that isn't much different than masturbating at the end of the day—it's all soulless and empty."

"Huh." I hadn't expected him to be so open and surprisingly honest.

It was nice.

And so freaking hot.

He lifted an eyebrow and then his water glass. "Never have I ever read a smutty romance book."

I picked up my glass and drank.

"I knew it!" Mal crowed, pointing a finger at me.

I flushed and looked away. I knew it was nothing to be ashamed about, but it wasn't exactly something I liked to talk about either. Especially with a hot guy.

Then Mal took a drink, keeping his eyes on mine.

"Wait...are you thirsty or have you—"

He waggled his eyebrows.

"Seriously?" I squealed.

He shrugged. "I was teasing my assistant because she left one in my office once. So the next time she came over, I had it open and was reading it in front of her. It started as a joke, but I gotta admit, I got into it. They had all the music industry stuff wrong, but the relationship and the sex scenes were enthralling. I might've finished it before I gave it back to her."

"Wait, so your assistant left a rock star romance book—a paperback—in your office?"

He shrugged. "Yeah. Like I said, it was good."

And he didn't see that as a blatant advance? Didn't get that she was clearly interested in him? Wow.

I wanted to probe deeper, but I didn't want to sour the mood, so I continued the game and blurted out the first question that came to mind. "Never have I ever...been arrested."

He took a sip. Then another. Then another.

"Okay, okay." I waved at him. "You can stop. But seriously? How many times?"

He narrowed his eyes. "Does a juvie record count?"

"Um, yeah."

"Then...five, no, six times. Twice as a teen for vandalism—our neighbor was an asshole. Twice for disorderly conduct, aka bar brawls, when we were first on the tour circuit. Once in the UK for assault. Kinda got into it with our opening act, but in my defense I was high. And of course, most recently for possession around...a little over nine-ish years ago."

"That's... That's a lot."

"It is." He stared at me over our long, cold dinner and gave me a sad smile. "That's also life with an addict. Regretting your choices yet?"

I shook my head. "Nope."

"Wow." He laughed incredulously. "Really thought I scared you off with that last one."

I lifted a shoulder. "The night's still young."

"It is." He surveyed me over the rim of his glass. "And so are you."

"Are me and my zero arrests making you aware of our age difference?"

"No, I'm pretty sure your endless optimism is doing it for me."

"What can I say? I'm an optimist by nature. Or I was before. Kinda hard to be optimistic when you're canceling your wedding and going on your honeymoon alone." I grabbed my water and hid behind the glass, wishing like hell I'd ordered some wine instead of water out of deference for Mal's sobriety.

And immediately I felt bad. He didn't ask me to avoid alcohol. I made that choice on my own.

"Right. I think that's the end of that game." Mal made a sound that could've been a laugh, but it was harsher than any laughter I'd ever heard. "How about a dance?" He pushed back in his chair then stood, holding his hand out to me over the table.

I looked around the room. There wasn't a dance floor that I could see. And now everyone was staring at us. "What? Where?"

"Right here. Right now. Dance with me, Saylor."

There was music playing faintly in the background. But it didn't make me want to dance.

That look in Mal's eyes did.

Shakily, I stood up and put my hand in his. And he very suavely led me to a wide gap between the tables that I hadn't noticed earlier. Turning me with a sure hand, he pulled me close to his chest, and we swayed together on his impromptu dance floor.

My heartbeat thundered in my ears as I took a deep, shuddery breath.

I was very much aware of all the eyes in the room being on us.

Mal kept one of my hands in his but held up toward his chest while he spanned my lower back with his other. Brushing his lips against my temple, he whispered, "Relax."

I laughed softly. "Never in the history of the world has telling a woman to relax actually worked."

He laughed with me then murmured, "Why are you so tense?"

"I don't know." I pulled back slightly so I could look into his eyes. They were gentle and intent on mine. "It just feels like one of those moments, you know? Important. Memorable."

He stared into my eyes for another beat then leaned down and kissed me. It was quick and gentle and almost over before it began. Then he gathered me back into his arms and we swayed some more.

It was easily the most romantic moment of my life. I didn't want it to end.

But of course it had to.

Several minutes later, Mal whispered, "You ready to head back?"

His lips brushed against my temple and I swooned again.

Sighing deeply, I finally pulled away and nodded.

And that was the moment I realized we'd started a little movement. All the other couples in the room were dancing too.

Shaking my head, I tugged on Mal's hand as I stepped toward the exit.

"G'night," Jone called as we walked past him.

I tried to ignore the leer he sent Mal's way.

Although judging by the huff he made, he'd seen it too.

We walked hand in hand down the beach path toward my treehouse and my heartbeat thundered in my ears.

This was it.

I was going to do it.

One vacation fling coming right up.

We'd have sex. And have fun for the next ten-ish days. And then when our trip was over, we'd go our separate ways.

I was an adult.

I was single.

I could totally have a fling.

Actually, I might puke.

"This is where I leave you," Mal said as he pulled my hand, urging me to stop walking.

I looked up and realized we'd walked to my place. We were here, and I hadn't even realized it. "Wait, what?"

He sighed. "You might not have said anything, but you're throwing all these signals. Clearly, you're not ready. Like I said, we'll go at your pace. Or who knows, maybe not at all if you're not ready." He shrugged. "I've been celibate for eleven months—what's one more?"

"Wait, you don't want to sleep with me?"

Chapter 6

Mal

"I didn't say that." I had to bite back my laughter. Not want to sleep with her? Had she seen herself? It was all I could do to keep my dick in my pants. The asshole really wanted to stand up and wave hello.

And make all my decisions.

Holding her on the dancefloor had been the best kind of torture. Feeling her satiny skin under my fingertips. Holding her in my arms. Feeling her body move with mine. I muffled my groan. It'd been foreplay as far as I was concerned.

"You think I don't want you?" I grabbed her upper arm and pulled her to me until her hips pressed against mine. "Do you feel that? That's what happens to me every time you're near. Hell, I just gotta hear your voice or smell that citrusy vanilla scent of yours, and I'm hard."

"You get like that because of me?" She sounded all breathless and disbelieving.

And it was seriously pissing me off.

"I don't know what the fuck was wrong with your ex, but clearly he was a jackass." I couldn't believe she'd ever doubt her worth. "Yes, *you*, Saylor. You're gorgeous. Sweet. You have a banging body and are so fucking quick and funny. I've enjoyed every second I've known you."

That was when she pounced. Her arms wrapped around my shoulders and her lips were on mine. I think I groaned when her sharp knee banged into my dick as she tried to climb me like a tree.

I definitely groaned when I grabbed her under her arms to help her climb up me. My palms came to rest under her ass and her supple—exposed—skin had me breaking our kiss with a muffled curse.

"Christ, baby girl. I swear you're trying to kill me. Please tell me you're wearing something under this dress?"

Her eyes shined in the moonlight as she bit her bottom lip and slowly shook her head. "Sorry, Daddy."

I felt those words in my balls. "Jesus Christ." Adjusting my hold and all but tossing her over my shoulder, I wrapped an arm over her body and ran up the stairs to her room.

"Eeek!" She squealed. "Oomph. This is way sexier in the movies." Followed by laughter.

I grinned even as my breath left me in puffs from the exertion. I loved hearing her laugh. She'd had more than her share of heartache lately.

I opened her front door and walked straight to the large bedroom without direction. I knew the floorplan from my last visit, and I wasn't going for subtlety.

Dropping Saylor onto the bed on her back, I crawled up between her legs. "Do you have any idea how fucking sexy you are?"

She leaned up on her elbows, her big blue eyes staring at me with wonder, before she shook her head mutely.

"Fuck me. That's my job for the next few days then." I settled between her splayed thighs, nudging her legs further apart with my shoulders until she made room for me. "I can't wait to see you all confident, knowing how easily you can slay me with a look."

She rolled her eyes like that was the most ridiculous thing she'd ever heard.

"Yeah. New mission unlocked." I shifted on the bed until I could get my hands on her thighs, and I rucked up her dress to her waist. Which was when I discovered Saylor had been a naughty girl indeed.

She wasn't wearing panties.

"Fuck." I breathed in her scent and about jizzed in my pants. "Someone's been a bad girl," I said and tsked in feigned disappointment.

"Oh my god, Mal. I can't, I don't..." She groaned and buried her face in her hands.

And yet she didn't try to roll away from me. Of course she couldn't hide how turned on she was, since I was between her thighs. I laughed darkly. "I thought we agreed on Daddy."

I'd never had a baby girl/daddy kink before, but something about Saylor brought it out in me. I wanted to protect her. Make sure she was taken care of. And give her screaming orgasms.

Christ, I was a sick son of a bitch.

Saylor sucked in a breath, and I didn't know if it was because of my words or the fact that I was nudging her very wet little pussy with my calloused fingers.

Probably the latter.

She was slippery smooth and so very wet. I ran a thumb along her seam and watched the way her soft sex wept in front of me. My fingers looked so big next to her opening. I couldn't wait to bury myself in her. Face. Fingers. Dick.

Fuck me.

"You still with me, baby girl?" I ran a finger along the seam of her sex and groaned when it was immediately wet with her cream.

It took me almost a minute to notice she hadn't said anything. I was so transfixed by her pussy. Definitely pussy whipped.

"Saylor?" I pulled back my hand and looked up at her, but she thrust her hips at me and whimpered incoherently. "Aww, is my baby girl impatient? You want something from me?"

She kept her hands over her face, but nodded vigorously.

I chuckled but went back to running my finger along her seam, learning the little touches that made her arch into me and the ones that made her breath hitch. Her clit was engorged and standing up, all but begging for attention.

"I'm going to need some help, Saylor. Be a good girl and hold your legs right here." I grabbed one of her hands from covering her face and guided it down until she was holding her leg behind her knee. "And the other one too."

She whimpered, her eyes wide and fixed on mine.

I could tell she was turned on but embarrassed at the same time. Like this wasn't something she'd done before. Like she'd never been talked to during sex.

"That's a good girl. Keep 'em open just like that." I ran a caressing hand down the length of her thigh to her spread open sex, and I set up camp.

I was going to be here for a while.

Slowly, I pressed a finger into her and dropped down so I could lick her at the same time. Her pussy gripped me tight. Images of burying my dick in her had me groaning and licking her faster.

She squealed as I licked my way up to her clit and flicked it with my tongue. I built a rhythm between my finger and my tongue—melody and harmony. A dance between the two like the best song. Teasing her opening with a second finger as I suckled her clit and flicked it with my tongue. Blowing on her clit when I plunged two fingers into her.

I built her to a crescendo, more tongue, more lips, faster fingers.

Her hands clutched her knees. "Oh my god. I'm gonna—"

She gave an anguished scream as she went over, her tight pussy clenching around my still fingers.

I rested my head on her thigh and panted like I'd been the one to orgasm. It'd been close. My dick throbbed impatiently in my jeans, strangled by the tight inseam.

After a few moments, I pulled my fingers free.

Saylor was still holding her legs.

Her body shuddered as I took another deep breath and blew it out on her exposed skin. "Sorry, baby girl." I tugged her hands free and wiggled up the bed until I rested on my side next to her. Pushing her hair off her face, I smiled at her. "Ready for round two?"

Her eyes were dilated, the sky-blue rim small against her large black pupils. She shook her head. "What?"

I laughed. "Nothing." I ran a thumb over her plump lips and wished I'd spent more time kissing them, but some women weren't keen on kissing after oral.

But then Saylor did something that shocked me. Her tongue pushed out and ran over my thumb. I'd used it on her clit at one point, so it had to still have some of her cream on it.

"Mmm." She moaned and arched her breasts toward my chest, my thumb still pressed against her lips. "So good, Daddy."

"Christ," I bit out. "Fuck it." And I swooped down and kissed her. Lips, tongue, teeth. It was the roughest, hungriest kiss of my life. I was hanging on by a thread, and if she didn't stop being so goddamned sexy, I was going to lose it in my pants before we got to the real fun.

Considering it'd been eleven months, it was a miracle I hadn't embarrassed myself yet.

Then Saylor bit down on my lower lip, and I lost it.

I leapt up off the bed like I could levitate and tore at my pants. I had to get them off now. I had to get inside her.

My boots went in one direction. My pants in another.

Saylor laughed at me from the bed. "You need some help?"

"Yes." I bent down and searched my pants for the strip of condoms I'd stashed in a pocket earlier. Finally finding them and holding them aloft, I pointed a finger at her. "Take that fucking dress off!"

"I thought you liked it." She fake pouted, blinking her long lashes exaggeratedly.

"I did. I do. But I think it'll look amazing on the ground next to the bed. Or bunched up around your neck—your call."

Her eyes widened.

"Fucking fantastic. Door number two it is." I unbuttoned my shirt partway, but that was taking too long. So I just ripped it off. A few buttons pinged as they flew off. "Leave the shoes on."

"Really?"

"Fuck yeah. I'm gonna love the look of them up by your shoulders with your dress pooling below them." I whipped my shirt to the other side of the room and pounced.

I was back between her thighs, on my knees this time. Tugging her dress, I heard a faint rip and then the material was above her luscious breasts, framing her body in the fire engine red material.

Her nipples begged for attention, all erect and quivering. But it was the look in her eyes that had me pausing. Luminous. Naked need. And maybe with a question mark.

Was I freaking her out?

I groaned and kissed her again. But gentle this time. With my hand cupping her cheek, my lips moved over hers with a softness I hadn't shown her in too long. Then I gave her a soft peck and another one on the tip of her nose. "Sorry, baby girl. Like I said it's been a minute for me, so I'm a little impatient. Are you still with me?"

"Yes, Daddy." She gulped, and I could still see the hesitancy in her eyes.

"Fuck me." I'd never felt so turned on and conflicted before in my fucking life. My shoulders slumped as I stared at her mostly naked in front of me. Those fucking tits, all perfect and plump. Her pussy all slick and just weeping for my dick.

But I couldn't.

Not while she looked so unsure.

"Wha-Why'd you stop?" She frowned and came up on her elbows. "Where's the condom? Did you forget how to put it on since it's been a minute since you've used one?"

"Hell, I've been using condoms longer than you've—you know what? I really don't wanna finish that sentence." I twisted around and sat on the foot of the bed. "Fuck. Fuck!"

Now I felt all kinds of dirty. Scummy. I vowed to never be *that* guy, but look at me now.

Shit.

"Um..." Saylor's hand brushed against my shoulder like she was afraid to touch me. "Are you okay?"

"Are you?" The words came out like an accusation. I groaned and buried my face in my hands. "Sorry. I'm an ass. Clearly, considering I was going to sleep with you when you're looking like that."

"Like what?"

"You've got question marks all over your face. You're clearly not sure about me—about this. And I almost..." I groaned again.

"You didn't almost do anything. You're not even wearing the condom, for crying out loud. You didn't get anywhere near almost fucking me... Unfortunately."

"What? No. You were looking all unsure. Clearly you don't wanna do this."

"Are you really going to make me beg? Please fuck me, Mal—I mean, Daddy."

I closed my eyes. "Christ."

"Look. If you were seeing uncertainty, it's only because I've never done this before." Her breasts jiggled as she gestured between us.

I tried really hard not to watch them.

And I mostly failed.

Shaking my head, I turned her words over in my head. "But you said earlier tonight that you're not a virgin...?"

Saylor rolled her eyes. "I don't mean sex. I just mean, I've never had a fling or whatever this is before. I've always been in a relationship when I've slept with guys...both guys."

"Two?! That's your number? Two? Seriously?"

She made a face. "So what?"

"Oh, I'm definitely going to hell. I mean, not that it was in question before, but this clinches it. I'm an old, dirty fucking man."

Saylor squealed as I pounced, taking her down in a tangle of limbs and that fucking dress.

Pushing it impatiently out of my way, I palmed her tit in my right hand as I kissed her. I wanted her to know that I wanted her. That she was so fucking sexy, it'd taken everything inside me to turn away from her. I kissed her for an impossibly long time.

I kissed her until I forgot how to breathe.

Breaking our kiss with a gasp, I nuzzled my nose along her cheek while my fingers kept playing with her nipple. "You still game? Need a little more foreplay?"

"Oh god." Her head fell back, and I kissed a path down her neck to her amazing tits. "Yes to all of it. More of that. And definitely more of the sex stuff. Anything really."

"Aww, baby girl," I murmured as I nuzzled her breast. "You're so agreeable when you're horny."

She moaned. "Anything you want, Daddy."

"Fuck me."

I scrambled across the bed to find the dropped condoms. And then I fumbled with the stupid thing once I unwrapped it.

Saylor sprawled back with a smirk curving her lips like she was so fucking proud of how flustered I was. Like it was because of her.

She was totally right.

Then I was the one grinning as I crawled up the bed on my knees with my dick bobbing in front of me like a dowsing rod seeking an underground spring.

What? I saw it on a viral video.

But Saylor's eyes widened.

"That—You're not, I mean, there's no way."

I grinned. "You're sweet, baby, but I don't need the ego trip. It'll fit. I'm not any bigger than the guys you've been with before." Once I settled between her thighs but still on my knees, I reached out and ran my thumb over her still wet folds. "And you're still dripping for me, baby. It's gonna be fine. Now be a good girl and give me a kiss."

Her breath hitched when I asked her to be a good girl. Noted.

I braced myself on either side of her and bent down to capture her lips again. In seconds, she was lost in our kiss again. She almost didn't notice me prodding her sex with my dick. Almost. She stiffened ever so slightly.

Breaking our kiss, I leaned on one arm and guided my dick into her folds with my other hand. She immediately clenched around me so tightly I had to stop with only the tip inside her.

"Ah, baby girl, you're killing me here. Fuck."

She winced and looked up at me with wide eyes. "I was serious. There's no way you're going to fit."

I checked my eyeroll before it began. "I'm gonna need you to take a deep breath."

Her eyes widened again. "Because you're going to push it in?!"

"Fuck. No. So you relax some. I couldn't even fit a finger in you right now with the way you're clenching. I swear, we're going to go at your speed, but you gotta relax a bit. We're not gonna get anywhere with you all tense." I reached out and feathered my thumb against her labia, feeling her stretched around the head of my dick.

Fuck, maybe she was right. I might've been the biggest she'd had.

Distraction. That was what we needed.

I shifted forward so I could kiss her while keeping one hand teasing her distended clit. She whined deep in her throat but kissed me back.

Little by little, I pressed into her as she relaxed around me until I was finally seated inside her tight little pussy.

It took everything inside me not to roar and just pound away. I'd never felt a pussy grip me so tight. It was the best and worst sensation all at the same time.

Saylor apparently agreed because she rolled her hips under me, trying to take control.

I gave her flank a playful, little slap. "Who's in charge here?"

She squealed, and her eyes flared. But I felt the telltale clench of her sex around me. Someone liked a little slap with their tickle.

I grinned down at her. "That didn't sound like an answer." I gave her another spank. "Who's in charge here?"

"You are, Daddy."

My dick flexed in response. "Fuck yeah. Now be a good girl and take my dick."

She moaned and tightened around me again. She might just come here and now without any more friction.

Fuck, I might too.

Without another word, I took over, thrusting into her wet pussy. The sound of our panting breaths competed with the wet slaps of our bodies. Saylor whimpered beneath me. Her hands clutching at my shoulders, urging me closer or faster or maybe just hanging on.

She was close. I feathered a finger between our bodies on her clit.

"Such a fucking good girl. Taking her daddy's dick." I groaned.

She squealed and clenched hard around me. Her grasping pussy strangling me so hard I saw stars for a second.

And a second later, I was following her over the edge.

Dropping down on my arms on either side of her, I groaned loud and long as my dick pumped the condom full of my cum. I'd never come so hard.

Fuck.

After a long, long minute, I grasped the condom at the base of my dick and slowly pulled free of her tight pussy. I wavered on my knees for a second. I know, I know I needed to get rid of the condom, but I couldn't really walk at the moment.

Spying a little trash can near the bed, I rolled off the bed and staggered over to it and tossed the condom. Then I stumbled back to the bed and collapsed on my back.

"That was fucking amazing."

Saylor giggled and rolled toward me, burying her face in my chest. "Thank you."

Her words were muffled against my skin, but I heard them all the same. And I felt an answering pang in my chest.

"Pretty sure that's my line, baby. Thank you, thank you, *thank you.*"

She murmured something back at me, but I was too tired to focus on the words. I just needed a minute, then I'd get out of her hair.

That was the last thought I had before sleep took over.

Chapter 7

Saylor

I woke slowly and peacefully the next morning. The chirping of birds and the soft sound of the tide lapping at the beach came to me first. I was so warm and happy; I didn't want the moment to ever end.

And then the arm over my waist flexed slightly.

Oh shit. I wasn't alone.

Mal.

Or was it *Daddy*?

I flushed, remembering all his dirty talk the night before. I never thought I had daddy issues. I mean, my dad died when I was two and I called my stepdad by his name, Alan, from day one—even when I was only three years old. He'd never wanted me to call him dad, and Mom hadn't pushed for it.

But it was different with Mal. It was hot to call him Daddy and seeing how his eyes flared. It felt empowering. *I* did that to him.

I did a lot to him last night. Starting with jumping him at the bottom of the stairs. But I loved the way he checked in with me, making sure I was still into everything, especially when he'd doubted it at one point.

But what was he still doing here?

I would've thought he'd be the king of hitting and quitting it.

Judging by the hard-on probing my ass, he wasn't gonna quit me today.

"Mmmm." His arm brushed against my side and came to rest, cupping my right breast.

My nipple immediately hardened and pressed against his calloused fingers.

I squeezed my thighs together. God, he was so sexy without even trying.

But I was very aware of my very full bladder and no doubt horrible case of morning breath.

So I rolled out of his arms and headed for the bathroom, hoping he was still asleep and not watching my very naked butt jiggle as I walked away.

Judging by his muffled curse, I didn't get my wish.

He was awake and no doubt regretting his little sleepover.

I couldn't piece together my emotions. I was so all over the place. Proud of myself for pulling the trigger with Mal. Glad I was moving past Trent and his bullshit. Maybe a little embarrassed over some of the things I said and did last night. Definitely a little hurt over his cursing just now and how he was most likely regretting staying the night.

But I couldn't control that.

I mentally shook it off, preferring to bask in my awesome sexual awakening instead as I went through my morning routine. I'd usually shower too, but I didn't feel comfortable taking one with him still here.

After pulling on the complimentary robe, I stood in front of the closed door for a few seconds and debated my options. Take a shower? Go out there and see if he was still here? What if he wasn't?

What if he was?

Ugh. This was too much turmoil so early in the morning. I really needed some coffee so I could think.

Almost like I thought it into existence, the aroma of coffee wafted into the bathroom.

Weird.

Followed by a strange buzzing sound I've never heard here before.

Jerking open the door, I found Mal *naked* and standing in front of the espresso machine with a cup poised under the spout while my favorite liquid poured into it.

"Hey baby. Got a cup for you already. Do you want to mix in milk and sugar or do you take it black? Pretty sure I can get the thing to make you a latte if you want your milk steamed. What'll it be?"

He was all jovial and just calm. Not at all like Trent in the morning. I'd never met anyone who woke up so crabby and mad. Made it hard to be around him in the morning…not that it got better later in the day, come to think of it.

But not Mal. He was all happy and unabashed about the huge erection jutting out from his body. Like he didn't care.

Like he wasn't ashamed.

I blinked a few times, totally taken aback by the whole scene. Especially all those tattoos all over his body. I hadn't had near enough time to explore them last night.

"Babe? Latte? Espresso?

I jerked back into the present. "Anything. If it's coffee based, just pour it into my mouth."

"My kinda girl. Here's one already made." He handed me a cup and pressed a kiss against my temple. "And I'm just gonna pop into the bathroom before I drink mine."

Then he was gone before I could even say thank you.

The machine in front of me sputtered black liquid into the cup under it.

I was definitely going to have to ask him for a lesson on operating that before he left. Taking a few gulps from my cup, I felt all my nerves drain away. Nothing beat a cup of my favorite nectar.

Spying a flash of red, I walked over and picked up my dress from the night before. I set my cup down and shook out the dress. Fortunately, it'd ripped along the seam so I should be able to fix it. Not here and now; it'd have to wait until I was home with my supplies, but at least it wasn't ruined.

Although what a way to go. I smirked. Kinda hard to mourn something that made me smile remembering how ardent Mal had been last night when he'd done it. I'd made him react like that.

Me.

The bathroom door opened, and Mal padded into the room. "Ah, it's done. Great." He grabbed his cup and sipped his latte while watching me over the rim. "Shit, I forgot I ripped your dress. I'll buy you another one. You like Chanel?"

I shook my head. "I can fix it."

"You shouldn't have to. It was my damage. Let me buy you a new dress."

"It's no big deal. I still have the thread, so it won't be hard to fix."

"Wait, you made that dress?" Judging by his expression, he was impressed by the fact.

I shrugged. "Most of the outfits I brought—minus my swimsuits—I made."

"Holy shit. I know you mentioned you were into design, but I had no idea you're so talented. That dress last night was banging. Why aren't you doing that full time?"

I tossed the dress in the general direction of my luggage. "Because no one makes money at being a seamstress or designer or whatever. It's one of those you-gotta-have-money-to-make-money deals."

"What if you went back to school for clothes designing? Or have you tried to apply to work for someone else? Like intern or whatever?"

"Yeah, that wasn't going to fly with my mom. And Vegas only has hooker boutiques or wedding dresses, and neither one appealed to me. So anyway…" I ached to change the subject. Talking about designing clothes was like probing an open wound. Because that pipedream was never coming true.

He shook his head. "Damned shame that someone with talent like that isn't using it to the fullest."

"Some hobbies aren't meant to be careers. Some things like eating and shelter take precedent." I took another sip of my espresso and mumbled, "not that you would understand."

"You seriously think I didn't struggle? That I came from money?" He laughed harshly. "Fuck me, that's the funniest thing I've ever heard."

"Okay, fine. You made your dream come true. That doesn't happen for ninety-nine percent of us."

He sobered immediately. Judging by that glint in his eye, I'd pissed him off. "I made my dream come true because I scrabbled, I scraped, I slept on couches and worked shitty day jobs so I could play in bars at night. I got by on minutes of sleep some days. Don't tell me that I don't know about the sacrifices it takes."

"I…" I swallowed as shame all but engulfed me. "I'm sorry. I don't know much about your band or your story. I shouldn't have assumed."

He nodded stiffly. "Okay." He took another gulp from his latte then walked over to grab his boxer briefs tangled up in his black pants from the night before. "I should get back to my place."

"Um, okay." This felt weird. Like our first fight or something. But I'd only met him two days ago. It was too soon to feel this deeply for someone.

Right?

He dressed in silence then grabbed his cup and drained the contents. After setting the cup on the desk, he turned to me and gave me a quick up and down. "I guess I'll see you around."

Dread pooled in my stomach. I hated this. I couldn't let him walk away.

"Mal, wait. I don't want to leave things like this with us."

He stopped halfway to the door but didn't say anything or turn around.

I wanted to make things right, but I didn't know what to say, really. After setting my cup down on a nearby table, I twisted my fingers together, searching for the right thing to say. Finally, I opened my mouth and words just fell out. "I'm used to people telling me what a pipedream being a designer is. I don't know how to handle someone urging me to chase my dreams. I mean, even my best friend tried to talk me out of taking design classes at college. Said it was pointless. My *best friend*. Coming from her of all people, that made *me* feel pointless."

He stared down at the floor for a second before nodding. "I get it."

I stood there, unconsciously swaying toward him. I didn't know why I felt this pull. I wanted to touch him, feel his arms around me. Almost like being in his orbit made me feel better.

But it was way too soon to have thoughts like that. And weird.

"Anyway." I shook my head. "Yeah, so I'm sorry. I shouldn't have assumed anything about you. I'm not like that. I don't do that. Usually." I winced.

Then I blinked, and Mal was standing in front of me. His hand came up and he hesitated like he wasn't sure if it was okay to touch me.

I took a step toward him and his hand cupped my cheek. His smile was pained as he stared down at me.

"I'm sorry too. I guess people assuming I'm a rich asshole is a sore spot for me too. I definitely didn't like knowing you thought I was that guy."

"I don't." Taking another step toward him, I wrapped my arms around him and burrowed into his chest. His skin was smooth and warm against my cheek. "I just…it feels dangerous to let myself dream like that. I'm so close to saying fuck it and chasing it. I mean, I'm not marrying Trent anymore. I hated my student-teaching experience. But I've done all the classes, I have the degree, all that's left is a few tests, but I really don't want to…and I don't think I've ever said that out loud before. I don't want to be a teacher."

"Fuck yeah." Mal's arms squeezed me before he pulled back slightly to grin down at me.

I laughed nervously. "That feels so liberating to say."

"I'm fucking proud of you, baby girl. You should chase your dream. What are your twenties about if not going all in on yourself?"

"You'd know since you've already done it."

He winced. "Yeah. Thanks for that. I love being reminded of what an old fart I am."

"You're not old, you're…vintage."

"Oomph." He stepped back and clutched at his chest in feigned pain. "I felt that one right in the feels."

"What? It's not an insult. It's what they call old wine, right?"

"Fuck me." He laughed and laughed, all while I stood there with a silly grin on my face, confused by what he found so funny.

"Anyways, I wanna take a shower. Pretty sure my labia is welded together after last night."

Mal smirked at me like he was proud of that. I rolled my eyes.

"All right. I'm in."

"Wait, what? You mean together? You want to shower *with* me?"

He cocked his head. "Are you sure your fiancé was straight?"

"Of course he was. He was also a degenerate gambler, but he was definitely straight."

A look came into his eyes, but he let it go to concentrate on what he no doubt thought was the more important fact. "And you two never showered together?"

I shook my head.

"Oh baby girl, are you in for a treat." He tossed me a cocky grin before grabbing my hand and pulling me toward the bathroom.

I groaned as we sped by my forgotten coffee cup, and I reached toward it desperately.

When the bathroom door closed behind me, Mal was already stripping out of his clothes.

I stared at him wide-eyed as more and more deliciously muscled and tattooed flesh was revealed. Wait… "Is that a tattoo of Plankton from SpongeBob?"

I pointed at the blur of green high on his left thigh.

Mal shrugged. "I lost a bet with G. But I got him back the next year. He has Handsome Squidward on his ass."

I snickered. "Is that what rock gods do? Make stupid bets and tattoo ridiculous things on each other?"

"Don't forget we get to sleep on buses." He shrugged. "These tats were before we made it big. The stupid shit you do once you have money goes up exponentially the richer you get. The stories I could tell you… Speaking of wild, weren't we about to get in the shower?"

My breath shuddered for a second. All of him, looking like that, offering me a wild time? I swear I'd had a dream like this once.

Let me tell you, the real thing is way better.

I was across the room before I even knew it. The robe slipped from my shoulders with the slightest tug from Mal. His eyes were intent on mine as he took my hand and led me into the huge shower stall.

I didn't even notice when he'd turned on the water.

Honestly, it felt like a dream.

He stood with his back to the spray, and once I stepped onto the smooth, river rocked shower floor, he shifted slightly so I got some of the water.

I didn't know what to do. Was I supposed to be sexy? Or just shower? How did we do this?

Instinctively, I reached out to the water and let a small amount pool in my cupped hands before splashing it over my face. I'd repeated it twice when I heard a distinct rumble.

My eyes flew to Mal, but his gaze was focused on my cheek. The one Trent's bookie had hit last week.

I didn't know it was possible, but I felt more naked than ever. Which was ridiculous. I mean, I was standing here totally nude and Mal had already seen the bruise.

Only now it felt different.

And it looked like it felt different to him too.

His eyes blazed, and he took a deep, shuddery breath. "You mind if I use your stuff?"

"Huh?" I blinked.

He shrugged like he wasn't affected, but I could still see that burning look in his eyes. "Your stuff smells better."

"Um, okay."

He grabbed my body soap and squirted way too much into his hand before lathering it up—no washcloth or loofa, just straight on his hands.

I watched spellbound as he moved his sudsy hands all over his body, but more perfunctory than seductive.

This wasn't what I thought showering together was going to be like.

Maybe the dream version was better.

Sighing, I turned so I could get my hair wet since I now had most of the spray.

"Fuck me," Mal muttered.

"Everything okay?" I asked as I reached down for the shampoo bottle on the small bench in the corner.

Mal's hand caressed my bottom.

I squealed and snapped to attention. "Mal!"

"I think you mean Daddy." His lips quirked like he was fighting a smile.

"I think you mean excuse me!" I snapped.

His eyes flared. "Fuck, I love that fire." He swooped down and kissed me, his lips hungry and urgent.

I'd wrapped my arms around his shoulders and was kissing him back before I could even form a thought. And then I didn't want to let go. His cock jutted out, pressing into my tummy, and his hands were slippery on my back. The soap perfumed the steamy air between us with a mango citrus freshness. And my thighs were slippery against each other for a whole different reason.

I broke our kiss with a gasp because I needed air. "Definitely better than my dream."

Mal grinned down at me. "You dream about me last night, baby girl?"

"Maybe," I replied coyly.

His rumbled laughter echoed off the stone walls around us. "Hand me the shampoo, baby."

I turned in his arms and gulped as I realized what that meant. It was the whole reason I'd ended up in his arms. If I reached out for the bottle then…yup, he grasped my hips in his hands, and I was perfectly lined up for him to—

I waited a beat, but he didn't move anymore.

Disappointed—and amazed that I felt that way—I grabbed the bottle and passed it to him, straightening up.

He took the bottle and squeezed some into his hand. Then both of his hands came down on my head and awkwardly spread the shampoo on my hair. Something about the way he did it, his movements, the concentration on his face, spelled out to me that this wasn't a practiced move for him. He genuinely wanted to wash my hair.

My breath caught and tears burned my eyes for a second—and the soap wasn't anywhere near my eyes.

I couldn't remember the last time someone touched me like this—all gentle and accepting. And for it to come from Mal…gah, it got me all emotional.

"Tip your head back." He'd grabbed the shower wand off the wall and held it aloft.

I obeyed and warm water ran down the back of my head. He carefully kept the suds from washing over my face. My heart thudded unevenly as he continued to gently rinse the shampoo out of my hair, turning me carefully this way and that.

This was so different from what I'd imagined we'd be doing that I was confused but felt taken care of at the same time. It was a weird juxtaposition. I was used to doing everything for myself and taking care of the people around me. This felt so weird.

Weird, but awesome.

Once he'd rinsed away the last of the shampoo, I grabbed the conditioner bottle and squeezed some into my hand. "I'm weird about conditioner. I only like it in certain parts of my hair."

I feathered the conditioner into the ends of my hair, aware of his eyes on me the entire time—like he was tracking all my movements so he could do it himself next time. But maybe that was just wishful thinking on my part.

By the time I turned around, he had already lathered up his hair and was elbow deep in suds.

"I wanted to do that."

"Sorry, baby girl. Next time." Mal grinned at me before turning to rinse his hair. "The hot water tanks aren't huge here, so we have a finite amount of time."

I shrugged. "I just have to wash up. I'll be quick."

His grin turned downright naughty. "I'm sorry, but I really think that's a service I need to provide for you."

Chapter 8

Still Saylor

I bit my bottom lip and tried to fight the ridiculous grin from spreading across my face. Nodding at the whirl of material hanging in the corner, I said innocently, "I usually use a loofah."

"Today, I'm gonna be your loofah."

My laughter over his silly offer was quickly joined by his deep chuckles.

But our laughter faded away as his large hands lathered up with my bodywash. That, combined with the intent look in his eyes, had me catching my breath. Now it didn't feel so silly and light.

Now I knew he had all kinds of dirty, dirty thoughts running through his mind.

And he was going to act them out with me.

I swayed toward him, like a puppet caught by its string.

He grinned smugly down at me. "I need you to turn around."

Something about the glint in his eye and his husky voice just made me weak in the knees.

His grin turned downright wicked. "You gonna be a good girl for me?"

My knees about went out.

I swayed full force at him, and he muffled a curse as he caught me. I clutched at his shoulders and hid my burning face in his very muscle-y chest. God, that was embarrassing.

His husky laughter echoed around us. "Fuck, you're about perfect, baby girl."

I shivered in his arms. "I feel ridiculous. Like I swear you could make me orgasm just with your dirty talk."

His chest rumbled under me. "As much as I wanna test your theory out, we gotta finish up before we run out of warm water here. It might be a luxury resort, but we're still on an island."

Then his hands moved over me, spreading the suds all over my body. His fingers lingered on my breasts, teasing the aching peaks of my nipples. Plucking. Rasping. Teasing.

I moaned, the sound so loud in our little echo chamber.

"Mmm, you feeling a little needy? Want me to do something about it?"

"Yes. Please." I groaned as his hands continued to wash my chest. Moving over my breasts like I'd soaked them in mud before showering.

"Filthy. Just so filthy," Mal murmured as his hands caressed my breast, passing over my nipples again and again. The soap was long gone. Just his hands and the water beating down on us as he teased the aching tips.

"Mal," I whined, moving my hips into his thighs. I need more.

"I thought we agreed on you calling me Daddy last night."

If it'd make him touch me where I needed him to, I'd call him anything he wanted. "Daddy, please. I need more."

"I agree. We need so much more soap. You're just filthy, baby. And so much of you still to wash." He reached behind him and grabbed the soap before lathering up again.

I whined in the back of my throat. "Not more soap. More of you. Touch me, Daddy. Please."

"I am, baby girl." His hand moved over my chest, lingering on my nipples to pluck and tease me more, before moving down my torso and skipping over my sex to wash my thighs and knees. "Can't you feel me?"

"No, Daddy. Please!" I couldn't even form words. I was so full of aching need and frustration. I arched in his arms, rubbing my breasts against his chest as I tried and failed to find some friction for my aching sex. He dodged my every attempt to trap his leg between my thighs.

"Almost done." He picked up the shower wand and quickly rinsed his hands before running the water all over me. "Now, turn, so I can rinse that conditioner out of your hair."

I thought about wrestling him for the wand so I could use it where I really needed it, but I knew I wouldn't win. Apparently this morning was about driving me crazy.

I pouted as I turned so my back was facing him and closed my eyes as the water washed over my head. So warm, it would've been relaxing but for this aching need thrumming between my thighs.

His free hand rubbed through my hair, getting all the conditioner rinsed out. He moved me slightly and ran the water down my body, over my breasts. He passed the wand over them again and again.

And then he moved lower.

I whined as he petted my needy sex with one hand while he did something to the wand with his other.

And then I felt it.

All the force of the wand against my aching clit.

I juddered in his arms, my whole body went taut, and I clawed at the arm now banded around my waist while he teased me with the wand in his other hand.

I couldn't—I didn't—

I screamed as I went over the edge.

CHAPTER 8

Wave after wave of pleasure crashed through my body. I would've gone down but for his arm around me. His steady body behind me held me up as mine shook and quaked until I had to finally turn away from the now harsh sensation of the wand's stream.

I was dimly aware of Mal turning off the water and hanging up the shower wand, but all I could focus on was staying upright as aftershocks shook me. Any time Mal touched me, another one wracked my body. When my nipples brushed against him, another one hit. When the towel he wrapped around me rasped against my clit, another one shook me.

It felt like my entire body was just one tender nerve ending.

It was amazing and agonizing all at once.

"Good?" Mal asked as he rubbed the excess water out of his hair.

I shook my head slightly, and his eyes darkened. "Amazing."

He smirked. "Good."

He grabbed a towel and moved to wrap it around his hips when I noticed he was still erect.

That whole experience had been about me. I hadn't touched him. I hadn't kissed him. I'd done absolutely nothing to reciprocate.

Like hell was that the way our morning was going to end.

I knocked the towel out of his hand, letting it fall to the wet shower floor, before tossing mine down on top of it.

"What...?" His question ended in a groan as I fell to my knees at his feet on top of the towels and grasped his cock in my hand. "Fuck. I really should tell you that you don't need to, but I can't. I really, really need to come. Once is nowhere enough with you."

It was my turn to smirk as I ran my hand up and down his cock while Mal's groans echoed around us. His fingers tunneled into my hair, but he didn't pull or guide me. It was more like he needed help to stay standing.

I felt so powerful on my knees in front of him. I was the one making him groan. I was the one teasing him now. I was the one controlling things between us.

But I didn't have the patience that Mal did.

I wanted to taste him. I wanted to feel him come.

My lips and tongue ran along his length, tasting him, making him groan and shudder above me. I didn't even think about the towel biting into my knees; I was so focused on him and his reactions I could've stayed down here for hours. Watching this man come undone was everything.

I'd built up a rhythm between my hand and mouth that had Mal's thighs tightening and his cock throbbing.

"Fuck, baby. Yeah, that's it. I'm almost there. Just need a little more."

The devil on my shoulder wanted me to hold back and tease him like he'd teased me, but my jaw didn't agree. I was way out of practice. But there was no way I was going to stop now.

"You gonna swallow me, baby? I wanna see you take it all. I'm not—shit. Swallow me, baby." He grunted, and his cum quickly filled my mouth as he gave a muted shout.

So much cum shot into my mouth that some of it dribbled from my lips.

I gulped then panted for a second, struggling to get my breathing back.

That had been so intense.

But so very hot.

My nipples tingled in the steamy air. And I probably could've come again with some friction, but I was also sated and just mellow.

This was easily the best day of my life.

"Fuck." Mal collapsed onto the shower bench and gave me a tired smile. "Someone's been a naughty girl. Come here."

I swallowed the cum in my mouth and climbed into his lap. His arms came around me, and he had an expression I couldn't quite place.

Contemplative? It was definitely serious. Way more than I'd expected from him, considering what we'd just done.

His thumb swept my chin and under my bottom lip before pressing between my lips. "I want you to swallow it all." He hummed under his breath as I obeyed, and I felt his cock flex under my bottom. His eyes were intent on my mouth. "There's a good girl."

I was just as sick as he was because I melted against him. I'd do anything to hear him talk to me like that more.

He pressed a kiss against my forehead and just held me for a minute.

It was nice. Comforting.

Finally Mal sighed. "I have good news, and I have bad news."

"Bad news first. Always," I murmured back.

"Bad news is I'm pretty sure we've missed breakfast."

My stomach gave a painful rumble just at the mention of food. Food I was going to miss out on now.

"What's the good news? How I just ingested my breakfast?" I rolled my eyes.

Mal laughed. "Nah. Good news is I think we're less than an hour from lunch. We slept in, after all."

"Good. Women cannot exist on semen alone."

Mal laughed louder as his arms tightened around me. "Love it."

Then his lips were on mine with no thought or worry about where mine had just been. He kissed me just as ardently as he had last night.

But it was over all too quickly. "I'm gonna head back to my place and change. Meet you back here in thirty minutes or so?"

I nodded, and he kissed me again before grabbing a clean towel to wrap around his hips before he grabbed his clothes. He tossed me a smile and then disappeared back into the bedroom.

Leaving me alone and shivering in the shower with way too many emotions swirling in my head.

That had been a lot. And I didn't know what to do with it.

I just knew I wanted to do it again.

And again.

Lunch was buffet style. Chaffing dishes lined the buffet tables with a selection of sandwiches, fresh fruit, and chips. I loaded my plate and followed Mal to a large table in the corner.

Sliding into the seat next to him, I looked around the dining area. It was…surprisingly empty. "This is kinda weird, isn't it?"

"Hmm?" Mal mumbled through the large bite of his sandwich.

"Just how empty it is. We're the only ones here. I'd suspect zombie apocalypse if I didn't know better. I mean, we're literally on an island. How would they get here?"

"Same as you, I suspect. Boat."

I snickered as I picked up my club sandwich. "Bet."

"On what?"

It was my turn to roll my eyes. "It means I agree, old man. But seriously, where is everyone?"

It wasn't a huge island, but there were usually a dozen or so guests around at any given time.

Jone came out of the kitchen to set out some water pitchers. "Ah, you back early?"

Mal shook his head. "Back from where? We literally just woke up."

"Yeah, where is everyone?" I asked.

"Oh, sorry." Jone crossed the dining room to stop at our table. "I didn't realize you didn't know. We did a tour of the Taveuni Falls. Samu took most of the guests over a few hours ago. Did no one mention it to you?"

Mal and I shook our heads mutely.

I could tell Jone wasn't pleased. "I am so sorry. That is a major oversight. I'll talk to Samu and see what we can do to make it up to you both. *Vosoti au.*"

Jone bowed over us then practically sprinted from the room. No doubt to lay into someone.

I turned back to Mal and gave him an innocent look. "Totally worth it. No regrets here." I surreptitiously looked around then finished in a whisper, "*Daddy*."

Mal's eyes narrowed on me. "Someone's acting naughty."

I caught my breath. His voice was so low and rumbly. All bass and just…yummy.

"You eager for a punishment, baby girl?" Mal tipped his head. "We'll have to see what we can do about that."

I opened my mouth to reply when Jone came crashing out of the kitchen doors again, muttering something in Fijian under his breath. He wasn't paying us the least attention, but still, the moment was broken.

Mal's hand slid onto my knee and gave it a little squeeze.

I smiled at him and turned back to my sandwich. "So you never said…what was the bet that left you with a tattoo of Plankton on your butt?"

Mal choked. Coughs wracked his body, and Jone came running over to make sure he wasn't dying. I would've been concerned, but I could hear him breathing.

"Choking to death isn't gonna get you outta answering the question," I said as he collapsed back into his chair after waving off a hovering Jone.

"Have some pity, woman." He groaned. After a few more shuddery breaths, he took a drink of water and coughed a little more.

"So judging by that reaction, I'm guessing it had to do with sex. Number of partners in what? A tour? A day?"

He groaned again and buried his face in his hands. "You're embarrassingly close. Is that answer enough?"

I raised my eyebrows at him as my answer.

"Number of threesomes in a year. And I'll remind you that I lost…by a lot."

I wrinkled my nose. Yeah, I didn't like hearing that. Or picturing it. Sighing, I took a few more bites. "And the Handsome Squidward tattoo? Was that a rematch?"

"Nah, that was a March Madness loss on his part. He shouldn't have bet against Duke."

I swallowed hard. The food landed like a rock in my stomach. "Do you gamble a lot?"

The buzzing in my ears made it hard to focus on anything.

My skin crawled, and I shivered.

"Saylor? You okay, baby?"

My throat was suddenly really dry. I grabbed my water and took a drink, nodding at Mal's question. Oh yeah. I was fine.

Totally fine. Nothing to see here.

It was my turn to cough. "Fine. It's…yeah. Fine."

I could tell from his expression that he didn't really believe it, but he let it drop.

"Anyways, I was trying to teach Gio a lesson. He was starting to get into it pretty deep. And making such stupid bets. Like, who bets against Duke's spread when they're seeded as number one for like the third year in a row?" Mal shook his head. "This was back before I joined NA and learned about addicts. So now I'd probably go about it differently, but I think I made my point."

"Yeah, gambling is stupid."

"And so is the tattoo." Mal laughed.

I smiled weakly and let Mal carry the rest of the conversation as I picked at my lunch.

Suddenly I wasn't very hungry.

Chapter 9

Mal

I'd never been accused of being the swiftest kid in school, but even I clocked Saylor's demeanor change when gambling had been brought up over lunch. That, plus her comment last night about a 'degenerate gambler ex' confirmed my suspicions about him.

Did he slap her around when he lost? How long had it been going on for?

I was proud of her for ending it. But I really didn't like the mental picture it'd given me. Or how she locked up as she got lost in her memories. Would she be okay when she went home? Would he be waiting for her?

Of course he would. I mean, look at her.

As we walked down the beach hand in hand, our hips bumping into each other, I took her in. Her blonde hair tousled in the breeze, her long legs showed off in her skimpy shorts that she'd apparently made herself, and her t-shirt molded against her firm tits that I wanted to taste again. She was the complete package.

"You wanna walk for a bit?" I asked, swinging our hands sillily.

She didn't even crack a smile. Or say a word. She just nodded and walked along with me, lost in her thoughts. Probably worrying about what was waiting for her at home.

I didn't have jack shit waiting for me at home. I didn't even have a dog since I was on the road so much. And that might be changing now.

Usually we took a month or two off after the tour ended to recharge then would get back into the studio. Or at least booked a few boutique shows—award shows, ritzy birthday parties, a music festival—something. Leif had always been pushing for more visibility.

But the end of this tour has been suspiciously silent.

The only reason I could figure was that he was lining up his own ducks to go solo.

Which left me where exactly? A forty-two-year-old guitarist with no band.

What was I going to do with my life?

Saylor tugged on my hand. "That was a mighty big sigh. What's going on?"

"Just wondering what I'm doing with my life."

"Ah, so just the usual existential crisis then. Gotcha."

"Yeah, no biggie." I laughed.

She laughed with me. "Same."

"Fuck, I can't believe we're here—" I pulled away to gesture at the gorgeous beach we were standing on and the beautiful blue ocean stretching out in front of us. "And we're being such sad sacks."

"You know what would cheer me up?" Saylor asked with a naughty smile.

My dick flexed under my shorts. "I have an idea, but you tell me."

"Sandcastles!" Saylor shouted, raising her arms over her head and wiggling her fingers. Which consequently made other parts of her wiggle.

I looked up from her swaying tits to give her an incredulous look. "Wait, are you serious? We're finally fucking and you wanna build sandcastles?"

The glee leached out of her expression, and her body sagged. "Oh." She shook her head. "I mean, no, of course not. That was totally a joke. Ha ha. Um, let's go back to my private pool. We can—"

"I'll go see what equipment they have on hand. I'm sure Jone can rustle something up for us." I turned back the way we came, tossing over my shoulder, "Find us a good spot. Preferably sandy, not too rocky, and no logs."

Saylor grinned and saluted. "Aye aye, Captain."

"I thought we agreed on Daddy."

She squinted. "I think that should stay in the bedroom." She gestured to the beach around us. "It's a little icky in the wrong context."

"Noted." Sandcastles and Daddy. I shuddered. I got the ick too.

But a thought at the back of my mind nagged at me. A dim mental picture of a blonde little girl, running around on the beach, splashing in the water, and calling me daddy.

But that was crazy.

I was an aging rock star. Not daddy material at all.

* * *

After an afternoon of sandcastles, another naughty shower, and a nap—twined together in Saylor's bed with zero naughtiness—Saylor and I headed for the dining hall for dinner, holding hands and enjoying the evening air. Unlike this afternoon, our silence felt comfortable. Companionable, even. Easy between us since we'd spent so much time together.

Sand crunching under our shoes was the only sound until Saylor piped up, "So what's the wildest thing that happened on tour?"

I laughed. "Seriously? Do you not remember what happened last time you asked that?"

"You're not in danger of choking now." Saylor gestured at the empty beach around us. "And for the record, I answered your reciprocal question, so you owe me."

"Yeah well I'd rather pay in a different way. And wait, you only asked that question to make a point about how I was prodding into your life about—you know." I gestured to my cheek. "And considering your answer was a non-answer, I don't owe you jack."

"Wait, give me a second; I'm trying to map out your reply in my head." She tilted her head and gave me a teasing look. "So are we back to tit for tat again?"

"Yeah, but new rules. I show you my tats and you—"

"Evening, Eva. Justin." Saylor drove her elbow into my stomach as she greeted the couple walking up behind me.

"Hey." Eva grinned, her eyes darting between me and Saylor. "We missed you two on the falls trip. Did you find something better to do?"

"Eva," Justin hissed, tugging his wife's hand. "That's none of our business."

Eva shrugged, her overly made-up face sparkling in the tiki-torch lit path. "I just think it's sweet how the two singles on the island are falling for each other. Almost like a reality show. Although come to think of it, I feel like I've seen you before. Are you a reality star, Malcolm?"

I shook my head. My smile felt so plastic. Brittle. "Sorry, Ava, no. No reality fame here."

Justin sighed. "Everyone looks like a celeb to her. I swear she spent the whole flight over convinced there was a rock star on board."

Saylor choked and tried to cover it with a cough.

I struggled to hide my smile. I thought they hadn't been on our flight since they'd arrived after us but on the same day.

"I heard the flight attendant!" Eva exclaimed. "She said the guitarist from the Long Licks was on our flight. You just weren't pushy enough to get us past her and into the first-class cabin. It's not like all ten people up there needed their own bathroom. Ridiculous."

Saylor became seriously interested in her sandal strap. I was just trying to keep my laughter off my face. I guess someone had recognized me after all—the flight attendant. Clearly not Eva. Or Saylor.

Justin rolled his eyes. "You know they never let people through that curtain barrier. Can we go eat now? I'm starving. I missed lunch."

"Yes, dear." Eva sighed. "I swear all this one ever thinks about is food."

"See you guys in there!" Justin hollered as he left us and his wife behind to hightail it to dinner.

"Justin! Wait for me! Sheesh!"

Saylor, fortunately, waited until they disappeared further up the path before letting the laughter fly. "Oh my god."

I sighed. "What? Some people just really like food, okay?"

"You know that's not what I'm laughing about. You realize you might've been able to talk her into the mile-high club? Did you see the way her eyes sparkled when she said guitarist?"

I shook my head and followed in Justin's path—leaving my woman behind. "She's not my type. Never would've happened."

"I can't tell if I should be flattered or not." Saylor panted as she caught up to me.

Fuck me. I couldn't help but smile. "Definitely flattered."

Later that night as we were eating dinner, Samu came up to our table totally apologetic about leaving us behind on the falls trip.

"And to make it up to you both, we'd like to comp you a private beach picnic tomorrow," Samu offered.

Saylor's eyes lit up. She'd no doubt read the brochure about the island's amenities displayed in every room. And I'd never done the private beach picnic.

"Sounds good." I smiled at Saylor.

She grinned back. "What time?"

She was cute when she was being all eager.

"We'll meet at the dock at eleven tomorrow morning and take you by boat. You can snorkel in the bay—it's totally private—have lunch just the two of you, and we'll be back to pick you up at three."

Four hours on a totally secluded part of the island?

"Sign us up." I reached across the table to hold Saylor's hand.

She smiled bashfully back at me.

We walked back to our rooms in companionable silence. Dinner had been delicious. The company great. I kinda felt like I'd known Saylor for forever. Most of the time I completely forgot about our age difference.

I wondered how she'd slide into my life back home. I might have a lot of free time on my hands when we got back.

Shit, what was I going to do with my life?

I blinked and suddenly we were standing at the base of the stairs leading up to Saylor's treehouse bure.

"Everything okay?" Saylor asked with a head tilt, concern twisting her eyebrows.

"Yeah, just thinking about home. I might have a lot of time on my hands soon, and I don't know what the hell I'm going to do."

She squinted. "I thought we put the kibosh on that thinking with the sandcastles."

"I can't help where my mind wanders."

"Well, that sounds like a problem for Future Mal to figure out. We're staying in treehouses on an island in Fiji. How about you try living in the moment?"

"Sometimes I think you're way too wise for your twenty-whatever years."

"Twenty-two years, thank you very much."

I winced. When I was twenty-two, I'd been making stupid decisions—sleeping with groupies and getting talked into ass tattoos. Damn, that made me feel old. So very, very, old.

Is that what I was for Saylor? Her poor decision ass tattoo—only she was sleeping with a washed-up rock star instead? Fuck.

Why did that bug me so much?

"Uh uh," Saylor tsked. "There's that face again. You're getting all grumpy. Not very sexy."

"Yeah, I don't know if I can do sexy tonight. It's hard to turn off my mind when I'm mentally spiraling like this." I sighed. I might need to call my sponsor.

"That's too bad." She pouted exaggeratedly then shook her head sadly. "Because *I* was feeling sexy tonight. Guess it's just going to be me and the collection of toys my bestie packed for me…"

"Toys?" I perked up.

Saylor tipped her head. "A whole suitcase full of them, practically. Paige was insistent. Said I needed to take care of me while I was here. I have vibrators, some flavored lube, and more that I haven't even seen yet. Paige bought out a whole store, I think. I don't even know what some of them do." She sighed. "Sounds like I need to dig into the bag since you're not up for the job."

"I'm up for the job. Who said I wasn't up for the job? What are we doing down here when you have a cornucopia of sex toys waiting for us?" I grabbed her hand and all but drug her up the stairs. "Let's go."

She laughed as she let me guide her to her treehouse.

When we got to the top, I bounced on my toes like a kid waiting on

Christmas morning. "Where's the bag? I wanna see it? Show me!"

Saylor cringed. "God, I don't know where I got the brazenness to even tell you about it. I mean, it sounded like a good idea at the time, but standing here now..."

I tugged her toward me and brushed the hair out of her eyes. "Look at me, baby." I waited until she did. Her baby sky eyes looked so uncertain and kinda freaked. I softened immediately. "Nothing is going to happen here tonight that you're not enthusiastic about. If you don't want to dig into your perverted sex bag, we won't. Simple as that."

"But you were so excited..."

"And I'm still excited." I pushed my hips into hers. "He's happy every time he sees you, I promise."

She bit her bottom lip and still looked unsure.

"And you can change your mind anytime. All you gotta do is say 'get out.' And I don't mean that as a safe word or whatever. I'm not into the whole 'no means yes' thing. You say no and it stops. End of conversation."

She nodded. "I did change my mind."

I dropped my arms from around her and took a step back.

"No, I don't mean about that—about you. I meant about the bag. I want to go through it with you. If that's something you still wanna do..."

"Oh, I sure as hell do. It'll be like the best Christmas ever. Let's do this!"

Chapter 10

Saylor

My heartbeat pounded in my ears as I took his hand and led him deeper into my room, through the lounge area to my bedroom and the walk-in closet in the corner. When my bags had arrived, I'd been adamant that I unpack them myself. I didn't want to think about someone else going through and touching the stuff inside.

Not that I really knew what was inside. Stupid, I know, but Paige had packed it for me. She gave me a whole lecture on discovering my body and my likes and dislikes now that I was single. The whole rah-rah sexual awakening lecture wasn't one I'd been in the mood for—I'd been too busy canceling the wedding.

I'd taken a tiny peek when I'd tossed my toiletries in the bag, but there could be a...um, insert sex toy here I'd never heard of. Because to be honest, I've owned one vibrator my entire life and never really used it. It was too intimidating. And Trent hadn't ever introduced toys in our bedroom. That would mean turning on the lights.

My hands were shaking as I approached the bag I'd flung into the corner. I'd been embarrassed by the contents. I almost hadn't brought the thing, but Paige had taken me to the airport, so I couldn't leave it behind.

All my earlier bravado was gone.

This was scary.

What would Mal think of me?

I tossed him a quick look, and he grinned back at me, bouncing on his toes.

Okay, so that wasn't an out. He was giddy.

Meanwhile I was freaking out.

But I knew Mal was the guy to do this with. I felt safe with him. He'd been amazing so far.

I pointed out the bag to Mal, and he skipped over to it, grabbed the handles, and carried it back into the bedroom. He tossed it onto the bed and dug in with zero inhibition.

"Gorgeous." Mal tossed a jeweled plug with a pink faux crystal on the end onto the bed. "Oh, this one's good. I haven't seen the pearled version before." A rabbit with pearls under the body of the bunny and wrapped around the base joined the plug on the bedspread.

My eyes widened. Which end went inside?

"Ooh, nipple clamps. Have you ever tried these babies?" He held up a gold chain that had what looked like tiny jumper cable prongs at either end.

I shook my head mutely.

"We might need to work our way up to those." Mal tossed them onto the bed. "Do you have a preference between cherry and coconut?" Two bottles of lube joined the collection of depravity on the bedspread.

"Either is good," I replied faintly.

"I like this one." A *whack* sound ripped through the room, then Mal tipped the end of a leather strap so I could see that Good Girl was carved into one side. "You wanna be my good girl, baby?"

I gestured helplessly. "Maybe?"

"I'll put that in the next time pile too." He emptied the bag. Two vibrators—one rabbit, one wand—a bejeweled butt plug, lube, nipple clamps, the strap, more beads—this time like a necklace, and a variety of batteries littered my bed.

"Oh wow." I blinked in shock at the pile. "That…That's a lot."

"How about you pick one thing? What one thing looks interesting to you?"

My eyes danced from one item to the next. Honestly, they were all scary.

How could those clamps feel good? They looked crazy.

And I'd never tried any butt stuff.

I wanted to point at the simple vibrator, but I remembered the way Mal's eyes had lit up when he'd pulled out the rabbit.

And wasn't this about pushing myself?

"The rabbit."

"Oooh! Good choice." He quickly tossed the rest of the items back into the bag and set the bag on the floor. Leaving the rabbit in the center of the bed.

The bright purple plastic was loud on the white sheets.

"Oh! Batteries!" Mal sat on the edge of the bed while he dug back into the bag for batteries and efficiently loaded them into the toy. "Your friend really did think of everything. Remind me to send her flowers."

I nodded mutely. I just knew my eyes were embarrassingly huge and scared.

Mostly because I was kinda scared.

This was so intimidating. Why did I ever think I could keep up with someone like Mal? He'd seen and done more than I could even imagine. Literally. I didn't even know what some of those things in the bag were for.

And how sad was that?

No. I needed to stop talking myself out of this.

I could do this.

I wanted to do this.

I heard a click, followed by a whirr, and Mal's giggle.

"Fuck yeah!" he hollered.

Oh god.

Mal looked up at me, and the grin fell off his face. "Okay. You looked freaked again. How about we forget the rabbit for now and just kiss?"

"No!" I all but shouted. Wincing, I continued at a normal decibel, "I mean, I want to do this. Play with you. I just..."

"You really don't have a poker face, baby." He wrapped his arms around my waist and buried his face in my boobs. His voice was muffled when he spoke again, "How about this? We'll work our way up to the rabbit. Fool around a little first. Maybe even fuck first, *then* I'll finish you with the toy."

"But...what's the point after? I mean, I thought it was about foreplay."

"Just because we fuck, doesn't mean we'll finish at the same time. You ever heard of edging?"

I shook my head.

"Remember how last time you kept almost getting there again and again but never coming? And how, when you did, it felt like your body was going to explode?"

"You did that on purpose? I thought you just didn't know how close I was."

"Oh I knew. It was so fucking hot." He nipped playfully at my top. "Sex doesn't have to be wham bam straight to orgasm, ma'am, then roll over and fall asleep. It should be about having fun. Exploring. Letting go."

The tone of his voice and that hungry look in his eyes had my whole body thrumming and swaying toward him. Almost like I was under a vampire's thrall. He could ask for anything right now, and I'd probably do it for him. *Anything.*

"Come here, baby." He nudged my hips, pulling me toward him.

"Climb onto my lap."

Heat flashed through my bloodstream when he called me baby. Why was that so hot?

I obeyed, climbing into his lap until both knees rested on the bed on either side of his hips. His arms supported my back, and I tried not to think about how my skirt was splayed, leaving absolutely nothing to the imagination. My blue lacy panties had to be the only thing he was seeing.

He rumbled his approval as he bunched my top up and quickly pushed my bra cup out of the way. His thumb rasped over my exposed nipple, making me shiver. "So fucking perfect, and you don't even know."

I caught my breath at the reverence in his tone. It was so different from his playful attitude that it caught me by surprise. This was supposed to be a fun thing. But maybe that was just Mal?

All thought fled my mind as he leaned forward and captured my nipple with his lips.

"Oh!" I gasped before I tangled my hands in his hair and just held on. He was so very good at this part. In seconds, I was unconsciously grinding against him. His cock hard under me. It felt like it was throbbing in beat with my pulse.

I tugged his lips from my breast and kissed him. I was just so amped up and hungry for more.

We tumbled onto the bed in a tangle of limbs and clothes. Mal tugged my top off and my bra went sailing across the room a second later. I pulled insistently at his shirt. I had to feel that masculine chest hair brushing against my aching breasts. But Mal was busy kissing a path down my neck to my exposed breasts.

"These would look so pretty with those nipple clamps on them," he murmured against my skin as his lips danced over my left breast. "First, I'd get them all hard and pulsing with need and then—" he nipped at the tip.

"Ah!" I shrieked as I felt the sharp tug of his teeth before he laved it with his tongue and more kisses.

"It'd keep you aching and so fucking aware of your body. There's nothing like that first bite of the clamp." He nipped at my other nipple, and I whined senselessly. He chuckled. "Next time, baby girl. Next time I'll get you so amped up with need that you're begging for the clamps. Teasing and edging you. It'll feel so good and torturous at the same time. Then we'll talk about that pretty little plug. I'd fucking love to take you from behind and see that diamond winking up at me, reminding me of the hole I still haven't used. Get you all slippery with lube, stretch you with the plug, and then fill you with my dick. Press into your body and feel you gripping me back. Fuck."

I whimpered at his words. They were so depraved and just... delicious. Damn, he could probably talk me into anything if he used that tone.

"I want you to lick it."

I opened my eyes and found him holding the rabbit in front of me. The purple silicone glowed in the room's light. I stuck out my tongue and flicked it against the rabbit. It didn't really taste of much—plastic-y really.

"That's it, baby. Lick it slow for me."

My eyes locked with his and my heart caught at the gleam in his eyes. Suddenly it felt really important that he know how much I wanted this. How much I was into everything he was doing.

I slowly ran my tongue up the rabbit. Well, not the rabbit since that apparently was an appendage. The base was shaped more like a penis but with the rabbit jutting out and a few strands of pearls just under the silicone about three inches down from the head. And the head was where I really amped up my performance—flicking my tongue under the tip, mouthing over the tip, moaning as I took it into my mouth until the rabbit ears prodded my lips.

"Fuck yeah, baby girl. Can't wait to feel those lips around my dick again, but for now..." He pulled the toy away from me then crawled down the bed until he was between my splayed legs.

I caught my breath as I watched him teasingly prod my sex with the rabbit. Then I jumped when a loud buzzing sound came from the toy immediately followed by a humming through my entire body. Oh wow. I couldn't even imagine what that would feel like against my clit.

"How you doing, baby?" Mal pressed a kiss against my labia then blew gently on my very wet folds. "Want to keep going?"

"Yes!" I all but cried. "Please?"

He chuckled then slowly pressed the vibrating toy against my clit.

I about came off the bed. It was so much and yet not enough at the same time. My sex squeezed against nothing, and I shivered as a...not really even an orgasm ...shook my body. Was it possible to get the aftershock before the event? Because that was what it felt like. A little baby orgasm. Good, but definitely not enough.

"Fuck, baby. You're like sexual napalm. I touch you and you go off like a fucking bottle rocket."

I could only moan as my body arched up toward his touch. I wasn't exactly capable of thought, let alone speech at the moment.

Then Mal gave me exactly what my body craved as he gently pressed the head of the toy into my aching sex. Slowly, an inch at a time, the vibrating toy entered my pussy, stretching me, igniting my senses until I almost couldn't take it. It felt like my entire body was humming, vibrating with the toy. So good. So much. It was...

The sound changed, and I felt something touch my clit.

I screamed. The orgasm slammed through my body and didn't stop. Wave after wave of pleasure kept slamming through my body. At one point it felt like it was rubbing against my g-spot at the same time as the bunny was vibrating against my clit. Maybe it was Mal? I couldn't tell. Just so much sensation I couldn't catalogue any of it.

Finally I had to roll onto my side to get away from the amazing agony.

Mal tugged the toy from my body and pressed a kiss against my naked back.

I shivered as another aftershock shook me.

He didn't touch me or say anything else.

After a long minute, I rolled back to my back and stared up at him with wondering eyes. "That was amazing."

He grinned at me then leaned down to kiss my wet cheeks. "That was fun as hell. Did you know it thrusts too? Does all the work for you. What the hell do you even need me for?"

I shook my head at him. "Having you holding the toy between my legs made it like a million times hotter. Especially knowing that you liked it too." My eyes flicked down to his lap and the huge bulge behind his clothes. "But I think it's your turn now."

"Okay, but we should probably wash it before you use it on me."

I laughed and rolled my eyes. He smirked back at me and tossed the toy onto the bed. Leaping to his feet, he was naked quicker than I could track. I still had my skirt wrapped around my hips. I don't even know when or where my panties disappeared to.

Less than a minute later, Mal was back between my splayed legs with his condom clad cock nudging my sex. His muscular arms were pressed against the bed on either side of my shoulders. And I had to catch my breath at the intensity in his eyes as he stared down at me. It felt like he could see inside my soul. Like he knew me down to an elemental level.

He pressed inside me, his cock stretching me in ways the toy just couldn't. Nothing could replicate the heady feeling of having a gorgeous, caring man on top of you, doing everything he could to make you come again.

"Fuck, baby." He breathed harshly. "You're so tight. Love that tight, sweet, little pussy."

I clenched around his cock without conscious thought, and he groaned again.

"You gotta stop being so fucking hot. Or else this is going to be over before we even started."

I laughed as I wrapped my arms and legs around him. "This is all about you. I've already had my huge, amazing orgasm."

"Oh, baby girl. You don't even know what's coming." His breath left him in a huge whoosh just before he bent down and kissed me.

I got so lost in his kiss and his thrusting cock that I didn't even notice the buzzing at first. Between my panting and his deep groans, the sound was lost in the mix.

And then I felt it.

Something solid—and not his dick—buzzed against my clit.

I about came up off the bed.

Between his dick inside me, pressing against the depths of my sex, that cocky expression on his face, and the buzzing of the toy against my clit, I was in sensory overload.

I shivered and my tight nipples brushed against his chest hair.

"Oh god. That's…I'm not—I can't—" I screamed again as I went over.

I distantly heard Mal's answering roar, but I was too busy with the shudders wracking my body to be aware of much. Then his limp body came down on top of mine and gave me another mini orgasm.

"Christ, woman. You squeeze me one more time—" He groaned.

I giggled. "It's not like I'm doing it on purpose." I shivered. And then I squeezed around him.

He groaned again.

"Okay, maybe that one was on purpose."

"Fuck, I can't even complain. My girl's pussy is too tight. Anyone I said that to would get out their tiny violin and mock me."

"Oh my god! You can't tell people!" I shoved his shoulder.

Mal rolled to his side and off me then pressed a quick kiss to my lips. "Never. Be right back."

I watched his muscular back flex as he walked into the bathroom. Okay, I might've peeked at his butt too…

Covering my face with my hands, I took a deep breath. I swear I hadn't had time to breathe the entire time I'd known Mal. He took up all the oxygen with his presence.

This was easily the best night of my life.

I couldn't believe I'd done that with him. And yet I also couldn't imagine doing it with anyone else. Mal was quickly becoming my safety net, and I didn't know what to think about that.

Although it sounded like Future Saylor's problem. I was too tired to overanalyze everything. After pulling off my twisted skirt, I decided to do something I'd never done before—sleep naked.

Shimmying into the bed, I pulled the sheets over my naked body and grinned. I could maybe get used to this.

"Good thinking." Mal tumbled into the bed next to me and burrowed under the sheets until his very naked body spooned mine. His arm wrapped around my tummy, and his large hand cupped my left breast. "This way I'll have unfettered access tomorrow morning. Although the condoms are…wherever my pants ended up. But that's Future Mal's problem."

I grinned into my pillow at his use of my favorite procrastination phrase.

"Is it okay that I'm still here?" Mal whispered.

"Of course," I whispered back.

He hummed happily.

Sighing, I relaxed into the bed and Mal's embrace.

And I don't know why, but a few moments later I whispered into the quiet room, "It wasn't Trent who hit me."

Mal's arm tightened around my waist.

"It was his bookie. He owes lots of people lots of money, and I didn't know anything about it. I'd been with him for years, and it turns out I never really knew him at all."

It felt like a weight was taken off my shoulders with my confession. That a large barrier I hadn't even realized was between us was now gone.

Mal pressed a kiss against my temple but didn't say anything, content for the moment between us to just breathe.

Chapter 11

Mal

It felt like something had shifted between us. After her confession last night, I spent some time thinking about all the ways her ex had no doubt hurt her and all the ways I wanted to hurt him because of it. She deserved so much better. I hoped she knew that.

It was now my life mission to make sure she realized her worth.

I couldn't remember ever having so much fun in bed with a girl before. Granted, it had been a minute since I'd been with a woman. But usually it was all about just getting off and moving onto the next. Something about being with Saylor changed that for me. It was intoxicating watching her discover what she loved about her body and mine.

And I don't think I'd ever laughed so much with a woman in bed before.

She was so giving and funny and just...perfect.

As I waited for her to get ready for our private beach picnic, I was practically bouncing on my toes. I couldn't wait to get her alone on that beach.

"Maybe we should pack something from your friend's bag for the beach!" I hollered at the closed bathroom door.

CHAPTER 11

Saylor was currently putting on a bikini and apparently needed complete privacy for the moment. Something about how if we ever wanted to leave, I had to stop taking her clothes off. I didn't really follow what she said. I'd been too busy staring at her gorgeous tits. So plump and just perfect. She should really be topless all the time.

Although I don't know how I'd ever get anything done.

"Mal?" Saylor called from the suddenly opened door. "You all right?"

I blinked then shook my head. "Sorry. Just got lost in my thoughts, picturing your tits."

She rolled her eyes and headed for the front door, her sundress hiding all the goods and yet swinging temptingly under her ass like a call to action. "You're ridiculous. And for the record, we're not taking anything from the sex bag to the beach. Salt water corrodes. But I've got sunscreen, my ereader, sunglasses...what am I forgetting?"

"Uh, condoms? And you should leave your ereader here. You're not going to be reading today. Plus, salt water corrodes," I repeated teasingly.

"But that's what I always do at the beach."

I widened my eyes at her. "Seriously? I plan on doing *you* at the beach. It's a private beach. No one around for miles. Totally something to scratch off your sex bucket list. Ditch the ereader. You're not gonna need it."

"Fine." She huffed and reached into her bag and tossed her tablet onto the small sofa. "But we can't bring condoms. Where will we put them after they're used? We can't litter, and I don't want someone to have to pick *that* up after us."

I shrugged. "They'll probably have a bag for trash. At the very least, they'll have our sandwiches or whatever wrapped up. We can use that."

She pulled a face like it was a gross suggestion.

Seriously? Were we really not going to have sex on our private beach picnic because she was squeamish about disposing the used condom later?

Saylor bit her lip for a moment then looked at me with a cautious expression. "I was thinking about that last night…after, you know."

"After the best sex ever? I think that's what you called it…"

She rolled her eyes. "Whatever. I'm only twenty-two, so there's plenty of time for better."

"Oh hell no." I tossed my sunglasses down then toed off my sandals. "Challenge accepted. Come on. Take off the sundress. Let's do this."

"Mal!" Saylor laughed and feigned like she was going to run when I crossed the room to take her in my arms. Despite her protests, she snuggled deeper into my arms. "No. We don't have time for more sex. We're going to have a once in a lifetime snorkeling session followed by a picnic on a private beach."

"Wherein we're going to have sex on said beach. Right?" I nuzzled the side of her neck. If she wasn't into it, I wasn't going to pressure her. But I couldn't deny that I was bummed. Sex on the beach! I mean, come on. Who cared about a used condom being seen by the staff? They knew we were fucking.

"That's what I was thinking about. I'm on the pill, and you said it's been almost a year since you were with someone else. Which means you're clean, right? Tested and everything?"

My heart stuttered in my chest. "Right…"

She hunched slightly. "I got tested once I found out about all the ways my ex was lying to me. I'm clean too." She bit her lip and looked at me with this uncertain expression. "So I think we can do away with the condoms. It's not like we're going to be sleeping with anyone else here, right?"

"Right. I mean, are you sure?"

"Yes, I'm sure." She bit her bottom lip and looked up at me through her eyelashes, her cheeks red.

I groaned and had to kiss her. My lips moved over hers like I was returning from war. I hadn't gone bareback with a woman since I was a stupid teen who thought he was bullet-proof. This was epic, paradigm changing shit.

Finally Saylor broke the kiss and pushed against my chest. "Again, we don't have time for this. Samu said we'd leave at 10:30."

"Samu will leave when we're ready." I ducked down again to kiss her.

She let me, for all of a second, before pulling away. "What about my sex bucket list? I think it just merged with yours. Bareback sex on a private beach?" She danced out of my arms and walked backward toward the door. "You coming?"

I groaned and dropped my head back. "Not for at least an hour, apparently."

Saylor's laughter had me grinning despite my aching erection as we walked out the door.

Not long after, we were bouncing across the waves on a small boat with Samu grinning as he operated the outboard motor.

"We gotta get you out here fishing!" he hollered over the sound of the engine.

Saylor squealed and burrowed into my arms at the cold spray from the ocean.

I raised my eyebrows at Samu as my answer. Seriously? I had this in my arms. Fishing could wait for when I was too old to get it up anymore.

He tipped his head at me like he got it.

Ten minutes later, the boat bobbed to a stop in the center of a large bay. The island was shaped like the Greek letter omega, and the bay we were in was the very center of the large loop. A horseshoe bay they called it. In the distance, a sailboat was anchored, but they couldn't come close since this was a privately owned island. And the sandy beach was deserted, ending in jungle growth beyond. The inhabited section of the island was a good hour hike away.

We'd be completely alone.

I grinned down at Saylor. I couldn't fucking wait. Literally.

She shimmied out of her sundress and applied sunscreen with some help from me. We listened to the quick safety lecture from Samu.

"And there's already a picnic blanket and basket on the beach for you. I'll be back in four hours to get you. Just leave your clothes here, and we'll keep them safe for you."

With our fins and masks in place, we sat on the edge of the boat. Saylor went in first and once she was clear of the side, I joined her with a big splash. We swam a safe distance back, and Samu waved as he slowly motored away.

And then we were alone.

We held hands as we swam along the surface of the water. Technicolor fish darted under us, twirling into the coral and seaweed. Saylor pointed out a bright blue starfish on top of the pale coral. I couldn't see much of her face, but I was pretty sure she was grinning the entire time. I know I was.

It was amazing and magical, and I was exhausted by the time we waded to the shore.

Exhausted but full of anticipation.

Saylor shivered, goosebumps breaking out over her body as the breeze picked up a little. I grabbed a towel and wrapped it around her small frame. Raising up on her toes, she pressed a quick kiss against my cheek.

"Thank you, Daddy."

I groaned and dropped my head down onto hers. "Fuck me. And here I thought you'd want to eat first."

"Who says I don't?" She blinked innocently up at me, her eyelashes and hair wet from our swim.

I groaned again. "Come on. I need some fuel if I'm ever going to keep up with you." I swatted her rear, and she squealed. "Let's see what they've put in the ole picnic basket."

While we munched on sandwiches, we talked about anything and everything.

"What do you need to go all in on your clothing designs?"

Saylor rolled her eyes. "Money. Connections. Experience. All things I don't have. I mean, I guess I could go back to school and make some connections while I get another degree, but that also requires money I don't have. I took out a student loan to pay for this trip."

"I think you're selling yourself short. You have experience. All the outfits I've seen are fucking awesome. You can always work for someone else at first. I bet if you put together a portfolio, you could get a job in no time."

"But all the best jobs are in New York or LA, which again requires money I don't have to get there, let alone survive once I'm there."

"I happen to know someone with money, connections, and a place in LA that you could probably use. He might want some quid pro quo in return though." I leered comically at her to lessen the huge step I was proposing.

Living together?

Did I seriously just put that out there?

Saylor rolled her eyes like I was teasing her. "What about you? What are you going to do when you get back?"

I paused for a second at the switch in topic then let her have it. I wasn't exactly ready to examine my feelings about the way she'd just blown off my offer to live with me.

"You mean when I get back to my band that's splintering?" I sighed and stretched out on my side. This wasn't a fun topic either. "I don't know. I could try to start my own thing, but honestly, that doesn't appeal—starting over, I mean. We worked so hard and for so long to get the band the attention we wanted. I love what we've built, and I kinda feel like anything else would feel like a cop out facsimile. I don't get why Leif would just chuck it all for his own ego trip. He's already the lead singer—what else does he fucking need?"

Saylor shrugged like I'd made her a little uncomfortable. Maybe I was yelling a bit at the end of my tirade.

"Sorry. Still pisses me off." My fingers traced a path in the sand on the edge of the blanket. "And I don't know what's going on with Gio. He hasn't returned any of my texts. Beau is wrapped up with his new bride. Ryker has also gone underground, so I don't know what the fuck is going on with him. Everything's just gone so fucking nuts."

Saylor laughed humorlessly. "Tell me about it."

"You have your own place figured out when you get home?"

She shrugged. "I stashed my stuff at Paige's place before I left. I might move in with her. I'm definitely not staying at our old apartment since his bookie knows where that is."

"Paige sounds like the smart and safe move."

Saylor moved her shoulders restlessly. "My mom is still pressuring me to make up with Trent. She's sent me a few texts."

"Even after what happened? She knows why you broke up with the asshat, right?"

"Oh, she knows. She just thinks it's a temporary slip up. That's what she called it—a slip up." Saylor scoffed. "I don't think owing money to the Russian fucking mafia is a slip up."

"He owes the mafia?" Fuck, that was bad. Like really, really bad. Those guys didn't fuck around.

She shrugged. "He had a Russian accent and said something about the Bratva. So yeah, we're very much never, ever getting back together. No matter what my mom thinks."

"Fuck yeah, you're not." I rolled onto my back and tugged her down on top of me. "You're mine, baby girl. No take-backsies."

"Mmmm, anything you say, Daddy." Saylor nuzzled into my

shoulder.

I wrapped my arms around her. "Christ, I'm a sick, sick fucking man. The way it gets me every time you call me that. I'm definitely going to hell."

"Mind if I ride you on your way down?" Saylor asked with a naughty little smile.

"Fuck, that's hot. I need to touch you." It was a struggle, but I eventually got all the wet fabric wrapping around her tight, little body free while she tugged my swim trunks down.

But before I could begin worshipping her gorgeous body, she shimmied between my legs and nuzzled my dick against her cheek.

I seriously didn't think there was a better sight on god's green earth. If I could've taken a picture, I would've.

Then she licked her way down my shaft to swallow me whole, and I wasn't capable of much thought after that. Fuck, she was good. Licking. Sucking. Humming. It was all I could to not blow my load all over her gorgeous face.

But I had the promise of a long-held fantasy to experience. "As fucking fantastic as you are at blowing me, baby, I gotta stop you."

Saylor grumbled as I pulled her up my body and onto my chest. "But you were almost there."

"Exactly." I grunted. "And you promised me bareback. Unless that's off the table now?"

She blinked in confusion then shook her head.

"Fan-fucking-tastic." I kissed her quick and hard even as my hands wandered over her body. I found with one touch that she was already soaking wet. "Ah, baby girl. Did sucking me get you all hot and bothered?"

She writhed against me, rubbing her hardened nipples against my chest. "Yes, I was thinking about your big, hard dick and how it'd feel inside me. And then I was thinking about watching you stand over me and jacking off all over me. And maybe you make me lick it up after."

"Fuck, baby, you gotta stop talking if you want this to end the way I want it to end." Her words got me all jacked up.

I pulled her body into place until her hips hovered over my straining dick. She rested one hand on my chest while she guided my dick with her other, her hand small and cold against my throbbing erection.

Fuck, I was going to come before I was even inside her.

But I also couldn't look away.

It was everything. The sound and sight of the ocean behind her. The total otherwise stillness around us. No one for miles. And Saylor's gorgeous naked body hovering over me.

If this was a dream, I definitely didn't want to wake up yet.

And then she slowly sank onto me.

Wet warmth gripped my dick. It was so much more than anything I'd thought. Not to overstate it, but it felt like a religious experience. This, this right here, was everything. Everything I wanted. Everything I didn't know I needed.

Saylor's eyes burned down at me, and I reached up to cup one of her tits. My thumb rasped against the tip, and she clenched around me.

"Fuck." I groaned.

Then she started riding me. Her tight, wet, fucking amazing pussy gripping my shaft. Up and down. It was the thing of fantasies. Her gorgeous breasts bouncing above me. Her tight, little pussy taking my dick so good. Her beautiful face tight with need.

"Fuck, baby girl. You're taking my dick so good." I reached down and flicked my thumb against her clit. I was so close, I needed her to come with me. I couldn't lose it before she did.

Suddenly, she slowed her pace. Her tits still jiggled with her slight motion, but it was the expression in her eyes that held me spellbound. So intent. So emotional.

I reached up and tugged her down to me. I had to kiss her. I had to let her know that I felt it too.

Then I totally took over, thrusting into her from below. I was so close, and I could tell she was too. Her little whimpers and gasps were driving me insane.

My balls tightened and just as I went over, I felt the tightest, harshest grip around my dick ever.

Saylor's screaming moan made birds in the trees behind us take flight in a sudden rustle of noise. But I didn't give a shit. I pumped my cum into her, totally lost in the sensation of her pussy gripping me tight.

She collapsed onto my chest, totally limp.

My heart thundered in my chest, and my breath left me in huge gasping pants.

"Fuck, baby. I think you almost killed me."

She didn't say anything in response, but I felt her smile against my chest.

As I held her close to me, I had a thought that but for her pills we could've made a baby just now. And oddly, it didn't terrify me. Once upon a time, it was the one thing I was determined to make sure would never happen. Back then I didn't have the time, attention, or energy to take care of a dog, let alone another human. But now…

God.

Now I think I wanted to go all in on Saylor Tate.

I just had to figure out how to convince her that I—unlike her ex—was a good bet.

Chapter 12

Still Mal

It was all I could think about the entire day. I was done obsessing about my bandmembers who didn't give a shit about me.

I was going all in on Saylor.

I held her close as we boated back to the resort. She sighed and snuggled close to me like she loved being with me. And I loved being that strong, protective person for her.

Her Daddy.

We spent the rest of the day together, hanging out in her treehouse, enjoying her private pool, and playing in the outdoor shower.

I finally broached the topic over dinner.

"So I was thinking…"

She looked at me with this open and soft expression that was just so sweet and totally her that I lost my train of thought. "Mal? Everything okay? Did you get too much sun today?"

"I think you should move in with me."

"What? That's crazy." She laughed incredulously. "We barely know each other. This isn't—I can't just…"

"But this feels right, doesn't it? Does time really matter when you know here—" I thumped my fist against my chest. "That you've found the one?"

"Mal, you can't—I mean, I'm not..."

"I saw your expression on the beach today, Saylor. You feel it too. And think about it—we make sense. Especially now. My band is probably breaking up, you want to break into the fashion industry. I have contacts. I have money. You could do it yourself with me standing behind you. I wanna go all in with you and your dream."

"That's—that's just nuts. I mean, you can't just promise something like that. You don't know—"

"We'll figure it out. Together. I'm going to have a lot of free time on my hands. I have more money than I know what to do with. Why not spend it on someone I..."

She waited a few beats then shook her head, disappointment clouding her features. "See, that right there. You can't even say it, Mal. I'm done pinning my hopes and dreams on guys that can't follow through. I deserve more, and I'm fine doing it all myself."

She was right. If I couldn't say it, why should she believe it?

Only I knew I felt it. And I knew that she felt it too. I saw it in her eyes today.

So why was it so hard to say the words out loud?

"I love you, Saylor."

She dropped her water glass. It crashed to the floor, spraying water and broken glass everywhere. But neither one of us moved to even look at it.

"What?" she whispered, her face suddenly pale.

"I love you, Saylor Tate." I stood and shoved my chair back with my foot. Grabbing her hand in mine, I moved to kneel down.

"No, you can't!" Saylor stood up and tugged on my arm to keep me standing.

"Yes, I can. I love you. I wanna be with you. I want to have kids with you. Nothing would make me happier than holding a tiny little replica of you. I've never said that before—kids were always the last thing I wanted or even thought about—but I want that with you. I want to make a family with you."

She dropped my arm and looked at me with wide eyes. "I thought you were going to get down on one knee and the glass…" She blinked a few times then shook her head. "This is crazy. We can't. I mean I don't even really know you. We can't just—whatever. This is crazy."

Jone came over with a broom and a mop and quietly cleaned up the mess from Saylor's water glass. I could tell from his pursed lips he'd heard our conversation.

Tossing a quick look around the room, we had *everyone's* attention.

I gestured helplessly. "I don't care. I know you. I know what's important about you, and we'll figure out the rest as we go. Because you're it. You're the one I want. You're the one who makes me want to be a better man. I love you, Saylor." As Jone backed away from our table, I took a chance and went down on one knee in front of her. Grabbing her hand, I held it in mine and grinned up at her. "I don't care if this is spontaneous or impetuous or whatever. I'll say it again, I love you, Saylor. I want to build a life with you. Will you marry me?"

"I don't—I can't…" She pulled her hand out of my grip. "I'm sorry." Then she turned and ran out of the room.

Leaving me on my knees in front of the entire island.

Fuck.

Pushing myself up, I didn't spare our audience a glance as I took off after her. "Saylor, wait! Please!"

I caught up to her on the beach path. My heart sunk as I realized she was crying.

Shit. I was totally fucking this up.

"Why did you do that?" She whirled around and stabbed a finger in my direction. "That was such a gross, demeaning joke. It's not funny."

"It's not a joke to me. I'm not laughing. I'm as serious as a fucking heart attack. I want you. I want to marry you."

"You can't just say things like that. You can't make me want..." She shook her head, tears glittering in the torchlight. She made a gasping whimper then turned and stomped down the path and away from me.

Like hell was I letting her run away.

"You can't just run when things get hard!" I yelled at her retreating back.

She whirled around. "You don't get to say that to me." Stomping back up the path, fire now glittered in her eyes even as her cheeks were still wet with her tears. "You don't know the shit I've faced. I don't run away. That's not who I am."

"Then stay here. Fight with me. Now. Tell me why it's such a bad idea—why you and I don't make sense."

"You, you, you...you're a rock star, and I'm a teacher."

"My band is breaking up, and you hate your job. Next."

She rolled her eyes. "You live in LA, and I live in Las Vegas. That's not exactly commuting distance."

"You said all the good jobs aren't even in Vegas. Pick a city you want to work in. I've been to most of the major ones. We'll figure it out. I got money. I got time."

"I-I-I don't know what to say to that. That's not how I live. That's not how most people live—how normal people live."

"But it's how you can live if you just pick me. Choose me. Choose us."

Her shoulders slumped. "This kinda thing doesn't happen. People don't just up and marry total strangers. It's not, I don't..."

"Does it make sense? Do we make sense?" I took a step toward her but didn't reach out for her yet. She was still a flight risk. "Despite the time, despite the distance, despite any other roadblock you think up to throw in front of us, don't you feel the same way about me?"

She sighed and looked away. After a few beats, she turned back to me. "But why does it have to be marriage? Why don't we just move in together or whatever?"

"Because you won't believe it. You're used to people letting you down—your ex, your mom, even your best friend when it came to you chasing your dream. But I'm not going to do that. I want to prove to you that I'm all in. I want to be your rock. I want to be your fucking everything. All you gotta do is say yes."

She bit her bottom lip, and I could see in her eyes she wanted to say yes. She wanted what I was promising her.

Finally she shook her head. "There's no way we can get married here. I mean, there's probably paperwork required that I don't have. I only brought my passport and driver's license."

I took a step closer to her and grinned wolfishly down at her. "You let me worry about the red tape. All you gotta do is say yes."

She stared at me for so long sweat ran down my back as the moment went on and on. I wanted her to say yes. I needed her to say yes. I felt like I finally found my purpose after the Long Licks—to be her husband and build a family and a fashion empire or whatever the hell she wanted.

"Yes. I'll marry you, Mal."

"Fucking yes!" I wrapped an arm around her and punched the other at the sky. *"SHE SAID YES!"* I shouted just before I kissed her with everything I had. As my lips moved over hers, I was vaguely aware of cheering in the distance. But all I could focus on was the amazing woman in my arms who'd just made me the happiest man on earth.

I could see she still wasn't a hundred percent sure, but I vowed to make it my life's mission that she'd never regret this decision. I'd do everything in my power to be worthy of this amazing woman.

Our hips bumped against each other as we walked down the path toward the treehouses with my arm still wrapped around her shoulder. I still considered her a flight risk so I wasn't letting her go just yet.

"Your place is better than mine, but we could go to my treehouse if you want?" I offered.

She shook her head. "If you don't mind, I'd rather sleep in mine. It's more familiar and won't freak me out in the morning."

"Sure, baby. Whatever you want."

Her smile looked tremulous and almost brittle, like she was hanging on by a thread.

Yeah, I had a lot of work to do.

When we got to the room, Saylor disappeared into the bathroom with a muttered excuse. No doubt to have a panic attack.

Even though she'd said yes, I still felt like I was screwing this up.

What I would've given for a landline so I could call for room service. Get some bubbly for her, create some ambiance in here.

Fuck it. I could do that. What did I have to work with…

When Saylor finally came out of the bathroom, the lighting was turned down, some low instrumental music was playing from my cell phone, I held two wineglasses —one white wine, one water—and flower petals were scattered from where she stood to the bed and all over the sheets. I might've decimated a few bouquets in the room she hopefully wasn't attached to in order to get the effect.

Judging by the way she gasped, her hands coming up to cover her lips, I'd done a good job. "*Mal*. This is…wow."

"I worked with what I had." I shrugged.

She crossed the room to me. I held out a glass for her, but she ignored it and went beeline straight into my chest, wrapping her arms around me and burrowing into my shirt. "Thank you."

I awkwardly hugged her back, despite the wineglasses in my hands. "Of course, baby girl. I don't have a ring for you yet, but I wanted you to see how serious I am. I meant what I said. I want to go all in with you."

"Thank you, Mal." She tipped her head back and blinked up at me.

"You might've guessed I was freaking out in there. I want to believe you—I do. I guess I'm just afraid to trust it. I've been let down so many times."

"I'm not going to do that. I know the real deal when I see it. You're it for me, baby girl. And I'm going to do everything in my power to make sure you believe it too."

She smiled at me, but I could see she still doubted me. Going up on her toes, she pressed a quick peck on my lips, and I quickly took it into a deeper kiss. She swayed unsteadily on her feet, and I juggled the wineglasses to try to stabilize her.

Laughing, I shook my head. "Maybe we should move this party to somewhere more horizontal."

This time, Saylor's smile was more authentic. Or maybe it was the eye roll. "It always comes to sex with you."

"Hey, I'm just looking out for you. It doesn't have to be the bed. We haven't played around on that sofa over there yet." I pointed with a wine glass hand toward the uncomfortable looking rattan based sofa.

Saylor winced. "Yeah, no. Not when you went to all that trouble of creating this lovely setting. Plus that couch looks like it'll poke us in the back."

"Whatever m'lady wants." I pressed a peck against her temple.

She took a glass out of my hand. "M'lady is imagining this is alcohol." Saylor tossed back the liquid like it was water. A second later, she was bent over hacking and coughing. "What the hell?"

"Shit, baby. Sorry. One was wine."

"I thought you were an alcoholic. What the hell are you doing opening wine bottles? Isn't that—" *Cough, cough, cough.* "Isn't that bad for your sobriety?"

"Wine isn't a trigger for me. I mean, I can't drink it, obviously, but being around wine drinkers isn't exactly the same as backstage before or after a show. Although you did toss back that glass like it was tequila."

"I haven't ordered wine this entire time because I wanted to respect your sobriety. I mean, I'm not a big drinker, but it would've been nice—especially when I first got off the plane."

I winced. "Sorry."

She shook her head, and I could tell it was one more hash mark in the 'marrying is a mistake' column.

We were literally minutes into this engagement, and I was fucking things up.

I cupped her face in my hands and gently rubbed her tears away with my thumbs. "It's okay that we're still figuring each other out. We'll get there, and it'll be okay as long as we continue to look out for each other. That you would forgo alcohol for my sobriety means the fucking world to me. It's just one of the many things I love about you."

She pursed her lips like she was fighting a smile then gave into the laugh burbling up inside her. "Is now a bad time to tell you that I don't remember what your last name is?"

I laughed with her. "Okay, it's a little crazy, but the best kinda crazy. And for the record it's Holt."

"Holt," she repeated. "Saylor Holt. I kinda like the sound of that."

"Fuck yeah. I do too."

Her eyes got misty, and I couldn't resist the urge to kiss her. So I did.

She groaned against my lips and wrapped her arms around my shoulders and held on.

We kept eye contact the entire time. Hers still full of questions but also wonder. Mine determined to prove my worth to her.

And when I came inside her, all I could think was 'what if.'

What if we made a tiny version of Saylor, with wispy white-blonde hair and gorgeous blue eyes? I wanted it more than anything, but it was too soon to say aloud.

Soon.

Chapter 13

Saylor

Mal moved quick.

The next two days were all about preparations and so much sex I barely had time to think, let alone doubt our plans.

He flew a jeweler in so we could pick rings. Despite his pressure for me to pick a gargantuan rock, I fell in love with a two-carat cushion cut diamond with a twisted rose gold band. When he saw the way my face lit up as I slid the ring onto my finger, Mal relented.

But he demanded that I pick out his ring. So I went with a matching rose gold men's band with a center inlay of brushed black zirconium. It looked masculine and whimsical at the same time. Perfect for Mal.

The way he grinned down at the ring made my heart skip a beat. He was just so happy. Giddy even.

It was contagious.

When he offered to get some dress options boated over for me, I asked for fabric instead. I'd never made a dress in such a short turn around before, but I'd grown up watching *Project Runway* and was naïve enough to believe I could do it.

It was close, but I'd forgone sleep last night to make it happen.

Which was how I found myself walking down a flower strewn beach path with a bouquet in my hands and a short, flirty white sundress flowing around me. At the end of the beach, Mal stood under an arch made from branches with topical flowers twisted around it.

It felt like a dream. Or an out of body experience.

Was I really going to marry this man?

I hadn't even told anyone back home this was happening.

I didn't want anyone to talk me out of it—because they would've.

In contrast to my heartbeat thundering in my ears, Mal looked so calm and just awestruck. Like he couldn't believe his luck that I was going to marry him.

Oh god. We were really doing this.

Before my doubts had a chance to multiply, I reached Mal, and he took my hands in his and grinned down at me despite the tears sparkling in his eyes.

A sense of peace enveloped me.

I could do anything with Mal looking at me like that.

"We're gathered here to celebrate the wedding of Malcolm Holt and Saylor Tate." Samu stood in front of us inside the arch with a mischievous grin. "And for some reason, Mal asked me to officiate this wonderful day for them."

The few people standing nearby chuckled at his cute expression. But I couldn't take my eyes off of Mal.

I jumped when Samu clapped three times. It felt like it was right next to my ear.

"The kava ceremony marks the official start of wedding celebrations in Fiji. During this ritual, we have both families gather in a circle as the village chief prepares kava in a tanoa bowl. Since it's just the two of you here today, Mal has asked me to prepare the kava." Samu turned and picked up a coconut bowl floating in murky water. "The ceremony strengthens bonds between families while seeking ancestral blessings for the marriage." He took a drink from the bowl then turned to refill it and passed the bowl to Mal.

Mal let go of my hands to take the bowl and took a deep drink before passing the bowl to me.

No one mentioned this part of the ceremony to me. I swapped my bouquet for the bowl and held it in both hands. After taking a deep breath, I took a drink.

It did *not* taste good.

Pretty much had the flavor I expected of murky water. But a weird sensation afterward had my tongue tingling and numbing a little. I passed the bowl back to Mal who gave me my bouquet and passed the bowl back to Samu.

Samu set the bowl back into the murky water then clapped once. Again in my ear.

I jumped and then scowled teasingly at Mal's grinning face.

"It's time for the *salusalu* <sar-loo-sar-loo> exchange. The *salusalu* symbolizes honor, love, and celebration." Samu turned to Mal. "I understand Mal has written his own vows?"

Mal nodded. Samu passed him a flower garland made from hibiscus and grass. Mal turned back to me and laid the flowers over my head like a necklace. "Saylor, I promise to be there when you need me, to fill your days with sunshine, to comfort and encourage you, to help you reach your goals, to be your best friend, and to love you all my life with all my heart."

The love and intensity in his eyes made tears well in mine. It was everything. Everything I didn't know I wanted. Everything I needed.

My tears streamed unchecked down my cheeks, and I laughed, so full of joy and love for this man.

He brushed my tears away then reached into his pocket and pulled out my ring. "With this ring, I give you my heart, my love, and my commitment. For now and for all our days."

He slid the ring onto my finger, and it was getting hard to see for all the tears blurring my vision.

"Saylor?" Samu asked from a distance.

I shook my head and turned to the arch where Samu stood, holding out a *salusalu* for me to give Mal. I accepted it with a teary smile, and he held my bouquet for me. I went up on my toes to drape the garland around Mal's shoulders. He bent down for me slightly and gave me a teary smile in return.

"Oh, the ring!" I turned to Samu and gently untangled Mal's ring from the ribbon holding my bouquet together.

As I faced Mal with his ring in my hand, I had a hard time remembering the words I'd wanted to say. So many thoughts jumbled in my brain. "Mal, I still can't believe we're doing this. Only you could make such an impetuous, spontaneous decision feel like the only thing that makes sense. You have become my safe harbor in an insane time, and I can't wait to see what crazy adventure you convince me to go on next. But I'll jump into it with you because I know I'll be safe as long as I have you at my side."

His eyes were misty as he looked at me, and I caught my breath at the naked love and devotion I could see in his gaze. He made me want to believe in everything.

I took his hand in mine and slid his ring onto his finger. "With this ring, I give you my heart. I choose you—today and always. I love you so much."

He laughed huskily. "You realize that's the first time you said it?"

"Really?" I shook my head slightly. "It can't be."

He blinked at me like he was waiting for my realization.

"Dammit," I whispered. "That's—That's crazy. I'm so sorry, Mal. But I do. I love you today and always."

Mal's eyes shone with emotion as he bent toward me to kiss me.

Samu cleared his throat. "Uh, we're not there yet. Give me one more minute."

Mal turned his head to glare at Samu while I tried and failed to swallow my laugh.

Samu grinned back at Mal. "*Rerevaka na Kalou ka Doka na Tui*. Fear God and honor the King. You may kiss your bride."

"About damn time," Mal mumbled just before his lips covered mine and muffled my laughter.

His kiss went on and on. My heart thundered in my ears, and I couldn't hear the ocean or the small crowd cheering for us.

I was too busy being loved by Mal. I don't know what I'd been so worried about. The promises he'd just made me were everything. And this was the best perk of our marriage by far. Mal seriously knew what he was doing when it came to kissing...and other things too.

Finally Mal broke our kiss and wrapped an arm around my shoulders.

"May I present Mister and Missus Malcolm Holt! *Vinaka*!" Samu shouted. "We have a *lovo* feast for the guests to enjoy back at the dining bure. *Bula*!"

It was at that point I realized that we actually had a crowd. It looked like everyone on the island had turned up. I don't know how I'd missed them on my walk down the beach. So many smiling faces greeted us as we walked down the beach, including Eva and Justin.

"I can't believe you two got married!" Eva squealed. "It's so romantic."

"Congrats." Justin smiled at us with his arm wrapped around his wife. They were both casual beach chic with his khaki shorts and polo and her bright, flowery sundress.

"Thank you," I replied, but Mal didn't do more than mutter something no one could hear as he tugged me down the beach.

"Someone's eager." Eva laughed in a loud aside to her husband.

"Yup, gotta fuck my bride," Mal returned as he fast walked toward the treehouse. "It's not legal until I've come inside her. Fijian law and all that."

"Mal!" I shouted before I slapped his shoulder. "Oh my god. I cannot believe you said that. I'm never showing my face at the dining hall. I'm so embarrassed."

"Come on, it's not like we're ever going to see them again after this trip. Who gives a shit?"

"But this trip isn't over!" I wailed as we hustled down the path. "We'll still have to see them for the next week or whatever."

"Nah, they're leaving tomorrow. Most couples only stay a week."

"Oh. Um, so does this mean we'll miss the feast or whatever? Because it smells amazing."

Mal stopped at the bottom of the stairs and bent down to pick me up in a bridal carry.

"Mal!"

"Well, you were taking too long." He puffed as he climbed the stairs with me in his arms.

"Because my legs are shorter than yours, and now you're going to screw up your back. Slow down."

"No, the faster we get to the treehouse, the quicker I get to see that gorgeous dress on the floor."

"Oh my god! You're insane."

He was only puffing slightly when he reached the door. "And it's tradition to carry the bride over the threshold."

He gave me this look so full of love and tenderness.

And I just melted. That look. I pressed a kiss against his chin since I couldn't reach his lips. "Now giddy up! We have a marriage to consummate!"

His laughter echoed around us as he carried me into the bedroom, which had pretty much become our bedroom the last few days.

"And for the record, I bribed Samu into leaving a picnic basket on our front step with all the fixings from the feast. I'm not gonna let you go hungry."

"Mal, you thought of everything."

"Just doing the job of taking care of my baby girl."

"For all of our days," I whispered.

Emotion clouded his eyes. "Nothing else I'd rather do."

Then he set me down on the bed and made quick work of my dress. And since I'd only worn panties underneath, the emotion in his eyes quickly turned to desire.

"Fuck me, baby girl. You really know how to get a man going."

I might've stolen one of his bandanas to make my own panties. The image of a tongue licking the neck of a guitar on the center of my panties was so suggestive and just perfect.

I shrugged. "I needed something blue. And we weren't doing the whole garter and bouquet toss, so…"

"Fuck me. I really wanna rip them off you, but I can't. They're so fucking perfect." He gently tugged them down my legs and off with me lifting my hips to help.

"I can always make some more."

"Oh, this is definitely going to be a thing. I'm going to need to see a whole line. The logo on the front. On the back. Maybe some bras, too." He groaned as he stared down at my sex. "But later. Way, way later."

I tipped my head. "I think you're wearing too many clothes now."

"Anything for my wife." He grinned playfully at me then stood so he could pull his shirt off and kick his shorts off.

"Wife," I repeated in a whisper. My ring glinted in the afternoon light, drawing my attention away from the strip show my husband was currently performing for me.

I was married.

Married!

That familiar feeling of panic and overwhelm threatened to swamp me.

"Hey, hey." Mal's soft voice drew me back into the present. "You all right, baby? What's wrong?"

"No, nothing." I shook my head and tried to convince myself that the words were true.

"I don't believe you. I'm over here performing a naked bump-and-grind and you didn't even notice."

I gave a wet sounding laugh. "Seriously? You did not."

"You don't know because you weren't even here. So seriously, what's going on?"

"I just, I guess I'm a little overwhelmed by everything. So much changed in a short amount of time. It's kind of a lot."

I was afraid to put my actual fears into words. Was this a mistake? Did I just marry my rebound guy? What was Paige going to say?

What was my mom going to say?

Was I really going to start a new life in LA?

Oh god. What was I doing?

"Hey, hey." Mal jumped onto the bed next to me and took me in his arms. "You are going to be fine. We're going to be fine. Because we love each other and want to be together, right?"

"Right," I repeated, but my weak tone didn't sound all that emphatic. Or believable.

Mal sat back on his heels. "Do you want to rip up the marriage license? Because we can. It's not official until it's signed, and Samu isn't taking it over to the main island until tomorrow."

He was referring to the document we signed last night that he'd jumped through a million hoops and bribed half a dozen people to get pushed through.

My heart felt heavy as I looked into his concerned expression.

I couldn't do it.

I couldn't break his already fragile heart. I couldn't be one more person who walked away from him.

"It's not that. I don't want to cancel it or whatever. I'm just...scared. It's a lot."

"It *is* a lot. But I promise I'll be standing next to you the whole way, holding your hand or holding you up if need be. We'll do it together."

How could I doubt this when he said things like that?

I sat up and kissed him, trying to put all my love and devotion into the action. He was just so special and wonderful. How was this my life?

Sensing I needed tenderness over hunger, Mal stretched out on his side next to me and continued to kiss me with a gentleness that made tears well in my eyes.

"I love you, Saylor, and I'm going to spend the rest of our life making sure you understand just how special and amazing and worthy you are."

Now the tears rolled unashamedly down my cheeks, and he pressed a few kisses to stem the flow before kissing his way down my body.

I threaded my fingers through his hair as he laved attention to my breasts. He was obsessed with them. I giggled at the thought.

"I'm trying to turn you on, and you're over here giggling. What the hell?" Mal grumbled.

"Sorry. I was just thinking about how you're obsessed with my breasts."

"I'm obsessed about every part of you, but your tits are a work of art."

I laughed more.

"Seriously. This body is the thing artists spend their whole career trying to get down in whatever medium they work in—paint, marble, text, lyrics. I could spend my whole life worshipping them, and it'd be a life well spent."

"Mal." I shook my head as tears welled in my eyes again. "You make it impossible not to love you."

He narrowed his eyes at me. "That's like a double negative right? So it's a positive?"

I laughed harder. "Yes. I love you, you crazy, insane man!"

"Fuck yeah you do." He bent over me and pressed a hard kiss on my lips. "And I love you too."

I urged him over my body, eager for that elemental connection we'd already had so many times.

But this time it felt deeper as he sank into my body.

He kept his eyes on mine, and all the love and emotion in his gaze made my heart clench even as other parts of me clenched around him.

I'd never felt so deeply, emotionally connected to a man.

But I had that with Mal.

He made me feel wanted. Needed.

Seen.

As my climax washed over me, I screamed so loud I was sure the whole island heard. His shout a few seconds later matched mine.

When he collapsed on top of me, I wrapped my arms around him and held him.

This wasn't a mistake. Having Mal in my life would be the best decision I ever made, not one I'd regret. Ever.

"I love you," I whispered into the sudden silence in our treehouse bedroom.

"Mmm," he hummed back. "Love you too, Saylor Holt."

Breaking News from the Babbler

Long Licks Drummer Gio Barone Dead at 45

Gio Barone Found Dead

Exclusive Details

stock image of Gio Barone

Long Licks drummer, **Gio Barone** was found dead in his LA home tonight *the Babbler* has confirmed.

A press release from the LAPD, which doesn't specifically name Barone says:

"Emergency services were called to an address in the Hollywood Hills at 10 PM today following reports of a man found deceased.

On arrival, officers found the body of a 45-year-old man who was pronounced dead at the scene.

The investigation into the circumstances of the death will continue, but as of now, it's not being treated as suspicious."

Barone famously battled addiction to drugs and alcohol and has been to rehab several times.

Last month, the Long Licks finished their two-year international

Infamous Tour.

He was 45.

RIP

Chapter 14

Mal

It was the persistent buzzing of my cell phone that woke me up. The thing almost vibrated itself off the nightstand. I'd moved into Saylor's treehouse before the wedding, so my stuff was strewn all over the place. Something I could tell bugged her—and I swear I was working on—but she hadn't confronted me about just yet.

About the fourth time the buzzing started all over, Saylor rolled over and nudged my shoulder. "Make it stop."

I groaned and blindly reached for my cell. Bringing it to my face, I grumbled, "What?"

"Fuck, man. I've been calling you all night," Ryker's deep voice muttered. "Nice to know you're still alive. Shit."

"Ry, it's…" I blinked blearily at the clock display on the nightstand. "Four in the morning. What the fuck are you calling me for?"

"Gio's dead."

"What?" I sat up, totally alert now. "Are you fucking serious?"

"As a heart attack." He coughed. "Sorry. That was…inappropriate. But yes, I'm serious. Gio's girl called it in tonight. Looks like he overdosed."

"I-I-I…" Tears clogged my throat, and it felt like I couldn't breathe.

The phone fell to the bed as I covered my face with my hands.

In the distance I was vaguely aware of Saylor's murmurs, followed by Ryker's faint voice. It all sounded like it was coming from a long hallway, all echo-y and distorted.

"Hello?"

"Who is this?"

"Who is this?"

"Look, baby cakes, give the phone back to my boy. We gotta discuss some important shit."

"I'm not baby cakes. I'm not sweet thing. I'm Mal's *wife*. So how about you tell me who you are and what the hell you just said to him to make him lose it?"

"Mal got married?"

"Yesterday. Sorry you weren't invited, but it was an impromptu thing. Who is this again?"

"Ryker. Ryker O'Keefe."

"Okay. And what's going on?"

"Gio ODed tonight."

"Shit." There was some rustling, and then Saylor was tugging on my arm. "Mal, baby, I'm so sorry." Her head nuzzled against my arm like a puppy, all wiggly warmth and impossible to resist.

I put my arm around her and pulled her into my lap.

"Girlie!" A small, tinny voice hollered. "Girl! Missus Holt, there's some stuff we gotta talk about."

I grabbed the phone and toggled the speaker function. After clearing my throat, my voice sounded froggy when I spoke. "What, Ryker?"

"Shit, man. I'm sorry for dropping it on you like that. But I thought it was better to just put it out there. Rip it off like a Band-Aid."

"There's no good way to share shit news, my friend. I get it. What else did you need to tell me?"

"We need you back here, Mal. G had you named as next of kin or beneficiary or whatever on everything, so we're having a hell of a time getting through all the red tape without you. There's only so much Danny can do."

I remembered him joking about how he didn't have anyone to leave things to—he'd grown up in foster care and pretty much spent all his time on our couch growing up—I just never thought he was serious.

"I didn't…I never knew. He's been ducking my calls for the last few weeks. I thought he was pissed at me."

"More like he didn't want the lecture about using again."

"Shit, I never even knew."

The weight of my failure almost broke me.

I couldn't breathe. My breath left me in gasping wheezes, and it was everything I could do to just hold on and get through this conversation.

Ryker coughed. "So listen, when can you get here? The cops will only release his body to you, and the longer it takes, the more likely we have of shit leaking."

"I'm in Fiji, so it's going to take me a day to get back."

"Getting married apparently. Congrats, by the way. She sounds like a feisty one. It's good you have someone in your corner to help you through this." He sighed. "Get your ass on a plane, boy-o. We need you."

"I'll text you the details once I have them. See you soon."

"Stay safe."

"You too." I ended the call and dropped my phone on the bed. Covering my face with my hands, I wept.

I felt so powerless.

So stupid.

How did I of all people miss the signs?

I couldn't believe he was gone.

Tears rolled down my face, and Saylor murmured something as she cuddled closer to me, trying to comfort me.

But some wounds just wouldn't ever close. And I had a feeling this was going to be one of them.

Everything moved quick after that.

I texted my assistant, Naomi—who I saw had also tried to reach me—and got her to work arranging our flights home.

We packed in a flurry. Having to put one foot in front of the other was the only thing keeping me upright. That, and Saylor's hovering presence. She never really asked too many questions, just got to work packing and arranging details on our end to get us to the airport.

I could tell from her expression she was stressed.

I was just numb.

Gio was dead.

Gio ODed.

The words looped in my brain until they almost lost all meaning.

I didn't get it.

How didn't I see?

I should've seen the signs. But I'd been too caught up with preserving my sobriety. I knew his girl was partying. Why didn't I think about him?

My shame spiral continued through the boat ride to the small Taveuni airport that looked more like a bus station than an airport.

Which might've been a joke from Saylor. I can't really remember.

I was too busy thinking about how Gio had been shooting up for the last time while I'd been making love to my wife. I'd been starting a new life while Gio had been ending his.

Fuck

Fuck!

"I'm sorry, but we don't have a booking for a Saylor Tate."

I blinked and found myself standing in front of an airport representative. I shook my head and turned, taking in the sleek white counter and the display screen behind the lady.

"We do have a second booking with Mister Holt's for a Saylor Holt, but I'm afraid you can't travel under that name if it doesn't match your passport." She stared back at us like an animatronic robot, all crisp diction and blank expression.

"Switch it to Saylor Tate then," I muttered.

"I'm sorry, sir, but I can't do that this close to departure. Our airline regulations state that—"

"I DON'T GIVE A FLYING FUCK!" I shouted. "We're flying back to claim my best friend's body. *MAKE IT WORK!*"

Silence fell through the entire airport.

Saylor nuzzled into my side. "Mal, please let me handle this. Go sit down over there."

But I didn't move. I kept my glare fixed on the bitch standing in front of me.

Three more agents came from behind a concealed door and judging by the walkie-talkie squawk behind us, security or police were standing nearby.

"We're sorry for your loss, Mr. Tate, but we can't—"

"Book another ticket then! I don't give a fuck. But the two of us have to be on the next flight out to the US."

Her head went down and after some tippy-tap on her keyboard, we magically had two first-class tickets to LAX.

We clunked our bags on the scale, and she didn't even murmur when Saylor's toy bag was over the limit.

Like I gave a fuck. I could afford the fee and then some.

Cops followed us from the check-in desk to security and hovered like I was some kind of security threat. I wanted to provoke them, pop off on how fucking ridiculous they were being, but I also needed to get on the damn plane.

Saylor passed our passports and tickets to the border agent when prompted, while I stared at the crowd around us with hazy eyes.

Gio was dead.

Gio ODed.

I blinked, and we were sitting in the first-class lounge. Saylor's knee bounced as she sat in the chair next to me.

I know I should probably say something to her. Comfort her or something, but I couldn't make the words appear.

Gio ODed.

Gio was dead.

I blinked again, and we were walking down the jet bridge.

I don't even remember hearing the boarding call or leaving the lounge.

As we settled into our seats, a flight attendant came over and buzzed about drinks or food or something. Saylor answered in her soft voice. I just stared back with blank eyes.

I grabbed a beanie out of my bag, stashed the bag in a compartment, and then sat back down. Pulling the beanie over my head and face, I blocked everything out.

I didn't want to see anyone. Talk to anyone. I just wanted them all to go away.

Leave me alone.

I must've fallen asleep because the next thing I knew, a voice overhead said, "Prepare for landing."

I tugged the beanie off and looked around blearily.

Saylor gave me a soft smile. "How are you feeling? You missed both meal services. I saved you a muffin if you're hungry."

"Oh, I'm hungry, baby girl, but not for a muffin." I leaned over to give her a kiss, but she frowned and didn't close the distance between us that I couldn't reach.

And then it hit me.

CHAPTER 14

Gio was dead.

Gio ODed.

I should've seen.

I should've known.

I was such a shit friend.

Gio deserved better.

Saylor deserved better.

What the fuck had I been thinking?

We stumbled through customs and immigration.

I didn't even know what time it was. Morning? Evening?

But it didn't matter.

They were waiting for us at baggage claim.

"Malcolm! Malcom! Did you know Gio had been using?"

"Mal! Over here! Look this way!"

Suddenly we were in a scrum of photographers. The clicking of their cameras, their questions, and the flashes surrounded us.

I held Saylor's hand in a tight grip and tried to get us away from them, walking so fast that she tripped a few steps later.

"Ah!" She went down on her knees, and I almost lost her in the scrum.

"Saylor!" I elbowed the guy on my right and lashed out on the one in front of me. "BACK THE FUCK UP!"

She was feebly trying to stand up.

"Is that an engagement ring?"

"Who are you?"

"What's your name?"

"Are you engaged to Malcolm Holt?"

"BACK UP!" I shoved one pap who was right in Saylor's face. "Let my wife stand up, for fuck's sake."

I might as well have chummed the water.

The questions and flashes came faster and more furious.

"When did you get married?"

"What do you think of Gio's death, Mrs. Holt?"

"Where were you when he died?"

I picked up Saylor and carried her away from the pestering fucking annoying assholes.

"I'm so sorry, Mal. I can walk now. Put me down, please."

I ignored her pleas. I wasn't letting her out of my arms as long as those vultures were circling.

I couldn't protect Gio, but I could damn well protect my fucking wife.

A few seconds later, police arrived and played interference between us and the paps.

"Where were you guys five minutes ago?" I snarled. "They fucking took out my wife."

"Sorry, Mr. Holt. We didn't see your arrival," one cop replied as we were ushered toward an office.

"Are you okay, miss?" another asked.

"I'm fine. I can walk. He's just protective and won't let go."

I was pretty sure I heard one mumble, "I wouldn't either," but I didn't know which fucker had said it so I couldn't swing on him.

"Is your transportation here? We can arrange your pick up at a secure location so you're not swarmed driving home."

I had to put Saylor down so I could get my cell out and text Naomi. She should be here somewhere.

Me: *Paps swarmed us at baggage. Where are you?*

Naomi: *I saw. I've got your bags. Where do you want me to meet you?*

I'd never been in this situation. Usually only one or two paps waited to take my picture if I was passing through LAX.

"My assistant is in baggage claim with our bags," I told the officer and he sent someone to arrange our pick up.

Fifteen minutes later, we met Naomi at a side exit and were motoring our way down the 105 in my Rolls-Royce Cullinan.

"How are you holding up? Congrats on the marriage, by the way," Naomi said from the front passenger seat since she'd engaged a driver for the trip.

I grunted in reply.

"Right." Naomi swung back to face forward with a sigh. "When do you want to meet with the authorities to make arrangements?"

"Let's do it now. Get it over with."

"We'll have to wait until they're open." Naomi tapped away on her cell phone. "It's only 6AM."

"I don't give a fuck. Just do whatever." I turned and stared out the window at the passing traffic.

I felt numb. Like there was a layer of cotton between my ears and all over me, muffling me from seeing and hearing what was going on.

And yet when I looked down, my hands were trembling in my lap, in much the same way they did when I was jonesing for a hit of something.

"Find me a meeting. I *really* need a fucking meeting."

"That's where we're going now," Naomi replied. "Crenshaw United Methodist Church has one starting soon."

"Good," I grunted.

"Um, meeting? At a church?" Saylor asked tentatively. "I didn't know you were religious."

My bark of laughter was harsh. "Fuck, no. It's an NA meeting. For addicts," I went on when it didn't look like she understood. "Because the one thing guaranteed to make an addict relapse is losing control."

"Oh." Saylor stared down at her hands in her lap and pursed her lips like she was trying and failing to find something to say.

I should reach out to her, let her know I still loved her, but I couldn't. I turned and stared out the window instead.

Breaking News from the Babbler

Long Licks Guitarist Malcolm Holt Married

He Said I Do to Who?

Exclusive Details

photo of Mal and Saylor at LAX

Guitarist **Malcolm Holt** proved there's always room for love, as he married a mysterious blonde beauty sometime after the end of the Long Licks' Infamous Tour.

As seen in the video below, Holt refers to the younger blonde bombshell as his wife.

video of tussle at LAX

No word yet on who the mysterious beauty is or when and where they got married, but considering they arrived at LAX from the international terminal it's safe to assume they were enjoying their honeymoon when word broke of the tragic death of drummer **Gio Barone**.

We broke the news a few days ago that Gio Barone died Saturday night of a drug overdose. The death was called in by his girlfriend, later identified as **Amaya Cahill**.

Barone was 45.

Chapter 15

Saylor

I'd never felt so lost in my entire life.

My heart ached for Mal, but every time I reached out to him, he pulled away. I didn't know what to do, how to comfort him. I didn't even know he needed a meeting, whatever that was.

We sat in the SUV in front of a church for over an hour after Mal went inside.

Naomi was nice enough, asking if I needed anything, but when I shook my head, she ducked her head back into her cell and that was that.

I pulled my phone out in sheer boredom, and after I powered it on, it pinged again and again with alerts.

"Looks like the news is out," Naomi murmured from the front seat.

Considering our greeting at the airport, it would make sense that people knew about Mal's friend's death.

But as I read my text messages, I realized that wasn't what she meant.

Paige: *Call me*

Paige: *Why are you on the front page of the Babbler?*

Paige: *Did you seriously marry a rock star and NOT INVITE ME?!*

Paige: *CALL ME!!!*

I didn't know what to say to her yet, so I couldn't call her. I opened another text thread.

Mom: *Trent says he's willing to go to counseling.*

Mom: *Ignoring me won't make it go away.*

Mom: *You're being so immature, Saylor. I raised you better than this.*

And yet not a single text from Trent himself. Clearly someone was deluded, and it wasn't me.

And then the weird texts started coming in.

Ping!

Angela: *You married Malcolm Holt! OMG! Call me*

Ping!

Emma: *You canceled your wedding to Trent to marry a rock star? How on earth did that happen?*

Ping! Ping!

Olivia: *Congrats on your wedding!*

Olivia: *Can you introduce me to Leif Eccles?*

People I hadn't talked to since college or high school suddenly started blowing up my phone.

Ping! Ping! Ping!

"Oh my god," I murmured.

"Yeah, you might want to power it off," Naomi muttered from the front seat. "Actually, hand it here." She held her hand out to me.

Just give her my phone? "Um, why?"

"We should lock down your social media accounts before the news goes mainstream." She wiggled her fingers in a gimmie motion.

"Okay." I shrugged and passed my phone to her.

"The trolls will be ruthless once they find you, given the timing with Gio's death and all. And you don't look like a girl who could hold her own with them. Better to lock them out."

That sounded like an insult, but I was too jet lagged to piece together a proper retort. Plus, I didn't know if she was snarky by nature or gonna be an issue—aka jealous about me and Mal. They seemed to have more of a sibling relationship, but it was too soon to tell really. And I was so, so tired.

I sighed and rubbed my temple. "Do you know how much longer he's going to be? I'd kill for a coffee right about now."

"There's a Krispy Kreme a few blocks away. Will that do?"

I shrugged. "Donuts and coffee sound awesome."

She tapped the driver on the shoulder. "Let's hit the drive-thru. We'll be there and back before Mal even gets to the serenity prayer."

As we bounced through the LA toward donuts, I sighed and asked, "So how often does Mal go to these meetings?"

Silence met my question.

I saw the driver—whoever he was—dart a glance at me in the rear-view mirror.

After a long moment, Naomi cleared her throat. "That, uh, sounds like a question you should ask Mal. I don't talk about my boss with anyone."

I sat back, stunned at the subtle clapback.

So we weren't going to be besties then.

"I want my phone back now." It killed me, but I purposely left the please off my request.

"Just a second." She tapped at the screen some more. Then she passed it back to me. "Here you go. I've turned off commenting on all your profiles. You might want to go back and delete some of those engagement photos, though. If we're lucky, they're not all over *the Babbler* yet."

"I've got nothing to hide."

"You say that now..." She gave a world-weary sigh.

Yeah, definitely not gonna be friends.

I sat back in my seat and thumbed through my photos while we waited in the drive-thru. It wasn't like I'd posted a picture in my wedding dress. I think it was still hanging up in my old closet. I hadn't wanted to pack it when I moved out. I didn't want to touch it.

God, that felt like a lifetime ago.

"Let's get a dozen assorted," Naomi said from the front seat, snapping me back to reality. "Is that okay with you, Taylor?"

"It's Saylor, with an ess." Like she didn't know since she was just looking at all my social media accounts and had booked my flight here. "As long as there's a chocolate iced, I'm good with whatever. And a vanilla latte with soy."

Again I left off the please. I was irritated over that Taylor comment.

Accepting my latte with a fake smile, I sat back with my drink in one hand and a donut in the other and counted the minutes until I could see Mal again.

I ached to call Paige and talk through all this insanity with her, but no way in hell was I doing that with this audience. Naomi might protect Mal's secrets, but no guarantees about mine.

I'd gotten to the bottom of my latte by the time Mal came around the side of the church. His face was still thunderous, and I sighed. Apparently the meeting hadn't helped. My heart ached. I really hoped he wasn't blaming himself. He'd told me days ago Gio was avoiding his calls. Clearly there were problems there, and Mal shouldn't take it all on himself.

He ducked inside the backseat with me and slammed the door shut. Naomi passed him a coffee I didn't even realize she'd ordered for him.

"Where to now?" She offered the box of donuts to him.

He waved off the donuts but sipped the coffee. "Let's head to the medical examiner's office. They should be open by the time we get through the morning traffic."

Naomi nodded at the driver, and we pulled out of the parking lot.

Mal stared out the window, his brows pulled together in thought.

I didn't know what to say.

"The pictures from the airport are already up on *the Babbler*," Naomi drawled. "Do you want me to put together a post for your socials? Something about Gio and your marriage?"

Mal closed his eyes and sighed. "Let's put together a post about Gio. Find a good picture of the two of us—preferably something from when we were kids. But don't post it until I vet the caption."

Naomi nodded, her thumbs flying across her cell phone screen. "And your marriage? That's the current headline on *the Babbler*."

"I don't give a fuck what *the Babbler* says."

I gasped. It was totally involuntary, and I knew he was going through a lot at the moment, but it still hurt to be so summarily dismissed.

I could feel Naomi's eyes on me, and Mal gave one of those weary sighs.

"It's not about you, Saylor," Mal muttered. "Hopefully, if we don't pay it any attention, the news will die off, and those fuckers will go stalk someone else."

"Not likely to happen if they frame it that she left her fiancé for you," Naomi muttered.

"Yeah well, I didn't ask for your opinion, so I'd appreciate it if you shut your trap." Mal scowled as he tugged on his beanie. "How long 'til we get there?"

"Fourteen minutes, sir," the previously quiet driver answered.

"Thanks," Mal grumbled. "Do you have my sunglasses, Nay?"

Naomi opened the center console and passed a pair of sunglasses back to Mal.

He slid them on then slumped in his seat. "Wake me when we get there."

I sighed and stared out my window.

And that was how the entire day went. Mal ran errand after errand to sort out the red tape of his best friend's death. Despite offering more than once, Mal didn't want me to help him with any of the appointments. I didn't get out of the car.

But Naomi did.

And she gave me a haughty little smile every time.

It hurt.

And I hated that I was making the most painful moment of Mal's life about me, but he was shutting me out. What was the point of having a spouse if you weren't going to lean on them in hard times?

He had no problem offering to be my rock when he'd convinced me to marry him. He said all those pretty words about loving each other and helping me with my career, but he clearly wasn't going to let me do the same for him.

What was I even doing here?

When we got to his lawyer's office, I didn't wait for him to order me to stay in the car.

I opened my door and hopped out, stretching my arms over my head with a groan. Tipping my head back, I tried to absorb a little vitamin D.

"What are you doing, Saylor? This'll be a quick meeting, and then we'll go home."

Like I knew that. He hadn't given me a hint about where we were going or what we were doing. "I assume they have a restroom? I'd like to pee."

Naomi muffled her laugh behind her hand.

I was so over her mean girl shit.

"Fine, come on then." Mal huffed like it was an annoying request, and unlike earlier, he didn't hold my hand as we walked toward the large building.

I tried not to let it bother me.

When we entered, we were immediately greeted by the slender and businesslike receptionist. "Mister Holt, welcome. Elizabeth is waiting for you in her office. Right this way."

"I know the way. Do you mind showing my wife to the restroom? She'd like to freshen up."

She was businesslike until she heard the word 'wife.' She swung her head to me, and it looked like she'd been slapped. Rubbing her bright red lips together, she nodded. "Of course." Her voice was hoarse. "Right this way, Missus Holt."

Mal didn't even spare me a glance. He just turned and walked down the hall on the left with Naomi trailing behind.

I followed the receptionist the other way and ducked into the room she waved me toward.

I avoided my reflection in the mirror and took care of my business, but as I was washing my hands, I couldn't miss the pain I glimpsed in my eyes.

Swallowing hard, I took a minute and tried to calm my nerves. This was just so hard. He had all these people around him who knew him better than I did. And he wasn't letting me in. I didn't know what to do.

I still ached to call Paige, but this wasn't the time. Or the place. This bathroom was seriously echo-y.

I touched up my makeup then gave myself a brave smile that I definitely wasn't feeling before I exited.

When I got back to the reception area, I stopped in front of her desk. "Can you show me to Elizabeth's office?"

"I'm afraid Ms. Chen made it clear she's not to be disturbed." She smiled wolfishly at me. "But you're welcome to take a seat and wait here." She gestured to the metal chairs lining the waiting area like it was a cozy spa.

Wait here under the watchful eye of Mal's fangirl, or in the luxury SUV with what's-his-name? Honestly, they both sounded like shit options.

But I was tired and these chairs were closer, so I collapsed into the nearest one then gave the receptionist a toothy smile. "Thank you."

She rolled her eyes and tapped her keyboard behind her tall desk.

This was officially the longest day of my life. The whole horrible emotion of the day was making my head pound behind my eyes. But I couldn't hide in my phone since everyone I ever knew was currently calling or texting me.

So I grabbed a nearby magazine and pretended interest in the Asian market.

"Is that her?" I heard someone whisper loudly from the other side of the room.

"Yeah, can you believe it?" a familiar voice replied. "Malcolm Holt finally married someone, and he robs the cradle to do it. She's gotta be young enough to be his daughter."

"I wouldn't mind calling him daddy."

Hushed giggles rang out from the other side of the room.

It took everything inside me not to stomp over there and tell them that I actually did call him daddy, and he loved it every freaking time.

Instead, I just sighed and turned the page.

"We'll contact his lawyer and get working on the probate right away."

"Thanks again, Elizabeth," Mal replied. "Saylor, you're still here."

I dropped the magazine and shook my head. "Yes, Mal. I'm still here. I wasn't allowed to join your meeting."

All eyes swung my way and the Asian woman next to Mal frowned. "Mal, who's this?"

"His wife," the receptionist piped up with a barely visible snarl.

"You got married, Mal?" His lawyer sent him a concerned look. "When? Where?"

Mal sighed and rubbed his face with a hand. "Two days ago, I think? In Fiji."

"I'm going to assume that means there was no prenup." Elizabeth frowned.

"Of course there wasn't a prenup." Naomi laughed.

"Nay," Mal bit out. "Go wait in the car."

Naomi swung an accusing glare my way before stomping out of the building.

"Maybe we should go back to my office and talk about this... situation." Elizabeth waved a vague hand to encompass me and Mal.

Mal shook his head. "There's nothing to discuss. We're married. Gio's dead. I've got shit to do."

"At the very least, we need a copy of the marriage license. A certified, legally filed copy of your marriage license. I assume all the proper paperwork was carried out?"

My heart froze at her statement. Were we really married? I know I signed something, but was it actually filed with the authorities? And legal?

"I'll get you a copy. The resort was going to take care of that for us, but if you could call them and follow up for me, that'd be awesome. One less thing for me to think about."

Elizabeth nodded. "Of course. I'll call your assistant for the details. Congrats on your marriage and our condolences on your loss." She turned to me. "It was nice to meet you. Hopefully next time will be under better circumstances."

"Thank you." I smiled at Elizabeth, honestly appreciative of her kindness and professional approach. It was a welcome difference today.

And wasn't that sad?

Mal walked over to my chair and gently tugged me up from my seat. "Come on, baby. Let's go home."

There was an audible sigh from the women at the reception desk.

I smiled up at Mal and let him lead me from the building.

And I tried to take comfort in the fact that he didn't drop my hand the second we were alone.

I just had to keep showing up.

Eventually he'd let me in.

Right?

Chapter 16

Mal

I don't know why I was surprised, but when we pulled through the gate at my house and I saw a familiar car parked in the driveway, I was shocked. "My mom is here?"

"Your best friend died. Of course your mom is here," Naomi retorted in her trademark snark.

I know she was close to Gio too, but I was sick of her sniping at me today. And following me around. She usually stayed in the car unless I specifically asked for her. "Right. You're done for the day. Don't come back until—what day is it?"

"Monday," Naomi replied. "And—"

"I don't give a shit. You've been annoying all day, and I'm going to chalk it up to grief for the moment. But it stops now. Don't come back until Wednesday. You officially have time off."

"But there are so many things we've got to—"

"I'll figure it out. I'll text you about the service once I've scheduled it. Go."

Naomi scowled at me then grabbed her bag and stomped down the driveway to the street where her car was parked on the curb.

Saylor coughed lightly. "So I guess this means I get to meet your mom?"

I laughed. Fuck, I loved how she just let it go and focused on the shitshow currently bearing down on us and not on the one we'd just shaken off. "Yeah, looks that way. Come on."

Trusting the driver to offload our bags, I put an arm around my wife and led her to the front door.

Which flew open before I could open it.

"Mal!" Mom shrieked, tackling me in a blur of gray hair and paisley fabric.

I went back on one foot but managed to stay upright. "Ma, you gotta calm down."

"I just can't believe he's gone. Gio had so many demons, but I never thought…" She shuddered in my arms and then gave a muffled cry.

I met Saylor's eyes over my mom's shoulder, and my heart clenched at the pain in her expression. She was hurting for me and my mom despite never even knowing Gio. "Let's get inside, Ma."

Saylor opened the door, and I made shushing sounds as I guided my wailing mom into my house. As we sat on the beige sofa with my mom burrowed into my chest, I watched Saylor curiously peer around the room.

I wondered what she thought. I hadn't decorated the place—it came with all this furniture. Beige on beige on beige. I mean the walls were white and the kitchen countertops were marble, but it was all just so boring and soulless.

Odd how that had never bothered me before.

And how detached I currently was.

Was that one of the stages of grief? Detachment? Maybe this was denial. Fuck if I knew.

After all the appointments today—between the coroner, the funeral home, and the attorneys—I just felt numb.

I sighed and patted my mom's back. "Uh, Mom, I know now's not the best time, but there's someone here I want you to meet."

"What?" She sat up and rubbed her eyes. "Who?"

"My wife, Saylor."

"*WHAT?*" she screeched before hitting me on the chest. "You got married, and this is how you tell me?"

I hunched and rubbed at my chest where she hit me in feigned pain. "It's not like I exactly had the chance. Shit hit the fan and you didn't exactly call me before showing up here."

"I called. If you'd checked your phone, you'd know I called." She sat upright and carefully rubbed at her eyes in that way women did. "Now where is she? Where is this pillar of femininity who finally made my son fall head over heels in love with her? You are in love, right?"

"Yes, Mom. We're in love. Saylor, come here, baby." I held out my hand to my perpetually hovering wife.

She smiled tremulously at me and took my hand. I pulled her to me until she sat on my knee.

"Mal! You can't—this isn't how I should meet your mother," Saylor protested.

"Oh, I like her already." Mom wiggled forward on the sofa. "She's not afraid to give you shit. Saylor is it?"

"Yes, ma'am. I'm so sorry for your loss. Mal has told me a little bit about Gio. He sounds like an amazing man." Saylor winced.

Mom smiled sadly. "Yes, he was. And you are just the picture of a gorgeous California girl. Where did you two meet?"

"She's actually from Las Vegas, Ma," I cut in.

"Makes sense you'd find a gorgeous local and elope without a word while in Vegas. Again," Mom retorted.

"I don't get married every time I go to Vegas," I protested before turning to Saylor. "Really, I don't. Just that one time."

"Wait, what time?" Saylor gave me an incredulous look. "I thought you were only married once before."

I tipped my head. "Technically, the wedding in Vegas didn't count because you need legal paperwork from the county before you do the whole little white chapel thing."

"You mean a marriage license?" Saylor gave a little laugh. "You didn't have a marriage license?"

"Right. That." I nodded. "We skipped that step, so it didn't count. Or at least that's what my lawyer said."

Saylor's eyes grew even wider.

"What? It was Vegas. I was drunk." I lifted a shoulder. "And high. In my defense that was way before I got sober."

"So like back when I was—what? In middle school?" She blinked innocently.

I groaned. "Fuck, you know the rule. It's not fair making me feel like a creepy old guy."

"Then don't hold back history like 'once I got married, but it doesn't count.' Like seriously." Saylor huffed and crossed her arms over her chest.

Mom gave a muffled laugh, reminding both of us of her presence.

A chagrined expression crossed Saylor's face.

I shook my head. "You hungry, Ma? I'm pretty sure the kitchen is empty, but we can order in."

"No, and don't think you can just change the subject that easily." She shot me a suspicious glance then turned to Saylor. "So tell me about yourself, Saylor."

"I, uh, met Mal in Fiji where I was on my honeymoon."

Mom's eyes widened.

"Alone! I was on my honeymoon alone because I broke up with my ex. Turns out he was lying to me for years, had a huge gambling problem, and owed people all over Vegas money. But anyways, I met Mal at the resort in Fiji and eventually we hit it off."

I appreciated that she'd left out our awkward first meeting on the airplane.

Kinda sad that we didn't get to recreate it on the flight home.

And then I remembered.

Gio.

My best friend died, and that was the reason we hadn't joined the mile high club on the flight home. I'd been too busy mourning my best friend.

I'd forgotten about him during that back and forth with Saylor.

I'd forgotten my best friend was *dead*.

Tears filmed my eyes and clogged my throat.

Grabbing Saylor by the waist, I moved her over to the couch between me and Mom and hightailed it out of the room with a mumbled, "Excuse me."

"Mal? You all right?" my mom called distantly.

No. Nothing was right. My best friend was dead, and I'd missed all the fucking signs.

I shut the bedroom door behind me and headed for the bathroom to splash some water on my face.

It didn't help.

My hands shook, and when I looked at my reflection, I saw the same red eyes and gaunt expression that I'd seen so many times when I was using.

The thought of not feeling anything but bliss sounded really good right now.

Just one little hit.

I bet with a few calls, I could get my hands on—

"Mal?" Saylor's tremulous voice came from the other side of the door. "Your mom and I are going to get some groceries delivered. Do you want to weigh in on the order?"

I closed my eyes and had to clear my throat before I could speak, "No, baby. I'm good with whatever. Ma knows what I like."

"Oh."

I winced at my less than stellar reminder that despite being married we'd just met.

"Okay. Let me know if you change your mind. Or if you need anything."

"Thanks." I couldn't bring myself to say anything else.

Everything about my life honestly felt like a colossal mistake.

What the fuck had I been thinking? I didn't know how to be married. But I also couldn't go back on it.

I felt trapped.

Like the walls were coming in on me.

My band was probably breaking up.

My best friend had died.

My assistant was being a bitch.

I was being a shit partner to Saylor.

Nothing was going right. Nothing.

What I'd give to feel nothing right now.

Fuck.

I pulled my cell phone out of my back pocket and made a call.

I expected voicemail, but surprisingly he picked up after only three rings.

"Mal, man, I heard the news," Caden Dawson, Hollywood A-list actor and my NA sponsor, answered. "How are you holding up?"

"Shitty. I, I'm afraid I'm going to break my sobriety. I just, I just really need…fuck if I know."

"All right. I'm in town. We're actually filming on the backlot at Paramount. Why don't you come to me, and we'll talk?"

"I didn't realize you're filming. I don't want to bug you at work, Cay. I can look up a meeting and—"

"Shit, you're so fucking hard-headed. I see there's a meeting in North Hollywood at noon. I'll meet you there since you're being a stubborn asshole."

"I already went to a meeting this morning."

"And you're going to go to a meeting at noon and get a coffee with me. And you might need to go to another meeting tonight. You're going to go to as many meetings as you need to if it'll keep you sober."

I sighed heavily. "Fine."

"I'll see you there. Don't make me chase you down."

"I'll be there. Thanks, Caden."

"Anytime, man. See you soon."

I ended the call and avoided my reflection as I put my phone back in my pocket. I already felt lighter just having talked to Caden. His Texan no nonsense tone always made me feel better, like having a big brother look after me. And I didn't need my bloodshot eyes or my haggard expression ruining that for me.

I left the bathroom and found my mom and Saylor in the kitchen, bent over a paper on the counter.

"Oh." Saylor looked up at me with a hesitant smile. "Did you change your mind? Because I was thinking of making chicken tikka tacos. I got the recipe from this actor's cookbook. I can't remember his name, but he's always the baddie in all the movies. Apparently he has few restaurants in LA."

"Robby Lopez?" I shook my head. "You realize we could just save all that hassle and order the tacos from the restaurant?"

"But…I wanted to cook for you." Her shoulders hunched, and she bit her bottom lip.

I knew, *I knew* I should reassure her or give her a hug at least, but I was just so tired.

And numb.

And, let's be honest, fucking selfish too.

So fucking selfish.

I realized it but couldn't drum up the energy to do anything about it.

I was just so fucking tired.

"Sure. Whatever. I gotta go meet Caden. We're going to a meeting, then I'm getting coffee or whatever with him at his trailer at Paramount. I might not be back in time for dinner."

"It's only eleven," Mom pointed out with raised eyebrows, clearly unimpressed with me.

I shrugged. "I might need to go to another meeting tonight. Look, I'm just trying to look after myself and not use again. Excuse me if my addiction is getting in the way of your mourning ritual or whatever. Sorry I'm such a fucking disappointment."

Mom pursed her lips and gave me the same glare that had made me get out of bed every morning and finish high school.

But I was an adult now, and this was my fucking house.

"Later."

So I left with my tail tucked between my legs, trying to look like my shit didn't stink when we all knew better.

I was an ass.

I pulled my black Benz into the strip mall and parked next to the metallic blue Porsche Panamera. Only one person would drive a car like that to a neighborhood like this.

I got out of my car and strolled over to Caden's. Scents from the Lebanese Grill warred with the gas pumps at the far end. I pulled open his passenger door before the disparate scents really got to me.

"Thanks for coming out, Cade."

Hollywood's go-to action actor gave me his trademark smirk. "It's what I get paid the big bucks for."

I laughed. Since it was an unpaid act of service, that wasn't true at all. But sponsoring other addicts made it easier to keep the demons at bay—most times. I'd had a few sponsees myself over the years, and helping them stay sober usually helped me stay sober too. But then these weren't usual circumstances. "Right, right."

"So tell me what's going on."

I let my head fall back against the headrest and closed my eyes. "You know what's going on. Gio ODed Saturday night."

"Yeah, man. I'm sorry. That's fucked." He sighed heavily. "Sorry to say that some addicts never break the cycle. When did he relapse?"

"I don't know. I pulled away from everyone at the end of the tour. They were partying pretty hard and the women..." I swallowed heavily. "I couldn't be around it. Gio said it wasn't like that—that he wasn't using—and I chose to believe him. Because it made it easier to distance myself from the whole scene."

"Okay, number one, I understand you're feeling guilt, but his actions are not on you. He knew that you were there for him if he ever reached out. He knew the program. He knew the steps. He had a sponsor to reach out to, too. But he didn't. And that's on him; it's not on you."

"Ryker said he tried to talk to him, but he wouldn't listen."

"*See.*"

"But Ryker's not in the program. He doesn't know what to say that would make the difference. He hasn't been here." I waved at the shitty strip mall we were parked in front of. Literally the bottom of the barrel—rock bottom.

"So what would've you said to him?"

"What?"

"To Gio. What were you going to tell him that would keep him from using again?"

"I, uh, I haven't really thought about it."

"So think about it now. What would you have told him? Let's play the what-if game. But this time, play it all the way through. What would you have told him if you'd known then that he was using?"

"I don't know. That he's being an ass. That he's throwing away his life to chase a high that's never going to feel like enough. That he'll lose his life if he keeps doing what he's doing. That he needs to work the program and really put his all into staying sober."

"Do you really think that's all that different from whatever Ryker told him? Or that he'd be more receptive to hear it from you because you know what it's like?"

I sighed. "No. Probably not."

"So maybe you need to give yourself a break. In my experience, he would've probably listened *less* to you than he would've to Ryker. Because he would've known exactly what you were going to say before you opened your mouth and he didn't want to hear it. He would've been closed off to you from the jump. So give yourself a break. What he did is not on you."

"I guess." I stared unseeingly out the window and sighed. "It's easy to say that, but it's hard as hell to believe it."

"Yeah, I get it, man. I've lost friends to this shit too. And it never gets any easier." Caden shifted in his seat. "So what's this I'm hearing about you getting married?"

"Damn." I winced. "I thought you, of all people would avoid *the Babbler's* bullshit."

Caden shrugged. "My assistant told me before I left. She keeps up to date on everything they post. Helps knowing when attention is coming your way."

Sounded like his assistant was more thoughtful than mine. I grunted. "Yeah, I got married in Fiji the same day as Gio died. Or the day before? Hell if I understand all that time zone bullshit."

"And what does she think about your sobriety?"

I bit my bottom lip much like Saylor always did, and then I softly laughed at myself. "She's supportive. She didn't order wine the entire time we were in Fiji out of respect of my sobriety. I didn't even ask her to; she just did it."

Caden hummed. "Sounds like just the kinda woman you need at

your back to get through this shit."

Maybe.

But it wasn't easy to open up under normal circumstances, and these were anything but normal.

"Come on." Caden clapped my shoulder. "Let's go inside and get a bad cup of coffee."

Chapter 17

Saylor

I flinched as the door slammed shut behind Mal.

Leaving me all alone with his mom.

Awkward.

Judy sighed. "That boy…"

I walked over and buried my head in his spice cabinet. Anything to get away from the uncomfortable moment.

"So what did your parents say about your wedding?"

I winced and dropped my head. "Which wedding?"

Judy laughed. "Touché. Either, I guess."

Sighing, I turned around and rested my hips against the sleek, glossy flat panel cabinets and equally gleaming countertop. "Well, my mom thinks I should patch things up with Trent and beg him for forgiveness since I was the one to cancel the wedding. I think she said in my last text that I was being immature."

"And your dad?"

"He passed away when I was little. I don't even remember him."

"I'm sorry. I know what a hole it leaves in a child's life not having a father figure."

I bit my lip at the 'father figure' call out. Some might argue that was why I was with Mal. I don't know, and I didn't really want to examine it that much, honestly. "Mom's always been big on financial stability, which makes sense since my dad died when I was two and she was a stay-at-home mom at the time. But instead of putting it on me to be able to support myself, she'd rather I find a good provider, and for some reason she still believes Trent is one. I'd argue that he's the opposite of stable, considering his bookie was the one to break the news of his gambling addiction to me. Almost literally. Fortunately it just ended in a black eye and not a broken nose. Or worse."

"His bookie hit you?"

I shrugged then nodded. Maybe I shouldn't have let that much slip, but I was feeling oddly vulnerable since Mal had run out on me again.

"Oh, you poor baby." Judy crossed the room and gave me a huge hug, rocking me slightly. "And your mom wants you to take him back? That's crazy."

"Thank you," I replied emphatically. It felt good to be heard. No matter how many times I reiterated to my mom what'd happened, she'd continued to gloss over it. Like it was a minor hiccup or something.

Judy stepped back and patted my shoulder. "I'm guessing that means you haven't told her about your wedding with Mal?"

"I've been avoiding her texts, and she doesn't know I'm back from Fiji yet. I was supposed to be there another week."

"Right. Well, I guess she'll find out along with the rest of the world once it's posted on the gossip sites."

I winced. "It kinda already is." I quickly explained the whole scene at the airport and how my phone had blown up with texts.

"My advice would be for you…" She sighed. "To do whatever you think is best. You know the dynamics between you and your mom better than I do. Mal wouldn't tell me. Didn't tell me, obviously. But then it wasn't the first time so—"

Ouch.

Judy waved a hand. "I'm sorry. That wasn't a dig at you. It was a dig at my thoughtless son." She gave me a warm smile. "How about we put in that order, and do you remember the recipe or do we need to look it up online?"

I let Judy change the subject, and soon we put in our grocery order with delivery promised in a few hours.

While we waited for the groceries, Judy showed me around Mal's place. It was annoying that Mal wasn't here to do that for me and just up and left me with a virtual stranger, but I tried not to let that show as we walked through the huge modern space.

But it was the view out the back that left me spellbound.

Past the glass doors was a teak deck surrounding an infinity pool with a view of downtown LA beyond. It felt like we were standing at the top of the world. Lounging chairs and a whole dining table were staged along the deck, but I couldn't take my eyes off the view.

Mal lived a *very* different life than I did.

My apartment had a view of a few local streets and some scrub dirt beyond.

"Yeah," Judy murmured next to me. "It's my favorite part of his house. Kinda helps since the rest of the place is so…"

"Beige? Boring?" I tossed out.

Judy laughed. "Exactly. I knew I'd like you, Saylor. Clearly my boy needs some color in his life, and I have a feeling you're going to be the one to help provide it."

Two days ago I would've said she was right, but now…

Now everything was so up in the air.

I wasn't confident I could say that we'd still be married a month from now.

Since it was starting to feel like Mal wasn't a hundred percent in anymore.

Maybe he just needed some time. A lot had changed in the last few days.

But then again, he wasn't the only one who'd had their entire life turned upside down. It would've been so much easier for both of us to get through all this turmoil if Mal would just talk to me.

A buzzer sounded somewhere in the distance.

"Oooh!" Judy perked up. "I bet that's the groceries."

I put my fake smile on and followed her to the door.

I was fluffing the Spanish rice when Mal came through the front door.

"You're just in time," Judy called out. "Dinner is almost ready."

I didn't look up, but I could feel the weight of Mal's stare as he took in the mayhem we'd unleashed in his previously pristine kitchen. Spanish rice, black beans, chicken tikka, shredded cheese, pico de gallo, and a spicy crema lined the countertops with varying levels of carnage of ingredients still strewn here and there.

"You guys actually cooked?"

I'd had so much fun buzzing around the kitchen with Judy. She was a hoot. We'd laughed and sang and told stories. It felt like I had a new friend.

But all that levity had been sucked out of the house with Mal's return.

I could feel his glower from across the room.

It was so hard to reconcile this angry stranger to the man I fell in love with in Fiji.

Although to be fair, we'd only known each other a week.

"Maybe this was a mistake," I murmured as I set the fork down with a soft click in the suddenly silent house.

"Saylor," Judy rushed across the kitchen to awkwardly stand in front of me. I could tell she wanted to wrap her arms around me, but my body language was very clearly warning her off. "Don't say something in the heat of the moment. You need to give the two of you some grace."

I shook my head and took a careful step back from her. "No, I just—" I turned and faced Mal for the first time since he'd returned. "I get that you're going through a lot. And I'm so sorry your friend died. But maybe this isn't the best time to try meld two lives together. You're going through a lot, and I'm avoiding a lot back home. Maybe this is just a case of right people, wrong time. Or hell, maybe it's also wrong people. What the hell do I know?"

I looked at Mal, silently begging him to say something—anything—to give me the slightest hint that he felt different.

But he just stood there.

"Right. I guess it's a good thing that I didn't unpack. I'm just going to go grab my stuff. It was nice to meet you, Judy, and I'm so sorry for your loss. Gio sounded like a good guy. I'm sorry I didn't get the chance to meet him."

I rushed out of the room and headed for the main bedroom closet where someone had conveniently stowed my suitcases. I'd noticed them during Judy's house tour. Maybe I should've taken pictures since it didn't look like this was going to be my home after all.

I was vaguely aware of Judy's high-pitched voice followed by Mal's low drawl in the distance, but I didn't stay to eavesdrop. I had to grab my stuff and figure out how I was going to get home. Uber to the airport and then... I didn't exactly have a home anymore. Paige's house, I guess?

I was hoisting a bag over my shoulder when Mal came into the closet—really it was bigger than Paige's whole apartment in Vegas so calling it a closet was disingenuous.

Again, I could feel the heat of his gaze, but he stayed silent.

I jostled two bags closer together so I could grab them. "Maybe you could stop Samu from filing the paperwork, and then we don't even need to get an annulment. But if not, just send me whatever you need me to sign. I won't block you or anything. So just text me for my address. I'm not exactly sure where I'll land."

"That's it? You're just going to end our marriage with a shrug and a 'send me the paperwork?'"

"Right." I slipped my ring off my finger and held it out to him. I loved it so much, but it didn't feel right to keep it when our marriage hadn't even lasted a week. "Here." I waggled it in front of him when he didn't make a move to accept it.

Mal scoffed. "You're fucking unreal. I can't believe you're just walking out."

"Are you serious? I get that today's been hard for you—that your best friend died and you're grieving—but have you even stopped for a second to see what today has been like for me? You ignored me the entire day. Aside from rescuing me from the paps at the airport, you've said all of three words to me today. I stayed in the car while you had appointment after appointment. You didn't introduce me to anyone unless you were forced to. You left me with your driver most of the time. You foisted me off on your mom with barely a word. She was the one who showed me around your tomb of a home. I don't even know where you've been for the last however many hours or who Caden is. You talked so much shit about my cooking I almost cried. I just...I don't see the point."

Mal gave a heavy sigh and stared at his boots. When he made no move to say or do anything *again*, I scoffed, set the rings down on the center display rack thingy, and loaded my bags onto my shoulders.

"Saylor, wait. I can't...I don't—" He groaned and scrubbed a hand over his face. "I'm shit with words. But you're right. This has been a shit day. I've been a walking zombie since I heard about Gio. I'd like to say that it's because I'm in pain, but honestly I've been thinking about using again. I haven't thought about anything or anyone else."

My bags fell to the floor with a thunk. "Mal..."

I wanted to reach out to him, but he was throwing clear 'don't come near' signals.

"It's whatever. My endless struggle, I guess. And apparently, sometimes it turns me into an asshole. I used to be better at this whole balance thing, but this shit with Gio has just thrown everything out of whack. I don't—I can't—I don't know what the fuck to do."

Then I watched, stunned, as he fell to pieces in front of me.

Tears rolled down his cheeks, and his shoulders shook with suppressed sobs.

I rushed to close the distance between us and wrapped my arms around him, holding him tight. He went rigid in my arms at first, like he didn't know what the hell a hug was for. Then he made this wail that sent goosebumps down my spine before he burrowed his face in my neck and just cried.

I don't know how long we stood there in the closet, me holding him and him crying. But I had a feeling this was the first time Mal had just let go and let himself actually grieve.

I felt bad for laying into him a few minutes ago. This wasn't about me. I should be here for him. That was my new job, right?

God, I was a jerk.

After a few minutes—or ten, I wasn't exactly keeping track—Mal stood upright and swiped at his face.

"Just...Just don't go, okay?" he mumbled, avoiding my eyes again. "I really do want to make this work."

"Of course, Mal. I'm so sorry for lashing out at you. I just really thought—"

"No, I deserved it. I've been an ass today. I'll try to do better, I swear."

"Okay," I murmured. "Um, how about you go wash up, and I'll heat up dinner?"

"Sounds good, baby. Thanks."

But he didn't even touch me as he left the closet for the bathroom.

And it was hard for me not to be hurt by it.

"Baby steps," I told myself as I headed for the kitchen.

He was probably just embarrassed for losing it like that in front of me. Some men were weird about crying.

We just had to give ourselves time.

Before I reached the kitchen, the gate/doorbell buzzed again.

It kinda felt like I'd fallen into a dark British comedy, and I had no idea what my lines were, while everyone around me continued like this was normal.

It was all just so surreal.

"Judy!" A deep male voice called from the living room.

Cue act two.

Chapter 18

Mal

It felt like all my emotions were bubbling just under the surface. Back in the day, it'd been easier to reach for something to dull the insanity. But I couldn't do that anymore. Now I had to face and feel my emotions like a regular person and just...cope.

It fucking sucked.

I really didn't know how to feel about having fallen apart in front of Saylor. I just knew I didn't want her to leave.

But I also didn't know how to deal with having her here.

Life was a bitch like that sometimes.

All my relationships previously, even my first marriage, had been very surface—all about sex or partying or fame. But partying was out and Saylor didn't seem interested in fame—especially after that scene at the airport. Her need to cook dinner and...nest, I guess for lack of a better word, was so far out of my realm. I didn't really know how to do real.

The program had given me some tools about confronting my feelings, but between my new marriage, Gio's death, and managing my sobriety, I just felt so lost.

How did I do this without Gio? He'd been my right hand since middle school. We'd been brothers for forever. I didn't know how life looked without Gio.

I didn't know how the Long Licks could survive without him.

It felt like I was standing on the precipice of monumental change, and I was the dumb fuck who'd kicked it all off by getting married to a stranger—a woman twenty years younger than me.

But she was also awesome and giving and sweet and so fucking gorgeous she could've been on magazine covers.

I was so fucked up.

Sighing, I tossed the towel I'd been rubbing against my head onto the towel rack and left the room, following the amazing scents down the hall.

Which was when I heard a few extra voices.

"This is the shit," Beau mumbled around whatever was in his mouth. My dinner, no doubt.

"Fuck yeah, it is," Ryker agreed.

"I see why Mal was quick to lock you down," Leif drawled.

"Oh, I've never cooked for him before," Saylor protested in her sweet as hell voice.

"Yeah, that's not what I'm talking about, darlin'," Leif murmured seductively.

That fucker.

I all but ran down the hall and skidded to a stop at the sight of my whole band gathered in my kitchen, plates in their hands as they scarfed down on the dinner my wife had made for *me*.

"Seriously, Leif? Do I have to piss in a circle around my wife?"

"Considering she can cook like this." Leif tossed his chin-length blond hair out of his face as he raised his plate. "I think you might need to."

I scowled at the asshat who'd been the source of more of my angst lately than I wanted to really think about. Stupid vampire looking asshole. He'd always reminded me of Lestat from *Interview with a Vampire*.

Just as devious, only stupider.

After crossing the room and glaring at Leif the entire way, I put an arm around Saylor and pulled her to my side. "Any food left for me?"

"I thought you didn't want to eat," my mom piped up from behind Beau.

The huge behemoth's eyes widened, and he took a big step away from the tension. He might look like a brawler, but Beau really didn't like drama. And my mom's tone clearly spelled drama.

He did however enjoy watching me get my ass handed to me by my mother, evidenced by the fact that he and none of the other guys left the room, despite the rising tension.

I groaned. "I'm sorry I was an ass. But in my defense, it's been a fucking week of a day."

Mom rolled her eyes even as she handed me a loaded plate.

I tipped my chin at her in thanks as I stared down at the burrito on my plate. It looked like every other burrito I'd ever had. Keeping one arm around Saylor, I put the plate down and picked up the burrito with my free hand and dug in.

The guys were buzzing about some new band hitting the charts, but my groan quickly drowned them out.

Once I swallowed the amazing bite, I nuzzled Saylor's head with my nose. "Baby, this is fucking fantastic. I'm sorry I was such an ass. You got skills, baby girl."

She blushed at my praise and shifted her weight, clearly uncomfortable with all the attention pointed her way.

"So, how did you two meet?" Beau, our bassist and the only member of our group currently married, asked with raised eyebrows. His wife, Phoebe, tucked close to his side but had no plate or food in her hands. She raised her eyebrows with a smirk as she subtly pushed her tits out when she caught Leif staring her way.

Leif quickly looked away.

Shit, they'd been married barely a year.

"Fiji," Saylor's soft voice brought me back to the conversation.

"Technically on the flight to Fiji," I interjected. "This one turned me down when I propositioned her to join the mile high club, and that was when I knew I had to lock her down."

The guys laughed as Saylor groaned.

"Malcolm Hendrix Holt!" My mom's harsh voice sliced through the laughter.

I winced and feigned hiding behind my wife. Honestly, I'd forgotten she was here.

"Saylor, did he really?" Mom asked.

Saylor lifted her shoulder and then nodded.

The guys laughed some more.

"Boy, you are lucky we have an audience," Mom scowled in my direction.

I continued to hide behind my wife and ate more of my burrito. Death would be the only thing that'd keep me from finishing Saylor's amazing food.

"So, uh, Mal, have you had a chance to make any arrangements for Gio's service?" Leif asked, shattering the levity of the moment.

My best friend's death would also kill my hunger.

My burrito dropped to the plate with a plop, and I grabbed a paper towel to swipe at my mouth. Swallowing hard, I shook my head. "Not really. I arranged for him to be transported to the funeral home, but I held off on making any plans beyond that."

"I'd like to help if I can," Leif offered quietly.

"I think it's safe to say we all would," Beau rumbled. "You shouldn't have to do it alone, man, just because you're the official next of kin."

"Yeah," Ryker agreed. "We wanna help."

"I can totally post the announcement on all my socials for my followers," Phoebe offered with zero irony, pressing a hand to her very impressive chest.

I exchange incredulous looks with Ryker.

"Uh, thanks. I think." I cleared my throat. "I guess that's the first thing we need to decide. Are we doing a private or a public funeral? Followed by burial or cremation?" I felt like a tool today when I was completely unable to answer any of the funeral director's basic questions.

"I can't speak to the first," Mom offered. "But Gio told me that he wanted to be buried. Fire freaked him out. Remember that time his apartment building had that fire in the middle of the night?"

"Right." I shook my head. "He said something like that when we had those pyrotechnics on our first tour. He didn't want any of that shit anywhere near him. Fuck the—"

"Encore." Ryker finished with a laugh. "You're not lighting me up like the Stay Puft—"

"Marshmallow Man in *Ghost Busters*," we all said together before breaking out in laughter.

We'd given him shit for years over his hysterics when it came to pyrotechnics. I don't know how I'd forgotten about that.

"Right, we're burying him then." I rubbed my sweaty palms on my jeans. "And the service?"

We spent the next few hours planning Gio's service while we traded stories and laughed about Gio's crazy antics.

It was simultaneously the best and worst night of my life. Gio would've loved it though. And having Saylor in my arms made it easier to get through.

After the guys left, and I got my mom settled in one of the guest rooms, I found Saylor back in the closet, staring down at her pile of luggage.

"I guess we'll have to arrange to have the rest of your clothes shipped here," I said, leaning against the doorjamb.

Saylor looked up with a tentative smile. "I was just thinking the same thing. And I don't have anything suitable for a funeral. I'll have to go shopping."

"I'll have Naomi set up some appointments."

She winced. "I'd rather go with Judy and handle all the details myself, if that's all right with you."

"Whatever you want, baby. I do want you to think of this as your home and settle in—unpack."

She opened her mouth like she wanted to object. But then she didn't.

Instead, she opened *the* bag in front of her.

Her whole body flushed as a dildo I'd missed the first time tumbled out. She grabbed it and shoved it back into the bag then grabbed her toiletry kit and quickly closed the lid on the suitcase. "I'm just gonna go brush my teeth."

Saylor galloped out of the room like hellhounds were nipping at her heels.

I shook my head. Given how things had gone in Fiji, I would've thought we were beyond all that timidness.

Or maybe it was an indictment on my dickishness.

Shit.

I slowly followed her to the bathroom and stood in the open doorway. Her face was still flushed, and she avoided my eyes as she stared at her reflection and brushed her teeth with alacrity.

Yup, this was definitely because of my dickishness.

I didn't know what to do or to say to begin to make up the past two days to Saylor. I didn't want her to leave, but I also didn't know how to make her want to stay.

Sighing, I entered the bathroom and grabbed my toothbrush and brushed my teeth at the sink next to her.

Saylor kept shooting me looks out of the corner of her eye but didn't say anything. Although fair, given she had a toothbrush in her mouth.

I smiled around my own toothbrush at my absurdity.

"What?" Saylor's question was muffled.

I shrugged and shook my head.

After she rinsed, she rested her hip against the counter and watched me. "So what's the plan for tomorrow?"

I spit in the sink and rinsed my mouth. "I guess Ryker and I will head over to the funeral home to make all the arrangements. You and Ma can go shopping if you'd like. I'm sure there's lots of stuff you'll need to make this your home."

"Okay." Saylor bit her bottom lip and nodded slowly. "I can do that."

"I'll leave the Benz for you. I want to arrange for a driver too."

Saylor shrugged. "I think an Uber would be easier."

"Yeah no. After that scene at the airport, I think I'd feel better if you had a driver or security with you."

"Oh. Right." She gave me an uneasy look. "Whatever you think is best."

"I'll arrange it myself."

"Oh. I—"

"It probably wasn't the best time to give my assistant a few days off. So I'll make the arrangements myself because your safety is important to me."

Her mouth closed with a click of her teeth and a warm expression came into her eyes.

"Plus my mom loves it when she has a driver and gets to hit the town like a starlet. She'll show you how to have a good time on Rodeo Drive."

Saylor frowned. "Your mom? The paisley wearing hippie who gave you the middle name Hendrix because of her love of Jimi Hendrix? That mom?"

"Okay, so that might've been an exaggeration. It might be more of a struggle than I let on. She actually hates the whole consumerism thing. So have fun with that."

She laughed. "Totally fine. Since we have a few days, I thought I'd hit some fabric stores and maybe make my own dress for the service."

"Only if you promise to go out and buy the best sewing machine money can buy. I don't want you bleeding for your craft." The memory of her sweating and literally bleeding over her wedding gown still bothered me.

"Fine." She sighed like it was a huge ask, but then a grin stole across her face. "The best that money can buy?"

I shrugged. "We can turn one of the guest rooms into your office or sewing room or whatever it's called. Workroom. That sounds like a thing. Let's go with workroom."

"You're giving me a bedroom?"

"To work in, *not* to sleep." I narrowed my eyes at her. "Your bedroom is in here. You sleep next to me in this bed."

She nodded slowly.

"Unpack whatever you have in the closet. This is your home. If you want to change shit—get new furniture, whatever—we'll do it. I want this to feel like your home too."

"So I can hang up some pictures? Maybe put some color into your beige?"

"Fuck yes. Whatever you want. I didn't pick out most of this shit as it is. It came furnished, and I've never really spent enough time here to get around to changing anything."

"Okay," Saylor whispered, her eyes darting around the closet. The eager gleam in her eyes when she turned back to me made me smile.

Maybe I was getting the hang of this whole marriage thing.

My cockiness was belied a few minutes later after we climbed under the covers in the beige bed, and Saylor was so tense next to me that the whole bed practically vibrated.

And not because of one of her vibrating toys in that way that had been so much fucking fun.

I sighed and reached over, pulling her closer to me until she finally rested her head on my shoulder and her hands on my chest.

"This okay?" I asked softly.

She gave a deep shuddery sigh and relaxed against me like this was where she'd wanted to be the entire time. "Yeah. I'm good. 'Night."

"'Night, baby." I pressed a kiss against her hair and relaxed into the bed.

So much of my life was in turmoil at the moment. But this, this right here, felt like everything.

And for the first time since I'd started seeing Saylor, I fell asleep with her in my arms without having sex.

Chapter 19

Saylor

The next morning while Mal was out with Ryker, Judy and I headed for the shops. She'd been excited at the mention of fabric stores and not the Rodeo Drive experience Mal had teased me with the night before.

I had a feeling I wasn't the only seamstress in Mal's life.

"So he made it up to you last night?"

I almost choked on my latte at Judy's not so innocent question. "Yeah, I'm not discussing my sex life with your son with you."

Judy rolled her eyes. "I didn't mean that, but it's not like it's a verboten topic. Everyone has sex. Talking about sex is healthy. But for the record, I wasn't asking for details. I just noticed the cute smile you had and assumed it had something to do with your husband."

I shook my head. "Yes, I was thinking about Mal. He was…sweet last night."

"Good, but like I said, I don't need all the dirty details."

"I didn't mean it like that!" I all but wailed. "We didn't even—" I broke off with a groan. "Whatever."

To escape, I pulled my phone out of my purse and powered it up without thinking.

Immediately, it rang in my hand.

The display read **Mom**.

And my heart froze.

Oh god.

Mom.

Given the way my phone had been blowing up yesterday, someone had to've filled her in on my wedding by now.

Dread heavy in my heart, I pushed accept and held my phone to my ear. "Hey Mom."

"*'Hey Mom?'* Seriously, Saylor?" She shrieked in my ear. "That's how you answer the phone after avoiding my calls all day yesterday?"

I flinched as her words hit me like a whip. "Uh, I didn't get any of your calls. I had to turn my phone off."

"Of course you had to turn your phone off. You married some *singer*? What is wrong with you? Did you seriously think that you could fix things with Trent by marrying someone else?"

"What are you even talking about? I'm not trying to fix things with Trent, Mom. Trent and I are done—I told you that when I canceled the wedding. And now I'm married to someone else."

"So you're not trying to make him jealous? Because I have to tell you he's absolutely shattered."

I huffed in annoyance. "You mean his kneecap is shattered? Did his bookie finally catch up to him?"

"That's not funny, young lady."

"Considering what his bookie did to my face, I kinda thought it was. Gallows humor and all that."

"He said he apologized. He wants to make things right with you, Saylor. But now you've gone and ruined it all." She did that thing where she blew an annoyed breath—the soundtrack of my childhood by the way. "Do you seriously think you're going to be taken care of with that musician? And are you going to get a job in California? It won't be in teaching—not any time soon at least. Your certification is in Nevada. You'll have to start all over. I just, I don't understand what you were thinking."

My head spun. I didn't even know which point to address first. But one thing was apparent—I was done with her shit.

I avoided Judy's concerned expression and hunched over my phone.

"I want to make it crystal clear to you, Mom. I am never, ever, *ever* getting back together with Trent—current marriage notwithstanding. Trent is a degenerate gambler who doesn't think he has a problem. That's a dealbreaker for me. Or maybe the dealbreaker was when his bookie *hit* me. We're done. It's not happening. Ever."

"I just think—"

"I don't care, Mom. This whole dynamic is just so toxic. You need to figure out that I'm an adult, and you don't get a say in how I live my life. And I'm sorry I got married without telling you, but if you don't get why I did, then I've got nothing else to say to you. Mal is a good man who only wants the best for me. End of discussion."

"I think you're making a mistake, Saylor. Musicians are—"

"Don't even think about finishing that sentence. Mal is an amazing man who just so happens to be a musician. A successful musician, by the way, who can take care of me beyond anything Trent could even think of promising. Not that I'm counting on that. I'm going into design. Mal is supportive of my dreams. He wants me to go after what *I* want. He believes in *me*. Which is why I locked him down. And if you like Trent so much, maybe you should divorce Alan and marry Trent yourself."

"Young lady. That is the most disgusting thing I've ever heard come out of your mouth. Apologize. *Now*."

"Yeah, well, that's how I feel about you continually taking Trent's side despite all the shit he's rained down on me. So I'm done. Until or unless you can let go of Trent the Superman Gambler being in my life,

I don't want to talk to you."

"Saylor, you're being immature. We haven't—"

"I'm done with this conversation. I love you, Mom, but I can't have all your toxic b.s. in my life. Goodbye."

I punched the red button on my phone and tossed it onto the seat next to me.

The whole cab of the fancy town car pulsed with tension. My panting breaths were the only sound as I stared sightlessly in front of me. I couldn't believe I'd finally done it. I'd dreamt so long about telling my mom exactly what I thought about her and our relationship. It felt so…scary. Oh god.

"Um, not that it's my place, but I just have to say that I'm so proud of you, Saylor."

Judy's quiet words had me blinking in disbelief. "What?"

"It takes a very strong woman to put up and enforce boundaries with your parents like that. I think you did a fantastic job."

Tears sheened my eyes and made it difficult to see. I would've thought she, of all people, would've been upset at how that conversation went. A mom should side with the mom, right? "I…I don't know what to say."

"You don't have to say anything, sweet girl. Just know that she might not see the light, so that might not be the only barrier you have to enforce with her. People with myopic vision don't change all that much in my experience."

I smiled sadly. "Mal's lucky to have you in his life."

"You should tell him that. Often."

And despite that trainwreck of a phone call, I broke out into husky laughter. "Anything for you, Judy."

Mal wasn't the only Holt I was falling in love with.

Later that afternoon, after a fabulous trip to the fabric store with Judy and getting the sewing machine installed in a suddenly cleared out guest room down the hall and while Mal was out at yet another NA meeting, I got up the courage to call Paige.

Paige, of course answered on the first ring.

"Where the hell have you been, bitch?"

I sighed. "I think you get that it's been a wonderful and weird few days followed by epic tragedy here, right?"

"What I don't get is how you could marry anyone—let alone a rock star—without telling me? Seriously, Saylor?"

"I was on the other side of the world. It's not like you could've been there in time to stand up for me."

"I still would've appreciated a phone call or text. I can't believe I had to learn about your wedding from the freaking *Babbler* of all places."

"In my defense, I would've texted you, but then shit hit the fan with Mal's best friend dying the night of."

Paige huffed in a totally different way as my mom had. "Hard to argue when you play the dead best friend card, but I think you still should've told me before the wedding."

"I didn't want you to talk me out of it."

"I would never—"

"You would've tried and you know it, Paige. It was impetuous, we hardly know each other, and there's a strong possibility this was a mistake."

"You already think it's a mistake? What did that asshole do?"

"Nothing really. It's just…it's a lot harder than I thought it would be. We were supposed to have another week in paradise before we came home. Another week to enjoy the beaches and our treehouse and each other, but then…" I sighed. "It's just hard. He has these moments of absolute sweetness—like how he cleared out a guest room overnight so I could have a workspace here for my sewing machine—but then he can also be so jarringly selfish."

"What do you mean by selfish? What did he do?"

"I... Nothing huge. Nothing like what Trent did." I groaned and rubbed at my forehead.

I felt kinda ridiculous harping about yesterday given all that Mal was going through. And he'd tried to make up for it.

I was just worried it was a sign of worse things to come.

"He just left me in the car all day yesterday while he went to appointment after appointment. I kinda felt like a neglected dog."

"Why didn't he take you with him?"

"I mean, some of them were private—like his NA meeting, and I get it. But then at others, his assistant went inside with him. And I'm totally getting mean girl vibes from her by the way. Nothing I can really put my finger on; she's just...cold, I guess. But I would've liked to have been the one who helped him get through this horrible ordeal. You know? I mean, isn't that what marriage is supposed to be about?"

"It is to people who give a shit. But you're in Hollywood, honey. Actors and musicians are a different breed. They don't think like you or me."

I sighed and fell back onto the bed. "Yeah, this is exactly why I didn't tell you before the wedding."

"Because you didn't want me to save you from the mistake you knew you were making?"

"Maybe..." I rubbed at my tired eyes with my free hand. "Probably."

"Is this a bad time to ask you to introduce me to Leif Eccles? I've had a crush on him for freaking ever."

"I remember the posters on your bedroom walls in high school. Which made meeting him last night totally weird, by the way." I laughed weakly. "Yeah, no. That's not ever happening. Pretty sure it would unleash a power that would undo the space-time continuum or something. Mal has some issues with Leif as it is. We don't need to add his breaking your heart to the list."

"What do you mean? Do they not get along?"

I hesitated. Which was rare. I always told Paige *everything*. But this info—Leif maybe going solo and Mal's feelings on it—felt deeply private. And like it would be a betrayal to my husband to tell anyone else.

I'd never chosen a guy over my bestie. Ever. We were ride or die as long as I'd known her.

But now I *was* choosing a guy over her.

"Saylor? You still there? You okay?"

"Yeah, I just...I can't really talk about that."

"Really? With me?" Paige asked, clearly offended. "You know I wouldn't run to the tabs or whatever you're worried about. I wouldn't betray you like that."

"And I shouldn't betray Mal's confidence."

Stunned silence met my confession. Followed by Paige's softly whispered, "So you really love him then."

"Yeah. Yeah, I do." I sighed again as a sense of peace settled in my heart.

I loved Malcolm Holt.

"I'd like to meet him. Once you guys are through all the craziness of the next few days. But I think I need to meet the guy who makes my bestie glow over the phone like this. Fuck the space-time continuum."

I laughed. "For the record, it would only undo the space-time continuum if you got with Leif. I think we're safe if you meet my husband."

Paige laughed with me. "Gotta say, it's wild to me that we're still using that word given all that's happened. How's the eye? I couldn't even tell in the pics I saw on *the Babbler* that you had a shiner."

"It's better. All the color is gone. Almost like it never happened, but for the horrible memory."

"Gotta say, it sounds like you definitely traded up, even with the selfish tendencies."

"I definitely did."

I then proceeded to tell Paige all the ways and reasons I loved Malcolm Holt.

I did not however tell her that I sometimes called him Daddy.

Some things had to stay between me and Mal.

Breaking News from the Babbler

Long Licks Stars Gather to Say Goodbye to Drummer at Private Funeral

Leif Eccles, Malcolm Holt and More Mourn Gio Barone

Exclusive details

Gio Barone's bandmates and friends celebrated his life on Friday during an intimate graveside ceremony in Los Angeles.

slideshow of photos from parking lot and drones

Barry Brooks, the KLAS rock radio host who was a close friend of Barone, shared reflections on the funeral and confirmed the bandmembers' attendance. "**Gio Barone** has now been laid to rest in LA. It has been an emotional couple of days to say the least, saying farewell to an icon and long-time friend," Brooks wrote on social media. "The service went as well as it could and was attended by a small group of family and close friends, including the members of the Long Licks."

Brooks also announced plans for a future tribute show to honor the drummer with the blessing of Barone's next of kin. "That's something I feel, and many others feel, is deserved and should happen," Brooks wrote.

Barone died in LA a week ago, at age 45. Barone's rep, Danny Conlan, attributed his death to an "unfortunate drug overdose," though a specific cause of death has yet to be filed by the LA coroner.

The Long Licks bassist, **Beau Benoit**, shared a sweet tribute on social media to the drummer shortly after his death. "Our hearts are broken. Gio is gone. But no one can touch his legacy," he wrote. "Lick up every moment because you don't know when it'll be your last."

Lead singer, **Leif Eccles** posted, "Gio was the eternal rock soldier. Long may his legacy live on!"

Guitarist, **Malcolm Holt** posted a throwback photo of himself and Barone from their childhood with the caption, "What an honor it was to call you best friend. The void you've left behind will never be filled. Lick it all up in heaven, brother."

Earlier that day, the band shared a joint statement, describing Barone as "an essential and irreplaceable rock legend." Barone's bandmates added, "He is and will always be a part of the Long Licks legacy. His loss leaves the kind of hole that will never heal."

Gio Barone was 45.

RIP

Chapter 20

Mal

The worst day of my life was finally here.

And that was saying a lot, given my history.

I'd been arrested six times. Overdosed in Thailand. Fell off the stage in Minneapolis and broke my leg in two places.

All that paled in comparison to the shitshow today was going to be.

We opted for a graveside service early in the morning for Gio, hoping to put off the media by scheduling it quickly and quietly.

I still hadn't been able to get ahold of Gio's girl, Amaya. Ryker and Beau were trying too. I hadn't heard from Leif since that first night at my place. Ryker was in charge getting the service details to the asshole. I didn't want to talk to him.

It felt like my entire life was fracturing, and I didn't know what or who to hold onto.

I was pulling away from Saylor. This wasn't the life I'd promised her.

But then maybe I'd sold myself on the same fairytale—that my band breaking up wouldn't also break my heart.

I sighed, staring sightlessly out the window of our hired car. Given the many ways this could all fall to pieces, I didn't want to trust the lives of my loved ones to my driving skills. I'd no doubt be arrested for manslaughter because I wouldn't even slow down if one of those asshole paps jumped in front of the car to get a good picture.

Fuck 'em all.

The strained silence in the cab of the car was broken only by the lilting tones of whatever elevator music the driver had put on. It was starting to feel like a special kind of torture. Seriously, who played easy listening when they were driving a fucking rock god around town?

"Hey!" I called as I leaned forward. "Could you at least put some decent music on?"

"Uh, sure thing. I mean, yes sir." A few seconds later the Tin Gods anthem '*Nowhere to Hide*' blared over the speakers mid-song.

I sat back with a dry chuckle. If that wasn't an apt theme song to the day, I didn't know a better one.

"Mal, have you noticed the dress Saylor is wearing? She put it together herself in just three days."

I jolted at my mom's pointed question. "Uh, yeah. You look nice, Saylor."

Saylor sighed, no doubt annoyed I hadn't even bothered to look her way.

Naomi's snort underlined the point.

I glared at Naomi. I hadn't needed to look at Saylor again. The visual of her in that black A-line dress with long sleeves and a collar like a man's button-up shirt but open to perfectly frame her lickable cleavage was imprinted on my brain. She looked gorgeous, which was fucked considering the occasion—not that I was blaming her. I just didn't want to rock up to the graveyard with a huge boner tenting the front of my pants.

And Naomi had promised if I let her come to the service, she'd behave.

This definitely wasn't her behaving.

I said as much with the look I gave her.

She blinked innocently back at me.

Sighing, I turned to my wife. "You look gorgeous, Saylor. I think it's fucking amazing that you made your dress so quickly. Do you need anything else in your workroom? Equipment or something you don't have right now?"

The words sounded stilted coming out of my mouth, but I blamed that on our audience and not that I hadn't spent any time with her lately.

She shook her head mutely and stared straight ahead like she was wishing she was anywhere else than here.

Same, baby girl. Same.

The car slowed to pull into a parking lot, and my stomach churned.

We were here.

In less than a heartbeat, we were surrounded. Shouted questions, camera flashes, and clicks rocked the stillness of our car, and I went from sad to pissed off in a heartbeat.

"What the fuck! Who tipped those assholes off?" I bit out.

We'd made everyone sign NDAs, from the groundskeeper to our drivers.

Fuck.

"Um, where do you want me to let you out, Mister Holt?" Our driver asked.

I groaned. "Pull around, so I'll be the first one out. They can't come on the property, but that doesn't mean they won't be assholes." Turning to the others in the car, I said, "If any of you would rather stay in the car, I totally understand."

"I need to say goodbye to Gio," Mom said tremulously.

Naomi shook her head. "I'm used to it. And I want to say goodbye too."

I nodded and turned to Saylor.

She gave me a wobbly smile. "My place is next to you. I'm going wherever you're going."

I grinned back at her and for a second, I felt lighter.

Then I flinched as someone's hand slapped our window as the driver tried to pull through the crowd.

Naomi sighed and fussed with her bag.

Out of the corner of my eye, I spied the encouraging smile Saylor sent my way, and I reached over to hold her hand. For the first time that day, I felt slightly grounded. Like maybe I could actually get through this shitshow in one piece as long as I had Saylor by my side.

She squeezed my hand, and I grinned as I squeezed it back.

Then the driver opened the door, and the worst day of my life truly began.

The buzzing of several drones overhead hummed annoyingly and competed with the constant click of the paps' cameras audible across the street.

I sighed and dropped Saylor's hand before stepping out into the mayhem.

I pulled my mom out of the limo and blocked the paps with my body as best as I could before helping Naomi out and then passing their hands to the driver to escort inside.

Then I reached into the car and helped Saylor out, and a few shouted questions competed with the clicking cameras.

"Saylor, over here!"

"Saylor, how's life as a newlywed?"

"Saylor, is it true that your ex beat you?"

It was that last question that made Saylor trip. She would've gone down but for my hand holding her up.

I moved from holding her hand to wrapping my arm around her shoulder before leading her away from the bedlam across the street and overhead as we walked to the front gate.

I nodded at our driver on his way back to the car and stood with most of our band on the other side of the gate, safe from the cameras across the street, but not from the ones overhead.

"Next guy who dies gets buried in a private plot. Fuck LA County," our manager, Danny, muttered as he scowled at the drone hovering above us.

"Fuck that," Leif snarked. "Next guy gets cremated and spread over the Pacific Ocean or some poetic shit."

"Pretty sure that's not up to you assholes, unless you haven't filed a will?" I asked with raised brows.

Both of them nodded their heads.

"Where's Beau?" I asked with a frown.

"Probably waiting for Phoebe to put on her face." Leif sighed.

"I had to spell out to Beau that no, she couldn't livestream the service." Ryker rocked back on his heels with his hands stuffed in his front pockets. "Private means no cameras."

"Fat lot of good that did," Leif muttered, glaring at the persistent drone. "These fuckers just don't quit."

"Should be a crime," my mom murmured with a frown. "Everyone deserves a peaceful, final resting place."

"Sorry, Judy, didn't see you there." Ryker stepped up to give my mom a huge hug, and despite his skinnier frame he picked her up and twirled her around.

"Ryker, you lunatic! Put me down. This shit isn't dignified." My mom squealed.

Ryker chuckled as he set her down. "We don't do dignified here."

"Maybe given the circumstances, you should try it," Leif said before cutting in and giving my mom a tamer hug. "Judy. Good to see you again. Thanks for coming."

"Always," my mom murmured back. "You all are my boys, you know that."

Danny stepped up and hugged my mom as they murmured something to each other I couldn't hear over the drone's buzzing.

Both guys nodded at Naomi but didn't approach her.

Ryker stepped forward and gave Saylor a more reserved and respectful side hug. "Hey Saylor."

She smiled awkwardly back at him.

Leif didn't even bother with that much of a greeting. He tipped his head at Saylor then stepped back to complete our half circle.

I tried not to let his aloofness bother me. But I could tell it made Saylor feel even more awkward. She shifted next to me and clutched my arm in a tighter grip than before.

Danny stepped up and offered his hand to Saylor with a grin. "Is this the infamous wife?"

"Saylor, this is our manager, Danny Conlan," I said with a barely concealed eyeroll. "Danny, this is the infamous wife, Saylor Holt."

Saylor shook his hand with a smile. "Nice to meet you."

"Christ, did you rob a high school, Mal?" Danny laughed. "She looks the same age as my daughter, Bette."

"Not funny, fucker. Only way Saylor has been in a school recently was to teach. Try to treat my woman with some respect."

Since Bette just finished eighth grade, it was a disgusting comparison.

"Oh, you teach?" Danny asked innocently like he hadn't just insulted me and her.

Saylor lifted a shoulder. "Not anymore."

"Ah, right." Danny nodded sagely. "You married this lug so…"

His implication hung in the air between us.

Fucker.

I put a hand on Danny's chest and shoved him away from my wife. "Back the fuck off. Saylor is going to go into fashion. She made the fucking amazing dress she's wearing. She's got talent and she wants to do something with it. Sound familiar?"

"Hey, hey, I'm sorry okay?" Danny lifted his palms in placation. "I heard about your quickie wedding and made a few assumptions. Clearly the wrong assumptions. You wouldn't be stupid enough to get talked into marriage without a prenup and vetting your bride-to-be. I just heard all those reports about her runaway bride thing and assumed... I'm sorry, Saylor."

She bit her lip and shrugged. But the fact that she didn't immediately accept his half-assed apology made me so fucking proud of her.

Danny nodded back and took a spot in our little circle far away from us.

We stood there and talked for another ten minutes.

Twenty minutes.

At half an hour, I begged Ryker to text them again.

"Where the fuck are they?" I grumbled.

"Maybe we should start the service without them?" Ryker offered.

"It's gonna be like ten minutes tops," I replied. "If we start without them, there's a good chance we'll finish without them too."

Almost like I spoke it into existence, the gate opened and a disgruntled Beau stomped into the cemetery, followed by his prancing wife who was wearing the hugest hat I'd ever seen.

"Beau! Finally!" Ryker crowed. "We were getting ready to start without you."

"Sorry, guys." Beau pushed a hand through his long brown hair. "You know how it is with women—can't show up until you're fashionably late."

"No, can't relate." I gave him a blank stare. "We've been here for thirty minutes. My mom, my wife, and my assistant had no problem getting ready on time."

Beau winced. "Sorry guys."

"Let's get this show on the road," I muttered.

CHAPTER 20

Holding Saylor's hand, we made our way down the path and toward the tent set up on the vibrantly green grass.

As we dodged the headstones, I remembered that horrible appointment when Ryker and I had to pick out his headstone and his epitaph. After Ryker brought up our first international tour and how desperate Gio had been to see Jim Morrison's grave in Paris despite our tight timeline, I knew there was only one thing we could put on it—only we tweaked for Gio's Italian heritage.

It'll read: *Fedele al suo demone interiore.*

True to his own demon. A fitting epitaph for the way Gio lived and died.

Only that kind of thing took time apparently. Carving stone wasn't exactly quick.

But it wasn't the basic placard provided by the cemetery that held my attention.

It was the gleaming casket sitting on metal rails and surrounded by fake turf to conceal the huge hole he'd be interred inside today.

Fuck.

I thought I'd confronted the reality of this moment when I had to claim his body at the coroner's. But even though his casket was closed, I knew it was him inside there. I felt the loss more keenly now than ever before.

I would've gone down on my knees but for Saylor next to me.

I staggered for a second and she swooped under my arm to hold me up, bracing a hand against my chest.

And I let her.

She didn't say a word. She just held me.

And later when we stood around Gio's closed casket, and I wept, she continued to hold me.

Breaking News from the Babbler

Malcolm Holt's New Bride Holds Him Up at Funeral

New Wife Is His Support System, Literally

Exclusive Details

As seen only on the Babbler, **Malcolm Holt**'s new bride, **Saylor Tate** was by side his at the funeral of his best friend and bandmate **Gio Barone**. They met the other members of the Long Licks and a few friends of Barone. Tate wore a classy black A-line dress with a collared neckline, perfect for the occasion and matching her husband who wore head to toe black.

photos of Mal and Saylor at the cemetery

But when it came time for the service, the Long Licks' guitarist stumbled, and Tate swooped in and helped him stay up. She stayed at his side the entire service. Was he overcome with emotion, or has Holt's infamous sobriety also stumbled? You be the judge in the pictures below…

more photos of Mal and Saylor at the funeral

Barone died in LA a week ago. Barone's rep, Danny Conlan, attributed his death to an "unfortunate drug overdose," though a specific cause of death has yet to be filed by the LA coroner.

Gio Barone was 45.
RIP

Chapter 21

Saylor

I sighed in relief as the door closed. I knew it didn't mean we were leaving Mal's grief behind, but at least the circus of paps, drones, and annoying managers were on the other side. Even Mal's mom had returned to her house, murmuring to me that Mal and I needed some time alone to heal and bond.

Mal retreated to his office/music room and soon the electric wail of his guitar echoed in the empty house.

I didn't know what to do. Mal and I barely knew each other. I wanted to help him through his grief. But I'd never been through anything like this. Even my dad's death was a dim, distant memory. Really, the only thing I remembered was sitting under the kitchen table and staring at people's legs and feeling so confused and just…lost.

And no, I didn't miss the parallel here.

Sighing, I headed for the kitchen and did the only thing I knew I could do—cook. Judy had mentioned a few days ago that Mal's favorite food was friend chicken, although he didn't eat it much anymore. I'd ordered all the ingredients to make it for him, it had just never felt like the right time.

Soon I had the chicken brining in the fridge while I got the dredge together.

Mal's guitar was drowned out by the popping and snapping of the oil as I laid the first drumstick into the liquid. While the chicken fried, I popped some biscuits in the oven and stirred together a quick slaw Judy had given me the recipe for.

Ten minutes later, Mal wandered into the kitchen, clearly led by his nose. "Ma?"

That should probably feel like a compliment, but I still blanched. "Uh no. She went home, Mal. It's just me."

"That's so weird. I swear I could smell her…fried chicken," he finished weakly.

I turned to face him with the tongs in my hand. "Um, she gave me the recipe. It probably won't taste exactly the same, but—ack!"

I broke off with a gasp as Mal swung his guitar behind him, bounded across the kitchen, and swept me up in his arms. Before I could blink, his lips were on mine, and he was kissing me passionately. The tongs fell to the floor with a clatter as I wrapped my arms around him and threaded my fingers in his hair.

He'd been so distant lately. We hadn't had this much bodily contact since Fiji, and I realized how very much I'd missed this. Missed him.

He pivoted and walked me away from the stove, but I pulled away from his luscious lips with a gasp. "Can't leave the oil on!"

He kept one hand on me while I quickly moved the frying pan off the burner, turned it off, and batted at the oven setting. Mal swept his guitar strap off and set his fancy looking guitar down amid the scraps of my cooking.

"Mal, is that—"

"Don't care," he mumbled as he pulled me back to him and kissed me again.

He kissed me as we staggered down the hallway to his bedroom. He kept kissing me as he picked me up and set me down on his bed.

I couldn't really think. I just knew I loved how he kissed me.

His hand moved over me with an urgency, tugging at my dress. I should've changed after the service, but I'd been too blinded by my need to help him somehow. Between the long sleeves and the narrow collar, there wasn't a lot of give.

"There's a zipper in the back." I sat up slightly to give him access, but he shook his head.

"No time," he muttered just before he ripped my dress.

I couldn't deny that at first I was seriously turned on. Having a man like Mal want me so much that he couldn't bother with a zipper, made me seriously wet.

A beat later, I deflated slightly. I'd worked so hard on that dress. "Mal—"

"So sorry, baby." His lips moved over my breast as he quickly thumbed the cup of my bra out of his way. "I'll buy you another one."

"But I didn't…" The rest of my protest was lost as he pulled my nipple deep into his mouth and suckled so hard, I felt an answering pang between my legs. "Oh god."

"Mmm," Mal hummed. "I like it better when you call me Daddy."

"Oh god. Mal. I don't, I can't…" I swear it'd only been three minutes, but I was already so close to coming, I couldn't think, let alone speak coherently.

"Yeah, baby girl. You're so fucking sweet. So fucking everything." His nimble fingers dove under my panties and teased and petted my aching sex until I was hovering over the precipice. "Be a good girl, baby. Give me just a little more."

His finger strummed my clit like a guitar string, and I lost it. Pleasure crashed through my body, and I wailed as I went over.

I was still shuddering from my climax when he thrusted inside me. My hands clutched at his black dress shirt as I wrapped my legs around his pant-clad waist. His zipper bit into my tender skin as he bottomed out. But I didn't care. I was already climbing to another climax. He felt so good inside me. So hard. So big.

"Ah! Daddy, please. I can't, please!" I gasped incoherently as my sex clenched around him.

He bottomed out again and twisted his hips. His pants rasped against my clit, and I screamed as I went over a second time.

My body was quaking as he thrusted one more time and gave a harsh cry.

Our panting breaths competed with my thundering heartbeat in the silent house.

Mal rolled off me onto his side next to me on the mattress.

We hadn't even taken our clothes off. My panties were still on my ankle and I don't even remember when he took them off the other leg.

"That was insane." I moved to cuddle into his side, but Mal jackknifed up and scrambled off the bed.

"I gotta clean up," he muttered before the bathroom door shut behind him.

Leaving me laying in the middle of our bed with my ripped dress still mostly on and his cum leaking out of me.

I was wrong.

It was possible to feel more alone.

That started a pattern over the next few days. Mal was either out of the house at meetings or in his office playing mournful riffs on his guitar. The only time he swam to the surface was to eat whatever I'd cooked.

Or to fuck me.

It was hard not to feel some type of way about it.

He hardly talked to me, mostly used grunts or minimal words to get his point across.

The only time I really heard him speak was when he was bossing me around in bed. And it was so hard to be pissed off at him when he was being everything I'd always wanted in a sexual partner.

It was the moments in between that I struggled with.

And I said as much to Paige when she called me one night.

"I don't know, Paige. I just wish he'd talk to me. Say something. *Anything*."

"I think you have to give him time. His best friend just died. He's clearly grieving."

"I know." I sighed. "He leaned on me at the service, but since then he's been so distant. I don't know how to reach him."

"Can I just say, you looked amazing? You totally looked like you belonged on his arm, and that dress framed your cleavage perfectly. You looked like a bang-able widow."

I rolled my eyes with a laugh. "That wasn't the look I was going for when I made the dress, but thank you, I guess."

"You clearly have talent, Say. I'm sorry I wasn't more supportive of it."

"Thanks." This time my response was heartfelt. It felt good to have someone from my tribe actually acknowledge it.

"So what are you going to do about it? Are you going all in on design? You're done with teaching?"

"I…I want to. I just don't know where I should start. Do I need to go back to school? Should I look for an internship or whatever with a label? Mal is going to help me with it once I decide on a path to take." And once he surfaced from his grief. Not that I was going to reiterate it to Paige. I was starting to feel like a whiny brat.

"Maybe you need to make a pros and cons list. Or make a list of schools and labels that are near you, and see if that sparks something. But you can't just sit around and wait for it to happen. You gotta do your part too."

"I get it. Unfortunately, I think part of the problem is that Mal's mood is contagious. I just feel…stymied, I guess."

"How would you feel if I came for a visit? I can bring some of your stuff, and we can tour schools or make lists or just research or whatever. What do you think?"

I narrowed my eyes. "Is this your attempt to get me to introduce you to Leif?"

"No!" Paige laughed. "I just want to see my friend. And if by chance Leif Eccles happens to be in the vicinity…what happens, happens."

I groaned. It felt like a mistake. I hadn't been kidding about being worried over the space-time continuum if they got together. But I also needed my bestie. "Okay. Let's do it."

Paige squealed, and we made plans for her to visit later that week.

I couldn't wait.

Mal was less excited when I told him after he surfaced for dinner. That I'd cooked again.

"I don't know, baby. It's kind of a hectic time. Everything's so up in the air and just…"

"I get that things are"—I didn't know how to describe it since he wasn't letting me in, so I finished vaguely—"whatever for you, but I'm alone for fourteen, fifteen hours of the day. I don't know anyone here but your mom and your assistant. Judy's busy with her life, and I don't think it's news to you that I'm never going to hang out with Naomi. I'm lonely, Mal."

"I wasn't aware you had a problem with Naomi. Has she been rude to you?"

I mean, if you called haughty silences and subtle snubs a problem, then sure. But instead of saying as much, I went for the indirect approach. "She's not being outright rude, but I could never trust her like I do my friends. Well, just one friend actually. The rest are more like friendly acquaintances. You know what I mean. Paige is my ride or die. We've been friends for ages. She's my person. Or she was my person before you."

A muscle flexed in his jaw, and I realized what I'd just said.

Mal had just lost his best friend, and my dumb ass thought a week after his funeral was the best time to swan my bff over.

"It's fine. Paige doesn't have to come. We can just talk on the phone and—"

"No, no, you're right. I didn't think about how these past few weeks had been for you. It's fine. She can come. We got more than enough bedrooms here."

"Okay. Um, thanks. Just one thing..."

Mal raised one eyebrow, and I lost my train of thought.

That was so hot. He looked all broody and mildly angry. He set his plate down on the coffee table and his forearms flexed.

I really hadn't spent enough time worshipping his arms. They were so strong and muscular. And the tattoos on them... I loved the little glimpses I got of them. Like now.

He rested his large hands on his knees, and the tendons on his forearms stood up.

Sigh.

"Saylor? What's the one thing?"

"Huh?" I blinked and had to look away from his sexy arms. His dark blue eyes twinkled at me like he knew exactly what had derailed my train of thought.

"You said there was one thing about Paige coming to visit?"

"Did I?" I tipped my head and placed my plate on the table next to his. "Huh. I don't remember what it was. It's like all thought just went—" I flicked my fingers in the air. "Poof."

"Hmmm," Mal hummed as he tilted his head. "Wonder what made you lose your train of thought." His dimple flashed in his cheek.

I grinned back at him just before I pounced.

And like most nights, we ended up christening a new spot in the house before retiring to the bedroom to play some more.

Chapter 22

Mal

Leif called a band meeting.

I was pretty sure I knew what he was planning to tell us.

The timing was shit. I'd wanted to be home to meet Saylor's best friend who was flying in from Las Vegas this afternoon.

But Saylor had waved me off with a tremulous smile and a, "No, it's fine."

I was picturing that expression on her face as I sat on Leif's sofa while we all waited for Beau to arrive—again.

"Having deep thoughts?" Ryker rumbled next to me.

I shrugged. "Just how when women say everything's fine that means—"

"Nothing is," Ryker finished for me.

I laughed and nodded. "Why the hell do they do that?"

"Fuck if I know, boy-o." Ryker sank back into the couch with a smile. "If I knew the first thing about women, I'd be a happily married asshole and not a single asshole."

"Committed relationships are overrated and pointless distractions," Leif grumbled as he bounced down on the opposite sofa with a highball glass in his hand.

I raised my eyebrows. "I'm taking this to mean things are done with you and June Gibson?"

"Ah, you must be the only one who doesn't read the tabs." Leif raised his highball in a toast to me then frowned and set his glass down with a click. "Shit, I'm sorry, bro. I didn't think."

I shrugged, although I eyed his drink like it might jump up and bite me. Lately it felt like I was barely hanging onto my sobriety. Losing Gio while I was on my fucking honeymoon—literally—had me all kinds of messed up.

But I couldn't control what other people did. I could only control what I did. Maybe. When I wasn't giving up control to my higher power. I had a hard time with that step to be honest. Especially at times like these.

I sighed and sat forward, rubbing my temple. "He's not bringing his wife is he? I thought this was a bandmember only meeting. I mean, Danny's not here."

"Yeah, I mean, he shouldn't be." Leif shrugged and tunneled his fingers in his long, blond hair. "I wanted to talk to you guys first. I don't know what's taking Beau so long. He literally lives only three streets away; he could've walked here and back home by now."

"Phoebe is livestreaming on social media right now, so it's not like he can blame her," Ryker said as he stared at his cell phone.

"You follow Phoebe on social media?" I chuckled. She was an influencer who posted beauty tutorials and diet bullshit. Not exactly Ryker's thing. "Are you looking for eyeshadow tips?"

"Fuck off." He pushed my shoulder. "I follow all you fuckers and the women in your lives so I can stay up to date on all your bullshit. It's what a good friend does. And now I'm unfollowing June Gibson." Ryker tapped at his phone screen with a flourish.

"Okay, now I feel like an asshole." I shook my head. "I don't even know who I'm following on my socials. I usually just have Naomi post shit for me. I don't really look at it."

"It's not my official account." Ryker scoffed. "What do I look like—a moron?"

"You have a finsta?" Leif pulled out his cell phone. "What's your handle?"

"Fuck no." Ryker scowled. "Having Leif Eccles follow my finsta kinda negates the whole purpose."

Leif frowned. "I'm not going to follow you on my actual account, moron. You're not the only one with a finsta."

"Clearly I'm not doing social media right." I rubbed at my temple. "You all have fake accounts?"

"It's what all the cool kids are doing, Mal. You should ask your child bride about it. I'm sure she could clue you in." Leif chuckled while he tapped away at his phone.

I rolled my eyes.

But I still got my phone out and started setting up a finsta too.

"How's that going?" Ryker asked, stowing his phone in his pocket. "She seems pretty cool. Not into the cameras at all, which is refreshing."

"It's…It's really good, actually." I smiled down at my phone. On a whim, I pulled up Saylor's account and grinned at the top picture of her and Paige, I assumed, in bikinis at some Vegas resort. "She's pretty amazing. You know she made that dress that she wore to the service? She wants to get into fashion."

"So not so much with the fame ducking then," Leif drawled sarcastically.

"What the fuck? What's with the judgement?" I looked up from my phone and glared at Leif. "Saylor actually isn't into the fame bullshit. She just wants to make clothes. She's going to go back to school or get an internship. What's that gotta do with fame?"

"Are you saying she's not using you? That she didn't marry you for your connections?" Leif sat forward and scowled back at me all confrontational. “Because unlike you, I actually keep up on the tabs, and I wouldn’t be surprised if Saylor wanted to cash in. She seems like that type of girl.”

I dove across the coffee table, fists flying. “You keep my wife’s name out of your damn mouth.” I landed a few punches, swinging at whatever I could.

Leif wasn’t one to back down though. He got in a few punches before Ryker waded in and pulled me off Leif.

“What the fuck is going on here?” Beau yelled from the doorway.

I stood up and wiped at the blood trickling from my nose. “Someone doesn’t know when to shut the fuck up.”

“Someone is being sensitive,” Leif mocked before grinning at me. Blood sheened his teeth in a maniacal grimace.

“Someone’s being an asshole.” I shook my head, my eyes on him the entire time. “You know what? I’m happy you’re going solo. And I’m glad that Gio’s not here to see it. Would’ve broken his heart the way you’re putting your ego over everyone’s interests. *Again*.”

“What?” Ryker gasped. “You’re leaving the band?”

Beau stepped fully into the room. “Are you seriously going solo, Leif? Is that what this is about?”

Leif ducked his head and rubbed at the back of his neck. “I was. Had all the contracts lined up and ready to execute and then…fucking Gio. He always had the best timing.”

“Way to blame our dead brother for you being an asshole.” I held my thumb against the blood trickling from my nose.

“So you’re *not* going solo?” Beau shook his head. “What the fuck is even going on?”

“I’m saying I don’t know.” Leif swiped at the blood on his chin and left a smear behind. “We only have one more album left on our contract with the label, but I couldn’t get any of you assholes to talk about what comes next while we were touring. You all splintered and went your own ways, so I decided to look after me."

"Like always." I shook my head.

Leif grimaced. "What the fuck is that supposed to mean?"

"Are you seriously going to stand there and pretend like you haven't been acting like a solo act the last few years? You do interviews solo half the time. You constantly get promotional deals that you don't cut us in on. You judged that stupid reality show and didn't even ask any of us to be on. You don't give a shit about any of us. Honestly, I'm surprised you'd noticed that Gio died. It's not like you care."

"I don't care? *I DON'T CARE?!*" His roar bounced off the walls. "I'm the only asshole here who does care. Where were you when Gio was spiraling out of control last tour? Because *I* was the one who talked to him. *I* was the one who tried to run interference with him. *I* was the one who sent his girlfriend to rehab after he died. Where the fuck were you? Oh, that's right. You were off in Tahiti getting married to a fucking teenager!"

I jumped forward to rip into Leif again, but Ryker and Beau both held me back, Beau literally holding onto my leg. I pushed at them, but they wouldn't let me reach the fucker.

Finally standing upright, I pointed a finger at Leif over Ryker's shoulder. "You want to know where I was? I was protecting my sobriety. Unless you want another drunk and incoherent asshole guitarist who can't even stand up—let alone play—I can't be around that shit. I knew Amaya was getting out of hand, but I didn't have the first clue about Gio. Because if I did…"

I choked.

"If I did—"

Tears clogged my throat, and it felt like I couldn't breathe.

"It's my fault. I should've seen. I should've…" I made a god-awful gasping sob sound and just lost it. I wrapped my arms around Ryker, buried my face in his shoulder and sobbed.

Leif was right. I should've seen it. I should've known. If I'd only stuck around more in the greenroom… I could've stopped him. I would've stopped him.

But I was too selfish.

Someone muttered, "Fuck." But I was drowning in my grief and couldn't even look up.

"It's not your fault, bro," Ryker rumbled in my ear. "You couldn't have controlled Gio's actions. He was too far gone."

"I didn't even see it," I mumbled. "I didn't realize. I'm the fucking dick here. He's been my best friend long before you fuckers knew him. I know him best. *I* should've seen. *I should've seen!*"

Tears ran down my cheeks and onto Ryker's leather jacket. I sniffled as the tears slowed somewhat. "You smell nice."

"Fuck, I'd ask if you were drunk, but we all know the answer to that. Thanks, I guess?" Ryker's laughter made me smile.

I stepped back from Ryker and swiped at my face. "I should go. Saylor's best friend is flying in, and I think we've all said more than we need to."

"I disagree." Leif shoved his hands into the front pockets of his skintight jeans. The mutinous expression gone from his face. Now he looked contemplative. Remorseful maybe? "We haven't even broached what I wanted to talk about tonight."

Ryker huffed. "We get it. You're going solo. Are you seriously going to make us sit here and listen to all your justifications? Mal's right; you've become a seriously unbearable asshole."

Beau choked, trying to keep his laughter inside. "Fuck."

"I'm not going solo!" Leif shouted. "Don't you fuckers listen? I said I was going solo. *Was*. But then Gio ODed, and I realized I didn't want to lose you guys too."

"Aww, that's sweet." Beau pursed his lips. "Weif woves us."

Leif rolled his eyes. "Fuck off."

"So why'd you call us here then?" Ryker raised his eyebrows. "Is it time for a group hug?"

Leif scoffed and shook his head. "Nah, clearly that's not going to happen anytime soon."

"Maybe you should try keeping my wife's name out of your mouth." I cocked my head. "And not blame me for Gio's shit. I'm doing a fine enough job of that on my own. I don't need your bullshit in my head too."

"Damn, son." Beau laughed, covering his mouth with his fist.

I shrugged then gave each of them a firm look. "Saylor is off limits. I don't give a shit what you think about her or me marrying her. We're together, so fuck off if you don't like it."

I'd be damned if any of the guys had anything to say about my wonderful woman. I'd put up with their current and ex-wives over the years. It was basic manners. Fuck.

"I got no problem with your woman." Ryker lifted the shoulder I'd just cried all over. "Like I said, she seems pretty cool."

Beau lifted his palms. "I would not now or ever talk shit about someone's woman. That's fucked up."

The other guys turned to Leif, but I stared down at the toes of my boots. I think we all already knew what he thought. *'Teen bride.' 'Only with me for my money. Or connections.'*

Little did he know how laughable that was. I'd had to talk her into marrying me. Literally got down on my knees. She wouldn't have wanted any part of this shitshow if she'd known what she was really getting into at the time.

Fuck, I really did have so much to make up for.

"Agreed," Leif muttered.

I rolled my eyes. That sounded so weak. And given the shit he'd already spewed, I didn't believe him anyhow.

"Yeah..." Beau drawled. "Something tells me that's not gonna cut it with Mal here."

"Like he gives a shit." I scoffed.

"What the fuck do you want from me?" Leif sounded aggrieved, like I was the one being unreasonable.

"Seriously?" Ryker rumbled. "How about you try starting with 'I'm sorry'? You talked so much shit about his girl, I'm surprised your lips aren't brown."

Leif made a gasping chortling sound like he found the whole thing hilarious. Like he was the one being wronged.

"Right." I shook my head and started for the door. I had way better places to be.

"I am sorry," Leif tossed out. "For what I said about your girl. And for what I said about Gio. I forgot what being around us when we're partying does to you. It's just…these last few years we've all kinda pulled away, and I hate it. I wish it could be how it used to be—back when we were first starting out. I miss all that comradery and fun we used to have."

I stopped and I rolled what he'd said over in my mind. I think there was a sorry in there somewhere. He'd just also wrapped it in a lot of other shit too.

"I think that's the best you're gonna get from him," Beau said out of the side of his mouth.

"It's the best apology I've ever heard from the bastard." Ryker collapsed on the sofa with a sigh. "Take it and run. But not literally, I think we've got more shit to talk about."

"Fine." I turned back around with a huff. "Apology—such as it was—accepted. Now what did you want to talk about?"

"Shit." Leif shook his head then tossed his drink back with a gulp. "Are you fuckers ever gonna stop bustin' my balls?"

Beau cocked his head. "Not likely. Now where's the booze? I have a feeling I'm going to need a drink."

"Maybe we should abstain for—" Leif nodded his head toward me.

"After you've already drank your shot?" Beau laughed incredulously. "Seriously?"

"I'm fine with this level of drinking. It's the partying in the greenroom before and after shows..." I waved a hand. "Anyway, whatever you all need to do to get through the next few minutes. But could you hurry already? Some of us have wives to get back to."

"I think you're the only one eager to get back to the missus," Beau grumbled as he stepped behind Leif's bar and played bartender. "I, for one, was happy for the break. If I have to be in the background of one more of her stupid ass videos..."

Ryker pursed his lips and sent me a look.

I shook my head back at him.

Like hell was I going to say shit.

Chapter 23

Saylor

Since Mal had to go to a band meeting, he'd put Naomi in charge of arranging transport for me to the airport to pick up Paige. LA traffic was intimidating, and I was afraid of another clash at baggage claim like the last time.

"You ready to go?" Naomi asked from the front door.

I looked up with a frown. She hadn't knocked; she just let herself in. "Yeah, no. I think we're going to have a talk first."

"Fine." She huffed before stomping inside the house like an annoyed toddler. She flung herself down on the couch with the grace of one too. And she didn't look at me once. She pulled out her cell phone and tapped away at the screen.

"Right." I blinked a few times. "I don't like you letting yourself in. This is my house too, so in the future, you need to ring the bell and wait to be let in. I don't mind you letting yourself in through the gate, but you don't enter the house unless or until one of us opens the door."

She sighed heavily, dropped her phone into her Prada bag, and then closed it with a quick zip. "Let's get one thing clear here. I work for Mal. I've worked for Mal for years. So I'm only going to listen to what he says. He's my boss, not you."

"And I respect that. I'm not trying to boss you around; I just need you to respect me and my place in Mal's life."

She scoffed like I'd said something ridiculous.

"What do you have against me?"

"I have no idea what you're talking about." She had the gall to roll her eyes at me like this conversation—and me—were totally beneath her.

"Right." I let out a little laugh. This was all so weirdly insulting. I honestly didn't know how to handle it.

"Is that the only word you know?" Naomi mocked.

"No, actually it's not. Let's go with bitch because that's what you've been to me since day one."

"Oh honey, you're not special. I've seen girls like you come and go." She flicked her long fingernails at me. "You're a dime a dozen."

"I beg to differ because, unlike those other girls, I have this." I held up my left hand and flashed the huge rock on my finger. "And something tells me that bothers you the most. Is that the problem here? If so, I'm sorry he didn't pick you."

She narrowed her eyes at me. "Fuck. You."

"Right." I laughed. "This is you being professional? Being all bitchy and snarky and disrespectful?"

"I don't know what you're talking about." If she lifted her nose any higher, she'd tip over.

"*Right*," I replied mockingly. I was so done with her bullshit. "Get the hell out of my house."

"What?" Naomi blinked up at me like I was crazy.

"You don't respect me. You don't respect my marriage. I don't want you anywhere near me. So you need to get the hell out of my house."

Naomi gave me the mean girl snarl. "With pleasure. And joke's on you because I didn't book a car. I was going to drive you myself. Good luck figuring it out on your own. I'm out of here."

She flounced toward the door but paused as she stood in the doorway. "And just so you know, it's not your house—it's Mal's house. I should know because I helped him pick it out. And unlike him, I see you for who you really are. You'll be gone way before he fires me. Toodles, bitch."

She fluttered her fingers at me, gave me her mean girl smirk, and then slammed the door shut.

I blinked a few times before breaking out in incredulous laughter. That was…something.

But that annoying voice in the back of my mind whispered maybe she was right about the length of my marriage.

Shaking off the insanity of the moment, I pulled out my phone and booked an Uber to pick me up.

Twenty minutes later, I was bouncing down the 405 to LAX and talking with my driver, Stella. "Did your daughter look at any other design colleges?"

Stella, I quickly found out, was a proud mama with a daughter who was going to FDIM.

"She toured PRISMA, but felt like FDIM had more of what she wanted."

I nodded as I stared out the window at the passing traffic. "That's good."

"It's not a little thing to change careers like you are. It takes guts."

"So does marrying a stranger." I laughed softly to myself.

"Wait, what?"

I shook my head. "Nothing. Just something I heard once."

"So you didn't marry a stranger?" Stella asked with raised eyebrows as she changed lanes, narrowly missing a Tesla who blared their horn.

I clutched at my armrest and wished for a guardian angel to save me.

"Saylor? Did you marry a stranger?" Stella prompted from the front seat.

"I might've..." I gasped as Stella quickly merged into the next lane despite the blare of horns behind us.

"Yeah, yeah, yeah!" Stella made a gesture to another driver before turning back to the rearview mirror and my reflection. "Gotta say if my daughter did that, I'd tan her hide. You should really know everything you can about your partner before you join your lives together legally. He could be a nutjob for all you know."

"Right." Speaking of nutjobs, I would've felt safer with Naomi driving me. "It's working out so far...for the most part."

"What does for the most part mean?" Stella asked before breaking harshly and honking at a car that cut her off.

"Uh, just that he's going through a lot. His best friend died the night of our wedding, so we kinda came back to a lot of craziness."

"Whoa. That's heavy."

"Yeah. Yeah it is." I went back to staring out the window and sighed as I contemplated the insanity of my life lately.

And this car ride didn't even make the top ten.

I really wished I knew how to reach Mal. But maybe he just needed some time. And clearly some space to sort through his feelings.

I just wanted him to lean on me a little—open up to me. What was the point of marriage if we were only there for each other during the easy bits?

And would he be there when I was going through something? Or would he retreat then too?

"Here," Stella called to me as we rolled up to the terminal at LAX.

I took the business card she held out to me.

Stella St John

Hell on Wheels

"I'll get you there early—no matter what LA traffic throws at us!"

Phone 323-867-5309

"I can't stand on the curb, so we'll settle up for this part of the ride, but I'll be over in the cell phone waiting lot until you're ready for me to pick you up. I'll give you a discount for the return." She pulled up to the curb then turned around to squint at me. "I like you, so fifteen percent off the return."

I blinked a few times then finally shook my head. "Um, okay. It'll be two of us, and Paige is supposed to have several bags."

Stella shrugged. "No problem." She flexed her arm. "I got you both."

I grinned, charmed despite my earlier fear. "It was nice to meet you, Stella. I can't wait to see what you think of Paige."

"I'll call my daughter while I'm waiting and see if she'd be interested in showing you around FDIM. She can use some good people for friends."

"Um, thanks." It felt weird to be set up by a stranger for a friend date, but then nothing about my car ride to the airport had been exactly normal.

"See ya soon!"

I climbed out of the back seat and Stella roared away before I'd even closed the door fully.

"Wow." I shook my head. That'd been… "Wow."

With a relieved sigh, I headed inside to read the arrivals board. I found Paige's flight and corresponding baggage claim carousel number with ease then followed the signs in that direction.

I got maybe fifty feet from the arrivals board when someone grabbed my arm roughly and shoved something into my back.

"Me and you are going to take a little walk."

It might've been a month since I'd last heard it, but I'd recognize Trent's gravelly voice anywhere.

He pulled my arm sharply. "Come on."

"Ow," the protest came out involuntarily when he wrenched my arm.

"Shut the fuck up!" he bit out. "You do get what's going on here, right? I've got a fucking gun."

I shuddered. "I'm very aware."

I could feel the cold metal pressing into the back of my dress right between my shoulder blades.

Oh god.

I looked around frantically at those passing around us, but we were just another obstacle in their path.

No one realized what was going on right in front of them.

No one was going to help me.

The weight of my situation slammed into me, and tremors shook my body.

"Come on." He shook my arm harshly again. "I've got a car in short-term parking. We're going for a little ride."

Oh shit.

I watched enough true crime documentaries to know it was a bad idea to let your abductor take you to a secondary location.

What should I do?

Trent shoved us in the direction of the short-term parking lot, and I stumbled.

"Um, Trent? I don't know what my mom told you, but I'm married. Happily even. So we can't—" I broke off as he laughed bitterly

"Fuck, I know that. Believe me, I know. It's all part of my plan."

"Plan?" I repeated numbly as I stumbled through the doors I'd entered only a few minutes before.

"Oh yeah. You're gonna get me a shit ton of money. More than enough to pay off my bookie and then some."

"You mean the Bratva?" The bundle of nerves squirming around in my stomach multiplied as I remembered the last time someone shoved a gun at me.

"Shut the hell up!" Trent snarled as we hit the sun strewn pavement.

"Everything okay here, folks?" An LAPD officer suddenly asked as he walked toward us with his hands resting on his vest just under his shoulders.

"Fine," Trent returned jovially. "Just helping the wifey stretch her legs. You know how they cram you into those metal tubes. It's like a cattle trailer, I swear."

Trent's tone was close to the one I'd known for so long I was having a hard time reconciling the insanity of the moment. It felt like an out of body experience or something I'd seen on tv. The jovial cop, the crazy ex, and the stupid girl who let herself be abducted.

I had the insane urge to laugh, but I bit it back. Barely.

Instead, I blinked wide eyes at the officer and shook my head.

His hands dropped to his belt and he quickly unclipped his gun but left it in the holster. "How about we have a conversation? I need to ask you two a few questions. Standard procedure, you understand."

"I'm afraid we don't have time for that right now." His smug voice suddenly sounded tight. Like Trent knew the cop was seeing through him. "We have an appointment we can't be late for."

"Well, you're gonna have to be, I'm afraid. Come with me, please."

Trent whipped the gun out from wherever he'd hidden it and pressed it against my temple.

"*GUN!*" the cop shouted before drawing his own and pointing it at Trent.

People screamed and ran away in chaos. The sound of mayhem and running feet joined a weird buzzing in my ears that made me sway in Trent's arms.

"*Let her go!*" someone shouted.

I couldn't breathe.

My chest was hardly moving, and no matter how hard I tried to calm down, my panting increased.

I blinked, and three more cops had joined the first one, fanning out behind him.

"Look, let's all calm down." The first cop lifted his gun away from us and pointed it harmlessly at the sky. "Nothing has happened here that can't be undone. Let's all just take a breath."

Hysterical laughter bubbled up, but I swallowed it down. Maybe he was psychic?

I locked panicked eyes on him, and he stared placidly back at me.

After a beat, his gaze darted from mine to the cement under me then back.

He repeated it again, and this time I almost laughed out loud.

Seriously?

He wanted me to dive to the ground?

He got that there was a gun pointed at my head, right?

He did it one more time, and I swallowed heavily.

Okay. I blinked once.

I was going to do it.

"I get that you're going through something right now. But for the moment, everyone's safe."

I mentally counted in my head.

One.

"Don't do something you can't take back. Don't make *me* do something I can't take back."

Two.

"All we want is for everyone to go home safe."

Three.

I dove for the pavement away from Trent.

Immediately, a gunshot rang out.

I clutched at my head and cried out.

Bang. Bang. Bang. Bang.

Four shots followed.

Then silence.

So still, I could actually hear the tweet of a bird.

And then more chaos.

"Is she okay?"

"Disarmed!"

"Oh my god."

"Was she hit?"

Someone touched my shoulders, and I whimpered.

"No visible wound. Looks like it's all his blood."

I finally opened my eyes, and the first cop was bent over me with his hands on my shoulders.

He smiled down at me.

"You were so brave. How are you feeling? Do you think you could stand up?"

I nodded disjointedly.

"Let's get you up." He gently pulled me up, careful to keep my back to Trent. "What's your name?"

"S-S-Saylor. Saylor Holt."

His smile belied the sadness in his eyes. "Nice to meet you, Saylor. I'm Luke. Let's walk over here and sit down. Is there someone we can call for you? Were you meeting someone?"

I looked over my shoulder, and the ugly sight of Trent's sprawled body with murky, bloody patches on his back and leaking under him would forever be emblazoned on my mind.

"Whoop. Let's go this way." Officer Luke gently guided me to a bench further down the way and far from Trent's clearly dead body. He sat next to me and frowned. "Were you meeting him or someone else today?"

"Paige. Paige Morris was on a flight from Vegas. I was supposed to meet her at baggage claim. She was bringing all my clothes from Vegas." The numb words fell from my lips and didn't even feel like they were coming from me. "I just got married."

"Was he..." Officer Luke cleared his throat roughly.

I shook my head. Despite the distance, my eyes were fixed on where more cops were gathered around Trent's body. Someone draped a sheet over him. "My ex. Trent Hale. We broke up a month ago. More than? I married Malcolm Holt."

"Malcolm Holt? As in the Long Licks' lead guitarist, Malcolm Holt?" Officer Luke blinked at me.

The buzzing was back in my ears.

I tried to swallow, but my mouth was so dry that my tongue stuck to the roof of my mouth.

Heat flashed over my scalp, making me dizzy.

"I don't feel so good."

That thought was immediately followed by, "Is this a bad time to mention that I'm late?"

Officer Luke's hand came down on the back of my neck as he forced me to lean forward and put my head between my knees. "For your friend? We've got someone trying to locate her now."

"No, I mean my period. I'm late. And maybe pregnant."

And then darkness swallowed me.

Chapter 24

Mal

Now that everyone finally had their drinks, I sat forward on Leif's sofa and clasped my hands between my knees. "So what's the deep, dark secret? Why am I here and not holding my girl right now?"

"Like I said, these last few years we've all kinda pulled away, and I hate it." Leif sighed, staring at his drink. "I miss the fun we used to have."

"So you called us all here to…what? Talk about the good ole days?" Beau raised his eyebrows.

"No." Leif tossed back his second shot of whiskey and set the glass down with a quiet click. "I called you guys to ask how you feel about continuing the Long Licks without Gio."

The statement slammed me in the chest with all the finesse of a sledgehammer.

Gio was the heart of the Licks.

Gio was the reason we called the band the Long Licks.

Gio was…gone.

"Fuck." Now I really, really wanted a drink. I needed to just get lost in oblivion and not feel anything for the next…eternity. Fuck. That wasn't what I needed.

"Shit."

Out of the corner of my eye, I saw Beau drop his head like he felt the weight of the world on his shoulders.

Same, bro. Same.

"What... How would that even look?" Ryker asked quietly. "I mean, it's Gio. It's, it's..."

"So fucking hard, I know." Leif shook his head. "And I'm not advocating for it to happen soon. I just...really need to know if this is the end of the Long Licks. Because that makes signing that solo deal a helluva lot easier. The label can always put together a 'best of' album to finish up our contract. But honestly, that's not what I want. I want you guys back in my life. I want the band back together. Like we used to be."

"It's not. It's never going to be the same again." The words shot out of my mouth like an accusation. So filled with pain because I was too. "Gio is gone, and I just can't...I don't know how we move forward without him."

Ryker leaned toward me with a concerned expression. "Regardless of what happens with the band, you are moving forward without him. He's gone, Mal. What exactly are you trying to say here? Are you... Are you thinking about hurting yourself?"

"What? No!" I shook my head, baffled that that was the conclusion he'd come to. "What the fuck are you talking about?"

"You sounded like a man at the end of his rope, honestly." Leif leaned forward, bracing his arms on his knees. "And we've already lost one brother. I'll be damned if we lose another on my watch."

I bit back the words that ached to escape because no matter how much I wanted to blame Leif for being a selfish dick, what Gio did had nothing to do with him. Or me. I *knew* that, but it was still so hard to let go of. Somehow it made it easier to blame someone, anyone, even me if it meant that I didn't have to face the fact that Gio was truly gone.

This whole meeting was a slap in the face—a reality check that I wasn't ready for.

Would probably never be ready for.

"It's just still so fresh." I ran a hand through my hair and tugged at the ends like I needed that small flash of pain to tell me I wasn't dreaming. "I swear I haven't had any thoughts like that. At most, it's threatened my sobriety. It'd be so easy to bury my head in a bottle and just not feel for the next month or year. But I didn't. I haven't. I've gone to so many fucking meetings that I have my own chair now. No one sits there but me." I gave a pained cackled. "Such a fucking loser."

"Good." Beau pushed his drink away with a sigh, not drinking a sip.

"You guys don't have to—"

Leif stacked his empty glass on top of Beau's.

After a beat, Ryker's joined the pile.

Leif grinned at me. "I think it's safe to say we've all lost our thirst after hearing that."

"Yeah." Ryker nodded. "And we'll totally be losers with you. Anytime you need someone to go to a meeting with, feel free to call me."

"Or me," Beau added.

"Or me," Leif echoed.

I looked down and shook my head, emotion almost overwhelming me. "Thanks, guys."

"Brothers now and always." Beau smacked my shoulder.

"Feels like we should toast that, but we've all just promised not to drink anymore tonight." Ryker laughed.

"I've got some soda behind the bar." Leif jumped up and rounded the bar top. He pulled four new Collins glasses out and filled them to the rim with cola.

"Just like in high school." Ryker laughed as we all gathered around the bar.

Leif lifted his glass as we grabbed our own. "Yeah, but Gio's not here to spike it with whatever hooch he nabbed from his ma's stash."

The levity of the moment stilled for a heartbeat. Then I shook my head. "Remember that time he couldn't find his drumsticks and tried to use chopsticks?"

"Which broke halfway through the first song." Beau grinned. "So he grabbed that nasty wrench and screwdriver that the venue left behind his kit?"

"Nah, it was a wrench and a grill lighter. Coz it kept sparking in his hand." I laughed so hard, remembering that look of shock on his face.

"Fuck, that was a shithole of a venue." Leif grinned. "But he didn't lose his drumsticks. Remember that chick in the greenroom *used* them before the show? And then stole every pair he had."

I shuddered. "Fuck, that was a memory I'd suppressed for a reason."

Some things were definitely better left forgotten. Gah.

"I miss his Muppet impressions."

Ryker's statement came from left field, considering the memory Leif had just inflicted on us.

"What?" Beau laughed.

"Remember how he could growl just like Animal?" Ryker shrugged. "Fucking got me every time."

"BEAT DRUMS! BEAT DRUMS!" we all hollered before breaking out into laughter.

Leif sighed. "It didn't hurt that he had a passing resemblance too."

We all giggled like school boys because Leif wasn't wrong. Like Animal, Gio was known for his stringy hair and wild beard.

"God, I'll miss that fucker." I stared down at my glass.

"To Gio, the best damn drummer the Long Licks will ever know." Leif held up his soda.

"To Gio," we all echoed before we clinked glasses and then drank.

My glass half full—I'd never been a chugger, especially with soda—I set it back down on the bar top. "I think you're right, Leif; I don't want to lose this either."

"Ditto." Ryker clasped my shoulder and gave me a little shake.

Beau tipped his head. "Me neither."

"Agreed." Leif looked at each of us individually. "I'll ask Danny to see who he knows and set up some auditions when we're ready."

I swallowed hard. It still felt like a betrayal to move on so soon, but I also knew deep down that it was the right decision for us.

Life marched on.

My voice only sounded a little froggy when I spoke. "Sounds good."

"Yeah, thanks, Leif," Beau rumbled.

"Thanks," Ryker echoed.

"And then we'll need to figure out the new guy's contract." Leif shifted his weight. "Only makes sense to do a trial run. Start out with a year and go from there?"

"If they're on a trial basis, we should probably wait to record anything with them." Beau pointed out. "Or maybe have Danny look into what rights we want to give the new guy? We don't want to end up with stupid restrictions on future royalties with some douche canoe who didn't work out."

Leif nodded. "Which brings us to the next point, what are we going to do after our next album? Find a new label or create our own?"

"I could ask Noah about the process." My NA sponsee just happened to be the drummer for the Tin Gods, a metal band that'd started their own label a little over a year ago.

"Or we could save the hassle and sign with them." Ryker rested his elbow on the bar. "They wouldn't screw us over."

"Would they be willing to take on a name like ours?" Leif asked with a frown. "So far, they've only signed unknown acts. And do they have the ability to give us the support we'd need? I don't want to trade one shitshow for another one."

I shrugged. "I'll feel him out without committing to anything. But given that they recorded and released their own album last year, I'm pretty sure they're up to the job."

"Okay, sounds like we have a plan." Leif's voice sounded tight. "We'll audition new drummers in the next few months, finish our contract with our label, and feel out the Tin Gods about joining their label."

"Fuck yeah!" Ryker shouted. "Sounds like another toast is called for."

"All hail the Long Licks," Beau said as he raised his glass, borrowing from the Tin Gods' trademarked slogan.

I shook my head. That bastardization wasn't going to fly with me. But I still clinked my glass with his and shouted, "Lick it up!"

"Every fucking drop!" Beau called back as he slammed his glass against ours.

"Every drop," Leif echoed before crashing his glass into ours, then shooting the rest of his soda.

"Fuck, it still burns, even if it's just soda." Beau gasped as he set his empty drink down.

"Coz you're shotgunning it like a moron." Ryker scoffed.

The door ripped open, and Leif's assistant, Zanna, ran into the room. "Answer your phones! What the hell is wrong with you all?"

I exchanged wide-eyed looks with Ryker. As long as I'd known Zanna—almost five years now—she'd never talked to Leif, let alone us, like that.

"We're in a meeting." Leif frowned at her. "You know better than to—"

"Saylor was taken hostage at the airport," Zanna spoke over Leif, coming straight to me. "It's all over *the Babbler*. Her ex grabbed her in baggage claim and was in a standoff with the cops."

"What the fuck!" I ran across the room to where I'd left my cell phone on his coffee table, powered off after our stupid finsta follow session.

Once I turned it back on, ping after ping of alerts came in.

Texts from countless people.

Twelve missed calls from Saylor.

Fuck.

Fuck!

I tapped on her name, and it took me a whole minute to toggle to speaker phone because of how much my hands shook.

"—not available. At the tone, please record your message. When you have finished recording, simply hang up. *BEEP!*"

"She's not answering!" I yelled before trying her again.

"Your call is being forwarded to an automated voicem—"

I killed the call again.

"What the fuck!" I turned back to the guys and Zanna. "Where is she? Is she okay? Is she, is she…" I couldn't even finish the thought, let alone say it.

"She's alive," Zanna answered shakily. "As far as I know she was unharmed. They haven't reported any ca—"

She cut herself off at Leif's nasty glare.

But I knew what she was going to say—casualties.

"I don't understand." I stared unseeingly at the hardwood floor. "Naomi was supposed to arrange security. I didn't want Saylor driving herself to the airport. She was supposed to be protected."

Shaking my head, I turned away and tapped at my phone's screen again. This time calling Naomi.

"Hey Mal," she answered, sounding all friendly and normal and not like someone answering from a hostage scene. "How'd the meeting go?"

"What the fuck? Where's Saylor? Why am I hearing from Leif's *fucking* assistant that she was abducted? Where the fuck have you been?"

"What? She was what?" She sounded legitimately shocked.

Like this was news to her.

"Where the fuck have you been? And where was Saylor's security? What the fuck have you been doing?"

"I didn't think—I didn't know..." Her voice was husky and tearful when she spoke again. "I didn't book any security. I didn't think she really needed it. I was going to drive her, but she gave me attitude, so I left."

"You left her? Where?"

"At your house!" she wailed. "She must've driven herself or booked a car service. I don't know."

"You are so fucking fired. I don't want to see your fucking face ever again. Danny will send you your final check. I—"

"Wait, Mal, please. Please don't fire me. I can't, I don't...I love you so much. You don't even kno—"

"And I don't wanna fucking know. I'm married. To Saylor. Who I fucking love. And who you put in jeopardy because of your bullshit. And I'm not putting up with it anymore. You. Are. Done!"

I punched the red end call button and flung my phone away in aggravation.

I don't know how I missed it. But I hadn't seen Naomi's weirdness until Saylor pointed it out this morning. And now this.

What the fuck?

I didn't know what to do.

Who to call.

How was I going to find my wife?

I'd never felt so powerless before in my entire life.

Then my phone rang.

I dove for it, thinking it must be Saylor calling again only the display screen read **Mom**.

I almost didn't answer it. I needed to find Saylor, but it was my mom so I did.

"Ma, I don't have time to talk right now. Saylor is—"

"I know very well what Saylor is. Why the hell aren't you here?"

"Here!" I yelped. "You're there? Where is there? I'll be there as soon as—"

"Okay, you gotta take a breath, Mal. I can hear the panic from here. And that's not going to help anyone, especially when I tell you where we are."

"What the fuck, Ma? Answer the fucking question! I don't have time for stupid platitudes right now. I'm going out of my mind here."

"I know. I can hear it in your voice. Promise me that you're not driving. I don't care where you are—who you have to call—do not get behind the wheel right now."

"I can't just—"

"We'll drive him, Missus Holt!" Leif called over my shoulder like the kiss-ass he'd always been.

"Leif! Thank god, you're there." My mom gasped in relief.

I was ready to strangle someone. Literally. I didn't care who. I was aching to get my hands on someone. "Where. Are. You!"

"We're at Cedars-Sinai Marina del Rey Hospital. There was some concern that Saylor..."

I didn't hear the rest of what my mom said.

My hand went numb, and I dropped the phone.

I swayed on my feet and would've gone down but for Ryker suddenly appearing to hold me up much like Saylor had at Gio's funeral.

She was at the hospital.

Hurt.

Maybe bleeding.

Because of me.

Because I hadn't been there for her.

Again.

I couldn't lose her. I just found her.

Fuck.

"Saylor," I whispered, my mouth barely moving. "I gotta get to Saylor."

"Right, I'm driving," Leif announced, waving my phone around. "You two good to drive yourselves, and we'll meet you there? Zanna, come with us in case we need some recon."

Ryker guided me the whole way to the car while he and Beau argued something about how he could get info out of the nurses easier than Zanna could. Or something. I don't know. I wasn't exactly paying attention.

I was too busy thinking about how I couldn't lose Saylor.

I just found her.

Breaking News from the Babbler

Bride of Long Licks' Guitarist Taken Hostage at LAX

Trauma at Terminal 1

Exclusive Details

stock image of Saylor and Mal at LAX one month earlier

Updated 1:23 PM

Our sources have confirmed that the assailant has been identified as Trent Hale, the ex-fiancé of Holt. As we reported earlier, Tate canceled their wedding five weeks ago, just a few days before the ceremony. And as luck would have it, ten days before she married Malcolm Holt.

Possible motive?

Updated 12:56 PM

Saylor Holt has been transported to a local area hospital with "superficial wounds," according to our sources.

Updated 12:38 PM

The assailant has been confirmed deceased. No information on the condition of Saylor Holt or the identity of the assailant.

Updated 12:38 PM

Our sources say Malcolm Holt was not at LAX at the time of the abduction.

Original Story 12:04 PM

Chaos broke out at Terminal 1 at the LAX airport when an armed man took a hostage near the Mojave Airlines baggage claim carousels in an apparent domestic dispute, law enforcement tells *the Babbler*.

Our sources say the hostage was none other than the bride of Long Lick's Guitarist **Malcolm Holt—Saylor Holt**. As we reported earlier, they married last month, the same day as the Long Licks lost their drummer, Gio Barone to an overdose.

No details yet as to the identity of the assailant or if Malcolm Holt was also present at the altercation.

This is a developing story.

Stay tuned...

Breaking News from the Babbler

Surviving Members of the Long Licks Band Together for Guitarist

Long Licks Arrive at Local Hospital

Exclusive Details

slideshow of Leif, Mal, Ryker, and Beau walking through hospital entrance

The Long Licks have arrived at Cedars-Sinai Marina del Rey Hospital where **Malcolm Holt**'s new bride, **Saylor Holt**, was taken after her traumatic hostage situation at LAX.

As we reported earlier, Holt was taken hostage at LAX's Terminal 1 by her ex-fiancé, Trent Hale. Hale was shot by responding officers and died at the scene while Tate was transported to Cedars-Sinai with superficial wounds.

No official word yet as to motive.

This is a developing story.

Stay tuned…

Chapter 25

Saylor

"I finally got ahold of your good-for-nothing husband," Judy snarked as she walked back into the curtained area where I was waiting with Paige.

"Isn't he your son?" Paige asked with a frown.

I sighed and shook my head. I understood the sentiment.

I felt that way too.

It'd been hours.

"Apparently he'd turned his phone off because they were having a band meeting. Like anything they were talking about was *that* important." Judy huffed. "How four men could get to their forties and still behave as teenagers is beyond me."

"Um, does that mean he's coming?" Paige asked when it became evident I wasn't going to.

"Yes. Leif is driving him."

Paige made a strangled sound.

And despite the whole ugliness of this day, I had to laugh.

"No." I turned to her and pointed my finger. "You are not to flirt with him. I don't need my whole world splintering any more than it already has."

Paige sobered and nodded. "No, I get that." Then she tipped her head. "But there's no harm in looking, right?"

Judy hooted. "I missed out on so much fun by not having a daughter."

"What happened to Mal's dad?" Paige asked with a frown. "He's not in the picture, I take it?"

Judy sighed. "That's a drama for another day. Although it might explain why Mal's still such an immature ding bat. I should've picked a stronger male role model for him than that asshole had been."

My eyes widened.

"Saylor Holt?" The doctor stepped back into the cubicle and paused when she saw my audience. "Would you like some privacy to discuss the test results?"

"I..." I looked helplessly at Judy and Paige. It felt wrong for them to hear the news before Mal, but I also didn't want to sit here alone.

"We'll give you a minute, honey." Judy patted my shoulder then walked around the bed I was sitting on. "I'll go direct that useless husband of yours in this direction when he arrives."

"And I'm going to go help Leif—I mean, Judy. Help Judy." Paige nodded resolutely then ran through the curtain before I could grab her.

I sighed and faced the doctor. "Okay. Lay it on me."

"You tested negative for pregnancy."

I sighed, expecting a wave of relief that didn't come. My emotions were all over the place, honestly. Or maybe I was just numb? I don't know. I was definitely tired.

So tired.

He tipped his head. "You should follow up with your regular practitioner or your gynecologist, but I would say your late cycle is probably due to a mix of stress and the missed pills while traveling. It happens more often than you'd think."

I nodded.

"And your abrasions should heal up in a few days. Like I said, the tetanus shot was just out of an abundance of caution. Better safe than, right?" He laughed weakly. "If there's nothing else, a nurse will be by with your discharge papers."

I shook my head. "Thank you, doctor."

"I'm just sad I won't be able to meet your husband. I've been a fan since—sorry, that's not appropriate." He shook his head then stared down at his paperwork, avoiding my eyes. "And again, if you experience any delayed trauma like we'd discussed, please reach out to someone. We have some excellent psychologists here. I'll include some pamphlets in your discharge paperwork."

"Thanks," I whispered before shuddering as I remembered the horrifying feeling of the gun at my temple.

And then the sight of Trent's lifeless body stretched out on the pavement.

"I hope you feel better." He gave me a vague smile then ducked out of the curtain.

I didn't even have time to breathe, let alone think, before I heard shouting.

"Curtain three! Where's curtain three?" I recognized the voice, although I'd never heard that panicked tone before.

A beat later, the curtain swept aside, and Mal lumbered through, anxiety twisting his features. "Saylor, fuck. Are you okay? Are you hurt?"

He crushed me to his chest without waiting for a reply, and I heard his heart thundering behind his ribs as I laid my head against him. His hands patted every square inch of my body he could reach.

"Shit, what's this? Were you shot? I'm going to kill that fucker." He pushed my sleeve up my arm after he felt the bandage beneath.

I weakly batted his hands away. "It's just a scrape. I wasn't shot." I looked up at his panicked face and gave a little laugh. "I'm fine, Mal. I swear."

"What the fuck happened?" He collapsed down on the bed next to me then pulled me onto his lap, wrapping his arms tight around me. "You were supposed to have security. Who took you hostage? I don't know anything."

I glanced at the curtain. I had medical privacy here, but I doubted that extended to conversations. And I'd had more than enough of my life splashed over the tabloids. I didn't want to add fuel to the fire.

"Can we talk about it at home?"

"Are you shitting me? No!" Mal hollered. "My wife was taken hostage at the fucking airport. What the fuck happened? Who was it? I'm going to kill the fucker!"

I gave a harsh laugh. "You're too late. LAPD already did the job for you. My ex is deader than a doornail. Why do they say that? How does a doornail die? Am I talking fast? It feels like I'm talking fast. My heart is pounding. Is that normal? It doesn't feel normal."

My breath came in harsh, wheezing pants, but I wasn't getting any air.

Oh god.

Oh no.

"Not again."

Then everything went black.

When I woke up, a nurse hovered over me. Her eyes were a gentle brown. So warm and nice.

"There you are. When's the last time you ate, sweetie?"

"Um…" I blinked a few times. I tried to put an arm under me to sit up, but the room swam around me again, and I fell back onto the bed. "Last night, I think? Dinner last night maybe?"

Mal cursed softly behind her and paced the short distance the curtain allowed. His hands tunneled through his hair as he muttered something to himself.

The nurse smiled at me. "Okay, well, since this is the second time you've passed out, we're going to put you on IV fluids and delay discharging you for at least an hour. Now lie back and keep your feet up. You'll feel better once we get some fluids in you." She stood up and turned to Mal. "And it wouldn't hurt to have someone bring you something to eat. I can order from the cafeteria, but take my word for it, you're better off ordering something in."

Mal nodded purposefully then stomped through the curtain, shoving it out of his way, clearly a man on a mission.

The nurse turned back to me with a smile. "It helps to give them a task. Makes them feel like they're in control of the situation a little bit. You're a lucky girl."

I gave an incredulous laugh. "Really? It doesn't feel that way."

I mean, I was lying on a hospital bed after being taken hostage. How exactly was that lucky?

The nurse winced. "I meant your hubby. He clearly loves you. You should've heard the hell he raised when you passed out again. Usually, guys like that are annoying assholes."

I raised my eyebrows and she laughed.

"But he's pretty to look at. It helps."

This time *I* laughed. She wasn't wrong.

"And he clearly loves you so much." She tipped her head. "Like I said, you're a lucky girl."

Again, it didn't feel that way lately, and this time I wasn't thinking about the abduction. My marriage hadn't been the easiest so far and considering we'd only been together a month, that wasn't exactly a good sign.

The honeymoon stage had felt like anything but.

My nurse patted my shoulder. "I'm going to start that IV for you. You try to get some rest. I'm only allowing your husband back since he's a handful, but we can bar him if you think it'll help. It's completely up to you."

I sighed and shook my head. Things might be bumpy between us, but I needed Mal here with me.

Mal was back—empty handed—before the nurse returned, and I blinked up at him in confusion.

He collapsed into the chair next to the bed with a sigh. "Ryker is getting you a burrito. Leif wanted to go, but he's creating enough of a stir here, sending him out for food won't help. The last thing we need is a bunch of Leif sightings. The place is a zoo as it is."

"Leif is here?" That was important, but I couldn't exactly remember why.

"And Ryker and Beau. The hospital arranged a private waiting room for them, since it was causing mayhem in the halls. Although to be fair, the press was already here, so they can't blame that on us."

"Press?" I repeated weakly.

Mal winced. "Shit. Sorry." He sighed and shook his head. "Yeah, it's a shitshow out there. *The Babbler*, KALI 14 news, the major networks, they're all out there. Considering you were taken hostage at a major airport, it's kinda headline news. And they all got pictures of us arriving."

The nurse came back with the IV and Mal waited tensely while she set up the IV stand.

"All right. I'll check back in on you in a few minutes."

After the curtain closed behind her, Mal sat forward on his chair, his hands clasped tightly and gave me this look so full of pain. "I'm so sorry, Saylor. I never should've trusted Naomi to handle your security. I should've called or gone with you. I just...I failed you. And I'm so fucking sorry. I should've put you first."

It was everything I wanted him to say, so why did it feel so wrong?

Tears sheened my vision, and I shook my head.

"I put my convenience over your safety, and that's going to haunt me the rest of my days. I don't... There's nothing I can say to make it up to you. I'm so sorry."

My whole body started shaking. "Will you hold me? Please?"

Mal's eyes darted from my bandaged arm to the IV sticking out of my other hand. And I knew he didn't want to hurt me anymore, but the puppy dog eyes I gave him did the trick.

He pushed out of the chair with a groan then walked around the bed to burrow behind me on the slim, hard twin-sized mattress. He spooned me, his knees behind mine but his pelvis nowhere near mine. His arm came around my waist and his hand rested just below my bra.

It wasn't nearly as tight as I wanted, but something about having his arms around me centered me. Suddenly all was right with my world, and I could breathe again.

I relaxed in his arms for a few minutes, but once I was calm again, I could tell he wasn't. From his rigid body to his heavy breathing, Mal was vibrating with tension and angst. No doubt he was still mentally beating himself up. And it hurt my heart so much.

"I know the first month of our marriage hasn't exactly gone to plan," I began, but had to stop when he shook the bed with his soft laughter.

"You think?"

I smiled at the sardonic tone in his voice. "Yeah. But I think as long as there's not a biblical plague on the horizon—although given our luck, there might be—we should be able to take some time and just be together now. Don't you think?"

I didn't need to see his face to read the heavy tension in the room.

"Mal? What's going on?" My stomach fell. Oh god. Was he breaking up with me?

"The guys and I might have agreed to continue the band tonight."

I blinked a few times, waiting for the hammer to fall. But when he didn't say anything else, I probed further. "Okay? Isn't that a good thing? I thought you loved your band."

"But it's not the life I promised you. I said I'd put my all behind you and your career. That we'd figure it out together, and I'd be the Stay-At-Home Dad supporting you."

'Stay-At-Home Dad.'

I had to catch my breath before I could ask, "Do you… We never really talked about it—which in hindsight is stupid—but do you want children?"

"I mean in theory, yes? But I don't see how it would work if I'm touring and you're either going back to school or starting your career. You're only twenty-two. That's not exactly fair to you."

My breath left me in a whoosh of relief. Which I realized meant I wasn't ready to have kids right now either.

But Mal kept going.

"And it also shouldn't take you getting abducted and passing out in a hospital for us to have a conversation. Especially one as important as this. I didn't even have the band as an excuse for my shitty behavior this last month. I failed as a husband again and again, and I wasn't even working. What's it going to be like when I am recording and playing and touring with the guys? How can this ever work then?"

His voice grew tighter and tighter the longer he spoke, and I knew he was blaming himself for way too many things.

"Okay, first, I want you to take a breath. We don't need them admitting you too, because then we'll never get out of here."

Mal gave a choked laugh that had me smiling in response.

"And second, I'm going to need you to give yourself some grace here. Your best friend died. Sure, this last month has been rough, but we're still here together. You tearing the hospital apart for me told me everything I needed to know about your feelings for me."

His arm tightened around me for a second, then he brushed his hand up to cup my breast. He nuzzled into my neck. "You are clearly the brains of this couple. Thank you for not giving up on us."

"Never. Not as long as you keep loving me like this." I sighed and relaxed into his embrace. "But third, and I think the most important thing here, is that we need to lean on each other. What's the point of this marriage if we're not there for each other in bad times as well as the good ones?"

"You have a point."

"It's like you said, it shouldn't take something catastrophic happening for us to have a conversation. You have to let me in."

"I am. I will." He sighed and burrowed his face into my neck. "Maybe you could come with me to my next NA meeting? See what I do every day?"

"I'm there, Daddy. Always for you."

"Fuck yeah, you are." His hands wandered a little north, and I sighed as a sense of peace washed over me. "And we'll figure out the rest of it in time. I mean, it's not ideal given your age, but I want to table the baby talk for a bit. Maybe revisit it in two years?"

"Did you just call me old?"

"Well, if the creased leather pants fit—eep!" I yelped as his nuzzling turned into a tickle fest.

"You two are disgustingly cute." Beau flung the curtain aside and stomped into the tiny space before plopping a greasy brown paper bag on the small table next to the chair. "Here's your damn burrito. Chicken okay? I forgot to ask if you're a vegetarian, and Mal here didn't answer his phone."

"Chicken is awesome, and I can totally relate."

Mal sucked in a breath, and I winced.

"Too soon?"

Beau lifted the side of his mouth in a smirk that no doubt would've made many a woman swoon. "Yeah, she's good people. You chose wisely, Mal."

I turned slightly to look up at Mal. "Did he just quote Indiana Jones?"

Beau cracked up. "Fuck, now I'm jealous." He shook his head. "I'll be back at our waiting room if you need anything else."

"Thanks, Beau!" I shouted at his large, lumbering Viking-esque form as he walked away.

He lifted a hand in response but kept walking.

Mal huffed before twisting out of the bed behind me and helping me sit up. He didn't say a word as he passed me the bag and collapsed onto the chair, folding his arms over his chest with a furrowed brow.

"What?" I finally asked, confused by his sudden change of behavior. And after we'd made up so much ground.

"I don't like him crushing on you. He should know you're my woman," he said, sulkily.

"Oh my god. You're ridiculous!"

He huffed again. "I shouldn't have to hear it. So disrespectful."

"Do you know what I've had to listen to the nurses say about you? And the doctor too!"

He perked right up. "What'd they say?"

I rolled my eyes and dug my burrito out of the bag. But when I looked up Mal was staring back at me with this expression in his eyes that made my heart skip a beat. Despite everything that'd happened today—his crazy assistant, the abduction, the trauma, the ER visit—I probably looked a mess.

And yet despite it all, he still stared at me like I was the most wonderful, gorgeous woman ever.

I smiled back at him then dug into the burrito with the gusto of a starving Dickens character.

And Mal had that look in his eyes the entire time.

If that wasn't love, I don't know what was.

Chapter 26

Mal

I don't think I slept the whole night. I couldn't take my eyes off of Saylor. Like I was afraid she'd just up and disappear on me because this whole day felt like a crazy fever dream or something.

I never knew it was possible to feel so strongly so quickly for someone, but here we were. That feeling I'd had of absolute panic when I didn't know if she was alive still made me nauseous. I'd happily live the rest of my life if I never had to go through that again.

Goddamn, she was so fucking beautiful.

After having a gun to her head, she still looked like an angel. My angel.

My baby girl.

I was a lucky fucker, and I wasn't going to forget it—ever.

"How long have you been staring at me, weirdo?" Saylor asked in a groggy voice.

My eyes darted from her tits to her sleepy sky-blue eyes, and I grinned back at her, totally unabashed. "Don't really remember even falling asleep. So all night?"

"Creep," she muttered before giggling softly.

"When it comes to you, baby girl, always." I pressed a kiss against the tip of her nose. "How would you feel about embedding a little tracking device? Microscopic, really."

She whipped the pillow out from behind her head and smacked me square in the face with it.

"Is that a maybe?" The pillow muffled my voice, but I thought I still got my serious point across.

"Ugh." She groaned as she rolled out of the bed, clutching her lower abs. "I've got cramps. Shoot, I don't think I have any supplies here. I was going to grab some yesterday, but then... Could you run out and get me some tampons? Or better yet, ask Paige if she packed any?"

"Sure I'll just call—" I bit my tongue because no, I wouldn't be calling my assistant now or anytime ever again. Shit. "I'll figure it out."

Maybe I should ask Leif's assistant, Zanna, for help?

I headed for where I'd left my phone charging while Saylor darted into the bathroom.

"Oh!" she shouted through the closed bathroom door. "Grab my purse, please? I have a few in there to hold me for now."

Clutching my phone in my hand, I turned and headed for the living room where I believe I saw her bag last. But before I could get there my phone buzzed in my hand.

Security Calling

Dread pooled in my stomach, but so much less than what I felt yesterday. Still, I pressed my free hand against my stomach when I answered.

"Yeah?"

"Hey, Mister Holt. Sorry to bother you," the security company Danny had arranged last night for us answered. "But we have an Erin Baker here. She says she's Mrs. Holt's mother. Her ID matches and she appears legit. Do you want me to escort her in?" The 'or send her away' was clearly implied and underlined when Erin hollered.

"I'm her mother, for crying out loud! What is all this drama for? Let me see my daughter!"

I sighed heavily. She sounded like a peach.

But it wasn't my call to make.

"Hold on, let me ask the missus."

I grabbed her bag off the ottoman where we'd dropped it last night then headed back to our bedroom. After knocking lightly, I called through the door, "Hey baby, I got your bag, and apparently your mom is at the gate. Do you want to see her?"

I heard her groan through the door before she opened it and stood in the doorway, still adorably rumpled from sleep.

She took her purse with a half-smile and a murmur of "thanks," then rubbed her eyes with her free hand. After a heavy sigh, she muttered, "Sure. Send her up."

Her reply was the definition of underwhelming.

"Hey, you don't have to see her if you don't want to. You control what happens now."

She lifted a shoulder. "She drove or flew all the way here, though."

"Who gives a shit? She's been pressuring you for weeks to get back with that punk ass bitch. And now she swans in all concerned for your wellbeing? Where was she when his bookie clocked you in that parking garage? Fuck that. Fuck her. Fuck. *Her*."

"Whoa-kay." Saylor dropped her purse and pressed a hand against my chest. "I get that you're feeling a certain type of way about my mom, and believe me I am too, but somehow I think all this—" she gestured at my clenched jaw and fists. "Isn't about my mom. What did they call it in my psychology class? Misplaced—no, displaced anger."

"Who the fuck cares? She screwed you over, and I don't want her in my fucking house."

She sighed. "I guess I can meet her at a restaurant or something then."

"Seriously? You're not going anywhere, except to the police station to give your statement this afternoon. And even then, we're taking at least two security guards with us."

She gave me this look like I was the crazy one. "Right. So where do you want me to meet my mom then? If she can't come in here, and I can't go out there…?"

"Fuck." I huffed in annoyance. "Fine." I lifted my cell and tapped the speaker button. "Send her in, but have someone standing by to eject her when shit hits the fan. Because it will."

I rolled my eyes at Saylor, but she just laughed.

"I love how you think ahead. Thank you, Daddy." She went up on her toes and pressed a sweet kiss against my cheek. "I love how you're always looking out for me."

Well, not always.

She shook her head. Apparently I didn't even need to say it out loud to get that across. "Do not take that on. We can't go back. Only forward. So take a note from Miss Swift and shake it off."

The doorbell rang.

Saylor stooped to grab her purse and moved to close the bathroom door. "Give me a few and please, please, please don't kill my mom in the next three minutes."

"No promises," I muttered as I turned away.

"I heard that!" Saylor shouted through the door.

I grinned at her sassiness the whole way down the hallway.

"What is going on?" Paige asked, popping her wild head of hair out her bedroom door.

"Saylor's mom has arrived." My tone implied that the devil was on our doorstep.

"Shit." Paige's eyes widened and she moved to close the door.

"Wait! Do you have any tampons?"

"What the—" she opened her door again and gave me a look like I was insane.

"Saylor is in need. I also need to organize a delivery of supplies for her. Do you know what kind to buy?"

She nodded. "Yeah, sure. I can take care of that."

"No, just text me the details. I want to do it."

"Aww. That's so sweet." Paige darted back into her room.

I continued down the hall. A beat later, I heard her door open again, then she scampered down the hall away from me to my bedroom and Saylor.

I tapped at the security panel next to the door as the doorbell rang a third time. I ripped the door open before the panel turned green and a screeching alarm joined Saylor's mom's bitching.

"Finally!" She scoffed, pushing past me. "Saylor!" her mom shouted.

I exchanged unimpressed looks with the security guard, who stepped inside and closed the door behind him. He went to tap at the security panel, and I grabbed Saylor's mom as she tried to run past me to the bedrooms.

"Whoa. She's not ready to see you just yet. We're going to wait for her in the living room."

"Oh, I don't know who you think you are, but nobody is going to get between me and my daughter."

I kept my grip on her arm and turned to the security guard. "What's your name?"

The enormous man shifted his weight as he crossed his massive arms across his equally large chest. "Lucas, sir."

"Nice to meet you, Lucas." I looked down at Saylor's mom. "I think me and Lucas have a difference of opinion about how you think this is going to go down. You are here at Saylor's invitation. If it were up to me, I'd a left you on the curb outside with the paparazzi trash. So you'll sit in the living room and wait for your daughter to put herself together. And maybe you and me will have a little chat, just the two of us while we wait."

Her lip lifted in a snarl, and she glared at me before stomping across the room to collapse onto the sofa with a huff.

"Charming," I muttered to Lucas.

"Oh you have no idea, sir," Lucas murmured sardonically back.

I choked back my laughter and made a mental note to get him on regular rotation around here. He was clearly good people.

I followed behind at a slower pace and took a seat on the oversized chair opposite her. "So let's talk."

"I have nothing to say to you. I'm here to see my daughter."

"Fine, then I'll talk." I sat forward and stared her down. "When Saylor comes out here, there will be no victim blaming. What happened yesterday is not on Saylor. I don't want to hear any 'poor Trent' bullshit from you. And the second Saylor gets distressed, you're out of here. I'll give Lucas over there the nod, and he'll drag you out by your hair if need be."

"You're disgusting. You can't treat me this way. I'm her mother."

"I don't give a shit if you're an amputee or a cancer survivor or her twin fucking sister. If you hurt Saylor, you're gone. End of discussion."

She huffed again as she turned away from me, hugging her arms.

But she also didn't protest again.

* * *

Saylor

A tap came again at the bathroom door, and I laughed at Mal's ridiculousness.

"Come in!" I yelled around the toothbrush in my mouth.

But it was Paige who ducked inside and not my husband. "Hey, I heard you needed some supplies." She passed a few tampons and some pads across the countertop. "That's all I have with me since it's not my time of the month."

"Thanks," I mumbled before spitting and rinsing my mouth.

"I heard the Wicked Witch is here. Did she come alone or is her monkey enroute?"

I sighed. "You sound like Mal. More creative, but he hasn't met her yet."

"Your husband is awesome, by the way. Like I haven't already told you that. He won't let me order your tampons—he wants to do it himself. So sweet!"

I grinned even as I hustled around her to grab some clean clothes from the closet. To be fair, I kinda led him in that direction. I'd learned a very important lesson yesterday at the hospital: give him a task to make him feel in control. I just hadn't expected Mal to run with it. Although he wasn't the type to get twitchy about anything body related, so I should've known better.

"Do you want backup out there, or do you want to me to stay clear?" Paige asked from the doorway as she watched me get dressed.

"I think Mal and I can handle it."

"Don't forget the security guy."

"What?" I paused with my head still buried in my shirt. "Who?"

"I'm pretty sure your husband has a security guard standing by the door like a bouncer at a club. Do you think Erin will actually bounce when he throws her out?"

I groaned. I had to get out there ASAP.

I quickly pulled my shirt on and grabbed a random pair of shorts. "Only come out if you hear screams. Or better yet, once the front door closes. Whichever happens first."

"Gotcha. And don't let her walk all over you, please."

I buttoned the fly and gave her a sardonic look. "I really doubt Mal will let that happen."

"I'm more worried about what you'll let happen." Paige walked toward me to wrap her arms around me and held me tight for a moment. "I'm so glad you're still here. I would've been so lost if anything happened to you. I love you so much."

Tears welled in my eyes for a second, but I determinedly blinked them away. "I love you too, chica."

"Once your dysfunctional family reunion is over, I'll cook breakfast for you all. Scrambled eggs in observance of your currently flushing uterus?"

I rolled my eyes with a laugh. "You're the best kinda of crazy."

"You know it!" Paige yelled at my retreating back.

I got to the end of the hall and paused for a second to take a deep breath.

I'd never realized how much anxiety I felt when I had to face my mom. Or maybe this time was different, given all that'd happened.

Straightening my shoulders, I calmly entered the room.

Chapter 27

Still Saylor

"Saylor!" my mom shrieked, jumping up from the sofa and racing over to me. She held my shoulders as her eyes searched me. "You're safe. Thank god."

Then she enveloped me in a hug that felt so different from the one Paige had just given me. Mom's thin arms tightened around me like a python as her sharp shoulder punched me in the throat.

Suddenly I felt so cold, despite the warm California morning sun pouring into the room from the glass wall next to us.

"Mom. It's good to see you too. Is Alan in the car?"

"Oh, he couldn't come on such short notice. They needed him at the bank. Kind of an all-hands sort of thing." She waved her hands in emphasis.

Given that Alan and Trent had worked at the same bank, I understood—kinda. But it was his stepdaughter who'd been held hostage. I guess it wasn't a big surprise I didn't rank an actual in person meeting.

It still hurt. But not as much as I would've thought.

I gave my mom a vague smile then crossed the room to sit in Mal's lap. I needed to feel his arms around me. I didn't even have to tell him as much. He just knew.

After a beat, Mom followed me and sat on the sofa opposite us with an uncomfortable expression.

"So, how are things?" I asked when it became clear she wasn't going to be the one to talk first.

She gave a weird sounding laugh. "Horrible actually. I've had to face some harsh truths lately and…" She sighed and wiped at her cheeks. "I'm just…I'm so, so, sorry, Saylor."

I shifted on Mal's lap. I ached to cross the space and hug my mom for real this time, but it still didn't feel safe. *She* didn't feel safe. "Okay."

"Okay?" she echoed, tears heavy in her voice. "Seriously? That's all you have to say?"

"Watch your tone," Mal barked, making me jump and look over my shoulder at him. "Saylor isn't the one in the wrong here. I told you I won't put up with any bullshit victim blaming, and this was exactly what I meant. Knock it off or get the fuck out."

The glare my mom sent him could've peeled paint.

But Mal didn't care. He gave me a squeeze and sat back into the chair, completely at ease.

She sent me an incredulous look. Like Mal was the one in the wrong.

"I don't know what you expect me to say, Mom." I sighed. "Yesterday wasn't the first time a gun was shoved against my temple because of Trent. And you didn't seem to give a shit. I told you all the dirty details of what his scary Russian bookie did, and you still chose to back Trent."

My mom looked away, totally abashed at the reminder of her failings.

"*'It's a misunderstanding, Saylor.' 'You should forgive him.' 'He's going to get help.'*" My laugh was harsh. It still pissed me off to remember all the ways she'd gaslit me. My own mother. "Trent Hale didn't give a shit for anyone except for himself."

"And the high he was chasing with his gambling," Mal chipped in.

I nodded, acknowledging his point. "Trent put me in danger back then, and you didn't care. You seemed more upset that I was canceling the wedding than the fact that I'd been attacked and held at gunpoint. What kind of mother does that?"

"A poor one," my mom whispered, staring down at her hands.

"So you see why it's hard for me to believe that you've suddenly seen the light? But I guess my side is more believable this time because I made the six o'clock news last night."

She raised her eyebrows and sent me a look. "I won't lie and say that it didn't hurt finding out about another life-changing moment in your life from the news."

Shifting the blame to me.

Again.

Mal twitched, and I clutched his hand to keep him from reaching for my mom.

"Do you know who I asked the police to call when it became clear that this moron turned his phone off?" I asked. Mal stiffened under me, and I ran a reassuring hand down his arm. I wasn't still angry about the missed phone calls; that wasn't the point here.

Mom shook her head. "Clearly not me."

"I asked them to call Mal's mom."

Mom jolted like she'd taken a bullet.

"Because I knew Judy would show up and just be there for me. She wouldn't come in with an agenda and make me feel like anything that'd happened was my fault." I leaned forward and pointed at my mom. "Because that's the kind of mother Judy Holt is. She loves her kids unconditionally, and I'm so freaking privileged to be one of them now."

Mom wiped at the tears streaking down her cheeks. "Like I said, Saylor. I've had to face some really harsh truths lately, and clearly I'm not done because all this is like a slap to the face."

"Me sharing my feelings is a slap to the face, Mom?" I blinked. "Seriously?"

She nodded.

"How do you think I've felt for the past…forever really? This isn't something new. This is just the final straw, actually."

"Saylor, no. Don't—don't say something you'll regret." She moved forward on the cushion and reached out to me. "Some words can't be unsaid."

"Like telling me my dreams were stupid? That designing clothes was a pipedream? Or how I was the irresponsible one because I canceled my wedding? I keep disappointing you over and over again, and I can't keep doing this."

"Now that's not fair. I apologized."

"While continuing to blame me in the same breath. Coming at me with a half-assed apology isn't making me feel any better about our relationship. Until or unless something changes on your end, I don't want to do this anymore."

"What does that mean?"

"It means it's time for you to go. And I don't know…see a therapist or something. I'll even go to a session with you. But you need to do some work that will make me believe you care about me and our relationship."

Mal tipped forward, peeking around my side to get my mom's attention. "PS, giving an interview to *the Babbler* or any news organization is not a sign of change and will only piss me off more."

Mom's eyes were wide and tearful as they ping-ponged between me and Mal.

After a beat, she nodded and stood up. She fussed with the wrinkles in her pantsuit for a few seconds then sent me a tearful smile. "I love you, Saylor. And I'm going to take what you said to heart. I am so, so sorry I didn't listen to you earlier."

I could tell she wanted a hug, but I couldn't do that.

"I do love you, Mom, but our relationship isn't healthy. And I refuse to be your passive-aggressive punching bag anymore."

She contorted like she'd taken a physical hit. Swiping at her eyes, she scurried from the room and out the front door with the security guy on her heels.

I felt so weird. Proud. Sad. Hurt. Relieved. It was the strangest mix of emotions.

"Fuck me. You're so fucking amazing, baby girl." Mal pressed me into the chaise lounge beneath me and kissed me like a solider returning home, so full of passion and life and joy.

It did so much to alleviate the ache inside that scene left me with.

"Ahem," Paige interrupted. "I was told to come out when I heard the front door close."

Mal sighed and rested his forehead against mine. "I forgot we weren't alone." Turning his head, he said to Paige, "We're busy. Come back later."

I giggled and pushed at Mal's shoulders. He was so ridiculous.

"Um, usually I would." Paige laughed. "I know you two are in the whole honeymoon stage and all, but I'm hungry and would really like to make breakfast now. I mean, I am a guest in your house..."

Mal gave a weary sigh and finally pushed off me and moved so he sat hunched over on the end. "Fine. I never get to have any fun around here."

I laughed at his exaggerated pout. "Um, not to rain any more on your parade, but could you call your mom and ask her to come over? I'd kinda like to be with people who care about me."

"Always, baby girl." Mal leaned over and pressed a kiss on my forehead. "In that case, I'll call the guys over too. They were almost as freaked out as I was last night."

I smiled. Mal's tribe was becoming my tribe too.

Until I saw the sparkle in Paige's eyes.

"Leif's coming over?"

"Oh, sweet baby Jesus," I muttered, shaking my head at Mal. "What fresh hell have we unleashed?"

Paige shrugged. "It's not like a portal to hell opened up last night when we…"

"Paige. Evelyn. Morris," I shouted. "What did you do in a *hospital* of all places?"

She sent me a mischievous look, then bounced into the kitchen and soon the sound of pots and pans clanging filled the charged silence.

Mal laughed. "Why am I suddenly afraid for Leif?"

"Because you are a very smart man."

Mal shook his head and gave me another long, lingering kiss before he left to make some phone calls.

I collapsed onto the chaise lounge with a sigh.

Crazy exes, besties, and mothers aside, my life was turning out pretty damn great.

But a sudden crash from the kitchen made me sit up with a start.

"Um, Saylor?" Paige called. "What are the chances that vase was a knock off and not a Baccarat?"

"Was it red?"

"Yes."

"And heavy?"

"Yes…"

"Shoot." I pushed off the chair and headed to a closet where we might have a broom. "It's coming out of your allowance."

"As long as everyone's okay," Mal called from down the hall. "I don't give a shit. I'll buy you another one, baby."

Like I needed one more example of why I loved that man.

"You're such a lucky bitch," Paige snarked when I entered the kitchen.

I grinned back at her. "I was thinking the same exact thing."

Epilogue

Mal

Six weeks later

Another day, another drummer audition.

It was starting to feel like we were never going to find our guy.

Maybe we were expecting too much from the guys.

Maybe there was simply no replacing Gio.

"I'm telling you, this one is the one." Danny was uncharacteristically excited. He was all but bouncing in place as he tapped at his cell phone's screen. Which was definitely out of character for our usually staid manager.

"Who are we seeing today, again?" Ryker asked from his sprawled spot on the couch next to me.

"Hunter Adkins," Danny replied.

"Never heard of him," Leif huffed, crossing his arms over his chest.

"I told you he was the drummer of a band I had my eye on. Shady Vortex," Danny muttered, his eyes still on his screen.

"Never heard of them," Leif repeated.

Ryker and I chuckled at his deadpan delivery. Someone was in a mood.

"You wouldn't," Danny replied. "Like I said, I had my eye on them. They broke up a few weeks ago. Creative differences."

"Let me guess." I threw Leif a derisive look. "The lead singer slept with the guitarist's wife's best friend then ghosted her like an immature asshole?"

Ryker clucked and shook his head like a disappointed papa, then ruined it by fake coughing while muttering, "douchebag," into his fist.

"You two are so immature," Leif grumbled. "But for the record, we never slept together. Just kissed and—"

"I don't need the fucking details, dude!" I protested. "I happen to see Paige on a regular basis. Which is what I told you when you came over. Please don't shit where *I* eat."

"Hey, I never touched your wife!" Leif shouted.

"That wasn't my point! Don't touch her friends. Don't touch her classmates." I gestured frustratingly. "This wife is the one. This is it. So please, *please* stop making my life harder, asshole."

"You're dating a schoolgirl." Ryker choked with laughter while he rolled on the sofa and accidentally kicked me with his boot.

"Fucking pervert!" Leif flicked a guitar pick at my head.

"I'm surrounded by children." Danny groaned, rubbing at his temple.

"Speaking of, where's Beau?" Lief asked, turning to Danny.

I frowned. "What does Beau have to do with children?"

"Didn't you hear?" Ryker sat up and straightened his shirt. "The missus is preggo."

"Oh." My eyes widened. I had a hard time picturing Phoebe with a baby. She was so selfish and honestly, kinda mean.

"Yeah." Ryker sighed.

The door ripped open and Beau stomped into the room, his long hair hanging wildly. "I got a call on the way over. I can't stay. I have a family emergency."

"Is Phoebe okay?" I asked in concern.

"What? Yeah, no. Phoebe's fine. It's, it's…shit. I have a kid."

"What the hell? How'd you go from pregnant to a kid already? I just found out about the pregnancy." And last I saw there was no way Phoebe had been that far along.

"What? We're not pregnant." Beau frowned.

Ryker sat up. "But you said—"

"I said we were *thinking* about starting a family. But we haven't. We're not even really trying—I just found out I have a full-grown daughter. She's twenty-two. Lives in Seattle. And her mom just died. I gotta get to Seattle ASAP." Beau turned to Danny. "Can your assistant arrange a flight for me? Whatever will get me there today."

"Yeah, sure. Of course." Danny gestured to the door.

After the door closed behind them, Leif smirked at me. "Dude, his daughter is the same age as your wife!" He cackled, wiping his eyes. "Fucking epic."

I scowled at the asshole. Unlike Leif and Ryker—who were also laughing at me—I didn't see the humor.

With impeccable timing as always, his assistant, Ethan, popped his head in. "Hunter Adkins is here for his audition."

I groaned. Like always with the Long Licks, the second everything started to look up, it all fell apart again.

***

That afternoon, after a surprisingly promising audition and jam session with Hunter, minus Beau, I stepped into my house and took in the delicious smells coming from the kitchen.

"Honey, I'm hoooome," I called out.

"In here!" she answered. "I'll be right out with your slippers and pipe."

I grinned and all but ran into the kitchen, so fucking eager to see my wife.

I wrapped my arms around her from behind as she stood in front of the stove, stirring a huge pot of bubbling marinara sauce.

She leaned back into my embrace with a hum. "How was your day, dear?"

"Really good. Well, first really weird, then good."

She turned in my arms, wound her arms around my shoulders, and gave me a smacking kiss. "What was the weird part?"

"Turns out Beau has a secret daughter he just heard about. He took off to Seattle to meet her."

"Wow," Saylor whispered. "That's, that's intense."

"Yeah, tell me about it." I might've spent some time today wondering if I could ever be in a similar boat. I hadn't exactly been a Boy Scout, but I did however always wrap it up, so the odds were small—but never zero.

I shuddered at the thought.

"And the good?"

"Aside from coming home to all this—" I pressed a kiss on the tip of her nose.

She huffed in feigned annoyance and rolled her eyes. But the small little smile told me everything I needed to know. That and the way she snuggled even closer to me.

"Aside from that. That's a day that ends in y around here."

"And I fucking love every single one."

"We're so disgustingly cute." She grinned at me.

I kissed her again. "I know. The guys were telling me all about it earlier today. But the other good part is that we might've finally found our new drummer."

"That's fantastic!" Saylor did a little excited wiggle in my arms that made all parts of me sit up and notice. "I have exciting news too."

I drug my eyes away from the hypnotic sway of her tits. "Hmm?"

"I loved my tour of FDIM. Stella and her daughter, Amber, were great. The campus was amazing, and talking to Amber made me so excited. I want to apply there next term."

"Fucking fantastic, baby. And I know the perfect way to celebrate."

"What's that?"

"By taking all our clothes off and rolling around our huge bed." I nudged Saylor, encouraging her to walk backwards toward our bed.

"Mal! But dinner is—"

"Will be fucking awesome an hour from now." Fuck it. I ducked down, tossed her over my shoulder, and took off down the hallway.

She squealed before her laughter echoed through the house.

I slapped her ass and she moaned. "Make that two hours."

The End

About A Lick of Sense

Want more *Long Licks Rock Stars*? The band's story continues in *A Lick of Sense* coming later this year!

Preorder your copy today

A Lick of Sense

I'm supposed to be getting to know my newfound rock star father—only I can't take my eyes off his drummer. Oh boy.

About Rocked

What happens in Vegas doesn't stay in Vegas. Not when you marry a rock star.

I went to Vegas to get married, only she married someone else, so why shouldn't I do the same?

It's the best way to stop public speculation about my jilted groom status.

But even better, something about Shay has flipped a switch inside me—suddenly I can write music again.

Only my new little wifey isn't thrilled about our marriage.

She says drunken mistake. I say best night ever.

Of course I'm right, and I'll use everything I've got to convince her.

Turn to page to read an excerpt from Rocked (Tin Gods 1)

Rocked Prologue

Shay Campbell

Las Vegas, Nevada

I opened my eyes and immediately regretted it. Everything was blurry, and the small amount of light in the room sent a shaft of pain straight to my brain. I closed my eyes and groaned.

Papers crinkled under me as I rolled to my back. What the hell? I wasn't going to open my eyes again to find out what that was—my curiosity wasn't stronger than my hangover. Raising my arms, I pressed my hands against my aching head. As the sheet fell away, I realized I was naked.

Naked. In bed. Surrounded by paper? What the hell had I done last night?

The last day or so came back to me in pieces.

Driving to Las Vegas with my cousin, Brianna, for her bachelorette party weekend.

Losing the coin flip and sleeping on the lumpy fold away bed.

Day drinking with Brianna and her horrible cronies.

The mean girl insults.

The tears.

The wedding?

It sounded insane, but I had a very vivid memory of trying on flirty wedding dresses in some boutique and holding hands with a handsome man.

Was I…married?

My thumb brushed against a ring on my left ring finger.

Oh no.

Oh my gosh!

Cue the nausea.

I leapt from the bed and ran for what I thought was the bathroom. Slamming the door open, I barely had time to take in the gleaming marble, tasteful stripped wallpaper, and luxe finishes before I was hurling the small amount of liquid in my stomach into the toilet.

My ribs aching, I flushed and sank onto the cold tile with my eyes closed. “I'm never drinking again.”

“You're not going to make it as a rocker wife with that kinda attitude,” a deep voice purred behind me.

I froze.

I wasn't alone.

And he'd just watched me puke.

Naked.

With a squeal, I opened my eyes and grasped for the nearest towel. When it gave with my second tug, a very nude—and amused—gorgeous man stood in front of me.

“Kinda thought you were too hungover for round three.” He chuckled and stood there naked and unashamed. “But I'm game if you are.”

Clutching the towel to my naked front, I sputtered. “I, uh… Who are you?”

“Clearly that last bottle of Krug was a mistake.” He shook his head as he grabbed another towel and twisted it around his waist. Then he bent down and pulled me and my towel into his arms. He easily carried me back into the darkened bedroom. “I'm Chase Robinson.”

He waited a beat. "Your husband."

This Adonis was my husband?

When I continued to stare stupidly at him, he scoffed and set me down on the side of the bed. "Damn, you are killer on my ego, baby girl. I kinda can't wait to introduce you to the guys and watch you eviscerate all their egos too."

"Guys? What are you talking about?" It felt like the room was spinning, and I was pretty sure only a little bit of that was due to the hangover.

He cleared his throat. "Uh, the guys I work with. They're going to shit themselves when they get a load of you."

I blinked a few times. What did he do for a living again? Did we even talk about that last night? I hadn't even remembered his name—and apparently my new last name—without his prompting.

A dim memory of us in a bar talking about writing came back to me. So he was an author…and worked with people? I'd assumed authors worked alone. Maybe he made enough to employ some people—like an assistant, maybe? I definitely remembered he'd had a bodyguard last night. Which would explain the opulent hotel suite. Was that a pool table?

Okay, so he was a successful author who could afford a killer Vegas suite. I was impressed.

The blare of my ringtone, George Strait's mellow voice, rolled through the suite and had me scrambling for my phone on the nightstand.

"We gotta talk about that, baby girl. I cannot have a wife of mine blaring country music. I'm gonna lose all my street cred."

His chatter fell to the background as a buzzing filled my ears.

I'd missed the call, but it was my phone's lock screen that had my heart thundering in my chest.

I had 112 missed calls.

367 text messages.

What the hell was going on?

My phone rang again in my hands.

Mom.

I didn't want to answer. What was I going to say to her? I was still trying to piece last night together for myself. But I had a feeling it had something to do with the gorgeous guy standing behind me and the ring on my finger.

My hand slipped on my phone's screen, and I accidentally accepted the call. On speaker.

Crap.

Crap!

"Um, Mom? Hey."

"Hey? *Hey?!* That's seriously all you have to say to me, young lady! Are we pretending I didn't learn from *the morning news* that you got married to a rock star last night?"

Morning news? I was morning news?

Wait, rock star?

My eyes swiveled to Chase, but he rubbed the back of his neck, avoiding my gaze.

And I knew.

My stomach lurched again.

Clasping a hand over my mouth, I dropped my phone and ran for the bathroom for the second time that morning.

Rocked Chapter 1

Shay Campbell

Desert Island Hotel Casino

Las Vegas, Nevada

24 hours earlier

For the first time in my life, proving my mom wrong didn't give me an ounce of satisfaction. But I was right. I hated this trip. I wasn't having *any* fun. And my cousin, Brianna, was still a witch.

Unfortunately, I was still on this bachelorette party trip from hell, and it wasn't ending any time soon.

Lord, give me strength.

At least I got to try day drinking. That was a first for me.

"Right, Shay?"

Brianna's question dragged me away from contemplating the bottom of my plastic martini glass and to the amazing hotel pool we were currently "enjoying." Brianna sat two chairs down from me on the partially submerged loungers with Leah between us. Meaning I was hanging alone on one end, while her two other cronies, Eva and Charlotte, sat on her other side.

All of us were in matching bikinis, but somehow I still managed to look frumpy compared to Brianna and her friends.

I was wearing the exact same thing, and I still didn't measure up.

"Shay! You're not listening to me!" Brianna's whine made my eyelid twitch.

"Sorry." I bared my teeth at her in a semblance of a smile. "I was thinking about work."

"Only you would be drinking in a pool in Vegas and still think about work!" Brianna did that husky laugh that sounded so alluring to men, judging by the way two were currently craning their necks our way.

"Sorry, Bree. I'll try harder to be present. I'm here. I'm excited for your big day." I tried to sound sincere, but considering Brianna's curled lip, I'd failed.

Look, this just wasn't my thing. I'd rather be inside curled up—fully clothed—with a good book and a Dirty Coke, preferably by myself. This trip had been an introvert's nightmare so far. And I'd paid for the privilege of torturing myself.

Eva huffed. "We're planning the rest of the day. Bree wants to hit that club Tidal after dinner. You're up for that, right, Shay?"

I bit back my groan and forced another smile. Fake it 'til you make it. "Sure. I brought some clubbing outfits."

"Mmmmm, I've seen what's inside your suitcase, Shay." Brianna wrinkled her nose. "I'm afraid I'm going to have to veto."

"You're vetoing clothes I haven't even worn yet?" I blinked. They still had tags on them. I'd bought them specifically for this trip.

Brianna pursed her lips. "They're just not...Vegas worthy. Maybe there's something in the boutiques here that are more appropriate."

"Yay!" Charlotte squealed. "I smell a makeover!"

"Please, let me do her hair!" Leah clapped. "I've been aching to fix that mess."

Mess? *Makeover*? We'd clearly entered the torturous portion of the trip. Taking a deep breath, I attempted to stand up for myself. "If my clothes and the rest of me aren't appropriate for your bachelorette party, maybe I should just stay in the room and read a book."

"Don't go getting all butt hurt, Shay." Brianna rolled her eyes. "You know we didn't mean it like that. It's just...maybe you'll feel better about yourself if you let us fix a few things."

"Like that awful side part." Leah snorted.

Charlotte waved a hand at me. "And something to cover her shoulders."

My shoulders? What the heck was wrong with my shoulders?

"You'll see." Brianna's lips curved in a piranha-like smile—all pointy teeth and thinly veiled venom. "You'll be gorgeous when we're through with you."

"I can't wait," I murmured, hunching my problematic shoulders. Of course, I folded like a house of cards at the first hint of push back by Brianna and her cronies.

I was so giving my mom a piece of my mind when I got home.

* * *

Two hours later I was regretting my need to people please.

Because nothing apparently pleased these people.

"No, not that one." Brianna huffed as she stood in front of me, surveying the eighth outfit I'd tried on. "It's all wrong. That hemline makes you look pregnant."

"Sure, the hemline," Eva muttered loudly. Leah chortled next to her.

My eyes burned, and I knew my face was bright red. "I'm done. You guys go out without me today. I'll stay in the room with my book."

"Aww, come on, Shay." Charlotte pouted. "Don't be a spoilsport. Try on one more. Please? For Bree? It means so much to your cousin, and it'll totally ruin our numbers if you don't come tonight. I already have everything booked, and I spent so much time planning all this."

"One more, Shay?" Brianna blinked at me. "Please."

And I caved like I always did. "Fine."

Swirling around in a sea of black tulle, I stomped back to the dressing room. One more and that was it.

Who was I kidding? I didn't even believe myself at this point.

"Try on that blue dress with the sequins!" Brianna yelled behind me.

"You're so bad, Bree." Eva giggled. "That one will make her ass look huge."

Brianna's reply was too soft for me to hear.

Why was I even doing this? I hated itchy, sparkly clothes. I hated loud music and other sweaty drunk people invading my personal space. How had I let my mom talk me into this trip?

Oh yeah. She'd played the Dead Dad Card and guilted me with how he would've wanted me to be close with his side of the family. He'd died before I was born, so I had no memory of him, but my mom knew I still somehow missed him.

All my life I'd felt like there was a hole in my soul. A piece of me missing. Stupid of me to think Brianna would help fill it. That girl had hated me since day one, and I still had no idea why. Only back then she would take out her anger on my Barbies—coloring on their faces and cutting their hair into weird styles.

Maybe not much had changed after all.

"Um, miss?"

I turned from the dressing room I hadn't mustered the courage to enter and found the saleslady hovering next to me with a blue dress in her hands.

"I think you'll find this one more...appropriate." Kennedy—I gathered from her name tag—held out the dress to me.

I frowned in confusion. "This looks like the same one I have in there."

"Yes, but this one is your size. I think your blonde friend accidentally grabbed the wrong size."

The blonde girl meaning Eva. She was worse than Brianna.

"Just a little friendly advice?"

I nodded, avoiding eye contact.

"Get yourself some better friends. Those girls are trouble and no friends of yours."

"I wish I could, but one of them is family. If I just cut and run, I'll never hear the end of it..." I smiled bitterly. "It's just not worth it. One more night, then I'll be free."

She nodded sympathetically. "Family is tough. Hang in there. But first—" She twisted and snagged a flame red dress from a nearby rack. "If you can't ditch them, make them regret bringing you here. This dress was made for a figure like yours, and with your skin tone, it will be amazing. Trust me."

This time my smile was genuine. "Thanks."

Kennedy dipped her head, smiling back. "Come see me if you need shoes. I'll hook you up."

* * *

Needless to say, Brianna and company did not appreciate me stepping out in my fabulous new dress and heels. And despite Leah's pleas, I wouldn't let that viper anywhere near my head with a pair of scissors.

I might've been a doormat, but I wasn't stupid.

My sushi dinner had been fabulous despite the company, and now we were pregaming at a bar near the club we were going to later. Apparently no one showed up until ten at the earliest.

This was going to be the longest night of my life.

I was coming back from the bathroom—alone—for the second time in so many hours. Just in time to hear them talking about me.

"Why'd you even bring her?" Leah sneered. "She's killing the vibe and won't even let me fix her hair."

"My mom made me." Brianna groaned. "Apparently Aunt Rebecca called her. She's worried that Shay doesn't have any girlfriends. Or any kind of social life, really."

Eva gasped. "She doesn't date guys? Is she...*gay*?"

"Oh my god, Eva!" Charlotte huffed. "You don't have to whisper it like that. You can say gay."

"I know." I could hear Eva's eyeroll despite standing around the corner. "But is she? You know...gay?"

"I doubt it. Aunt Rebecca's husband is ultra conservative. Religious. The kinda religious that wouldn't accept a gay stepdaughter."

"Really? That's crazy." The fake sympathy in Charlotte's voice made my skin crawl.

Brianna went on. "I guess they sent her to a private religious high school, and he even paid for her college as long as she attended an acceptable Christian school. That's why she went to BYU when she's not even Mormon. I don't think she's ever dated, let alone had a NCMO sesh."

Heat flashed through my head at Brianna's implication. For her information, I'd had a Non-Committal Make Out session. Once. And I'd been on dates! Not that I said a single word or let them know I could hear them. Everything about this moment was mortifying.

"Wait, you can't mean... You think she's *still a virgin*!" Eva all but shouted.

"Seriously, Eva? You whisper gay but yell virgin?" Leah huffed. "What the hell is wrong with you?"

"I'm drunk." Eva giggled loudly. "We've been drinking all day. What do you accept? Accept. Expest. Whatever. Barkeep! Another round, lickety-spit. Spilt. Argh."

"I think so." Brianna's harsh whisper was so loud it easily carried through the bar. "I suspect Shay is waiting for her wedding night. Like a *good girl*."

They all cackled like it was the funniest thing they'd ever heard.

Tears burned at my eyes again. I swiped under my eyes, determined not to let any fall.

"Oh barf. What a moron." Charlotte sneered.

"Are you sure she's related to you?" Eva hooted. "I mean didn't you lose your virginity under the bleachers sophomore year of high school?"

"Whatever, bitch. At least I was getting me some." Brianna scoffed. "And now I'm getting the best for the rest of my life. Brock's dick is..."

I didn't stick around to hear the rest.

I'd swallowed so much crap these past few days. I'd tried to find some common ground with Brianna and her cronies despite their nastiness, but I didn't have any more grace left inside me. It was official. I was done.

Done with their fakeness and the digs about me, my body, and my lack of experience.

Done with this whole craptacular weekend.

I spun and crashed into someone.

"Ommph." He staggered and clutched at his stomach where my elbow had apparently collided with him.

"Oh my gosh!" I reached out without thinking and patted his very firm stomach. A zing of electricity traveled up my arm, and I gasped before jerking my hand back. "I'm so sorry. I wasn't looking where I was going, and I just..." I trailed off as I looked up into the deepest green eyes I'd ever seen.

He was gorgeous. From his tousled short brown hair to his dark green eyes and the sexy stubble trailing up his jaw, he was easily the most attractive man I'd seen in my entire life.

Who I was still standing in front of and gaping at like a moron.

I knew the flush reddening my cheeks had nothing to do with my alcohol intake today. "Again, I'm sorry. I'm gonna start looking where I'm going. Or something. You know, I'm just gonna go now. So… thanks."

Closing my eyes in humiliation, I ducked around him but froze when his hand clasped my elbow.

"Don't go rushing off now, baby girl. We didn't even have a chance to exchange information. Maybe I want to file a claim with your insurance."

I snorted and then was immediately mortified. But still I was me, so I couldn't help myself from replying, "Really? Does that line usually get you any traction?"

He shrugged. "Usually I don't have to say anything."

"Right. You just let all of that—" I gestured at his body. "Talk for you."

He raised an eyebrow and tilted his head. "How drunk are you?"

"Not drunk enough. Clearly."

"Huh." He blinked a few times, then a large smile spread across his lips. "Okay. Let me buy you a drink then."

"Uh, Chase?" A tall, muscular man stepped over to my gorgeous guy's side. "I don't think that's a good idea. The crowd in here is—"

My guy cut him off. "I'm sure we can find a table out of the way. In a little secluded corner."

"Oh. Are you here for a bachelor party too? I mean, I'm not here for a bachelor party. I'm not a stripper. It's my cousin's *bachelorette* party. Not that there's anything wrong with being a stripper. I'm just…not."

I really had to stop babbling. Something about having his full attention just flustered me to no end.

And his husky laughter did crazy things to my nerve endings. "I can't wait to hear more. You're so damn cute when you start rambling like that."

"I, uh, I don't…" I couldn't make my brain work when he turned all his attention on me. And seriously, that was my one claim to fame—Book Smart Shay. Not so much with the athletics or the grace or…anything else really.

But no, this guy either had me losing my trail of thought or babbling like a crazy person. I had to get it together. He could be the one to—

"So? Can I buy you a drink?"

"I, uh, yes. Yes, please."

Yes, please? Seriously, just kill me now. That was so pathetic.

"I got you a table over here, Chase," Looming Tall Guy said over Chase's shoulder.

"Right this way, Shay." Chase grabbed my hand and tugged me in the direction of their table.

I tottered after him, relishing the feeling of his rough hand holding mine. This guy had some serious callouses on his hand. So freaking sexy.

Wait. He'd called me Shay.

"How do you know my name?"

He stopped next to the booth and winced as he turned to face me.

And then it clicked.

"Oh my gosh. You heard that? What they were saying about me? About my…"

"Virginity? Yeah. They weren't being exactly discreet with their gossiping. Pretty sure most of the bar heard them cackling."

"Oh, kill me now." I buried my face in my hands. "This has got to be one of the worst nights of my life."

"Really, baby girl? Even though you met me? It's still the worst night of your life?"

I had to smile at that. Dropping my hands, I gave Chase a little smile. "Well, no. I mean it's just…" I shook my head. "Still pretty horrible, honestly."

"I can respect that." He tilted his head, his eyes narrowing on me, making my heart race. "So are you? Waiting for marriage?"

Also By Gillian Archer

Long Licks

Lick It Up

A Lick of Sense

Tin Gods

Rocked

Refrain

Ballad

Encore

Holiday Mode

This December

That Summer Festival

Burns Brothers Series

Build

Fast

Spark

Torque

Grind

Star Studded

Falling for Rome

Fighting for King

True Brothers MC Series

Ruthless

Rebellious

Resilient

ALSO BY GILLIAN ARCHER

Rough Ride

HRH Series

Reluctantly Royal

Standalone Short

King of Hearts.

About Gillian Archer

GILLIAN ARCHER has a bachelor's degree in engineering but prefers to spend her time on happily ever after. She writes the kind of stories she loves to read—the hotter the better! When she's not pounding away on the keyboard, she can be found chasing her kiddo, or surfing the couch while indulging in her latest reality TV fixation, or reading awesome romance ebooks by her favorite authors. Gillian lives in the wilds of Nevada with her amazing husband, brilliant daughter, and goofy dog. Please visit her at gillianarcher.com

Gillian@GillianArcher.com
Facebook.com/GillianArcherWrites
Instagram: @gilliarcher

Sign up to receive important news, new-release info, and giveaways from Gillian Archer straight to your inbox with her newsletter.